Book Of Favours

By

Mary Gladwin

Lionheart
Publishing

First published in Great Britain in 2003 by:

Lionheart Publishing
Amscot House
Waterfall Road
Dyserth
North Wales
LL18 6ET

ISBN: 0-9546450-0-6

Printed by Gwasg Helygain Ltd
68/70 Kinmel Street, Rhyl LL18 1AW
01745 331411

Cover Design by Sarah-Jane Waller

single cigs and the more that he sold the more he could buy. He found it difficult to keep up with the demand for the games until he came up with the brilliant idea of copying the tapes. Twin cassette decks had just come out so he bought one which enabled him to copy his games so that he had even more to sell.

He got his punters to bring in games of their own for a discount of ten pence a night on his copies. Then he just taped loads of copies of each game he got from his punters which gave him all the more copies to go out on loan. Jimmy gained respect from the older boys both at his school and out who sometimes got a discount from him and who all admired his sheer bottle and entrepreneurial skills.

By the time that he left school at the age of sixteen Jimmy had managed to save over three thousand pounds which he put into bigger stock that he started to sell from a lock up on the estate. He progressed to selling fake perfumes along with other goods and within six months of trading he had over twenty lads on the streets selling his goods. He could also lay his hands on most things that people asked him for. He had contacts with petty criminals who brought him a couple of video recorders a week and when he was asked for drugs he had no qualms about getting involved. Jimmy however would never take any of the shit that he got other people to sell for him. Jimmy would oversee everything but he had never put his name to it. He used to tell people that he knew a man who knew a man so people had just respected the fact that he had good contacts.

He was a local lad who had survived and made good on what fast became known as a rough estate. Along the way Jimmy had managed to pick up favours like most lads his age had picked up a bit of skirt.

He had known what he wanted out of life and he had also known that girls could wait. The fact that Jimmy's brains had not been in his underpants had been the reason that he had grown to be so successful and he had known that. He paid debts for people who could not afford to pay them and he had given credit with a ten percent interest rate. Jimmy had never pestered for the money that he was owed for he knew that he would be repaid one day one way or another. He also would never have grassed on anyone nor would he had ever have divulged the identity of any of his suppliers. Jimmy Mack received a lot of respect for that.

Jimmy had been just fourteen years old when Lee Won-king had joined his school. Lee and his mother had fled from a nasty uprising in China in which his father had been killed. Lee's mother had brought him to England in search of his uncle who would protect him from any evil that might try to follow them. His father had been a very important leader who had been instrumental in the uprising in China. It had been his involvement that had sadly resulted in the loss of his life there. Lee's mother had just bought the Chinese chip shop on the estate and she had known that she would get racial abuse for it was a part of their lives they had come to expect. She had not however expected it to happen quite so soon at school for she had not expected such cruelty from young children. In class on that first morning Jimmy had known that Lee would not be made to feel welcome for he remembered only too well his own first time as an outcast there. Mark Skelton was the school bully and Jimmy had known from the attitude he had shown when Lee had been introduced in class that day that he would be out for Lee's blood. Skelly was an out and out British bulldog that disliked any race but his own. Jimmy had been right to be worried for sure enough after school Skelly had chased Lee and he had thrown him down a big embankment at the back of the estate. He had taken Lee's new bag and he had emptied the contents onto the ground then he had placed the bag over his head and he had started to beat him with a baseball bat. Lee's first taste of British hospitality had been with a reign of blows that he had been able to feel but not see. Jimmy had heard the cries and he had raced to the scene of the beating.

He had thrown his chopper bike down onto the ground and he had jumped down just in time to stop Skelly from delivering the final blow to the new boy's head. Skelly had screamed out in anger as he had turned round to face whoever was crazy enough to try to stop him from killing the yellow bellied chink that lay quivering on the ground. Skelly was the school bully and he was not used to anyone getting in his way.

He had shut up when he saw that it was Jimmy for although Mark Skelton was hard he was nothing compared to his big brother who had warned him about messing with Jimmy Mack. Skelly threw the blood stained bat to the ground causing Lee to jump in fear as if expecting another reign of blows. Then he had sneered at Jimmy before climbing up the embankment with his mindless morons following closely behind him. Jimmy had bent down and he took the bag from Lee's battered head only to find two slanted eyes full of hate and despair staring right through him.

"Are you okay? It's alright they have gone now"

Lee hadn't said a word instead he had picked up a piece of glass from a broken bottle and he had lashed out at Jimmy and cut his wrist with it.

Then before Jimmy had been able to move his hand away the young Chinese boy had grabbed it and had pressed the cut wrist firmly against his own savaged arm. As their bloods had mingled together Lee had uttered just two words before passing out.

"Bwud bwuvvers"

Jimmy had picked up Lee's school things that were scattered over the ground. He had dusted them down and put them back into the schoolbag that he had taken from off Lee's throbbing head.

Then he had got Steve Smith to take both school bags and his bike home for him whilst he and Mark Flood struggled to drag Lee's unconscious body back up the embankment. From there they had taken the bloodied body of the new Chinese boy back to Jimmy's gaff to get him cleaned up before taking him home. Lee had come round to find Jimmy washing the blood from his arms and he winced in pain.

"My muwwer will kill me"

was all that he had said but Jimmy had assured him that he would be okay. Jimmy had also loaned him some pants and given him a clean shirt and he had wiped Lee's tattered bag down so that it didn't look half as bad as it had done as it lay on the ground at the embankment.

Lee had been grateful to the brave boy who had stood up to the bully and had probably saved his life which was why he had joined blood with him. Only his pride had been injured for Lee had learned to endure pain in his old country. His father had shown strong beliefs that others had not always believed in which had caused his family much trouble. Throughout his young life Lee's father had taught him how to dismiss pain. The beating that Skelly had given him had been superficial and had been no comparison to what had happened to his family in China. Lee's mother had brought Lee to England to find a safe haven. Yet on his first day at school he had made an enemy but in finding the enemy he had also made a very good friend. Lee had told Jimmy that an old Chinese saying was that 'an unasked for favour is the greatest gift of all' Jimmy had given that favour to Lee who would be eternally grateful to him. He also knew that one day he would be able to return the favour. By the time that Lee had eventually left Jimmy's house for his own it had been hard to detect that he had ever been involved in a scuffle at all. Only the slight limp that showed as he walked awkwardly home had indicated to anyone that Lee had hurt himself. Lee had managed to convince his mother that he had got his injuries playing football. Lee's mother seemed happy to find that Lee had fitted in with the new school so quickly even though she had been surprised that he had.

Jimmy and Lee had become great friends after that day which they had remained until Lee went to live with his uncle at the age of seventeen. Lee's uncle owned several clubs in Chinatown and had agreed that Lee was ready and old enough to go and live and work with him. Just before he left Lee had hugged Jimmy tightly then he took the hand that he had cut with the bottle and held it up in front of him.

"Wemember Jimmy awways bwood bwuvvers"
then Lee had held his fist above his heart to make the sign of a Chinese promise.

"Goodbye my fwend and thankyou"
Lee had said before he had walked over to the swankiest car that had ever been on the Hattersley council estate and managed to keep its wheels. Lee had got into the long white limousine with the blacked out windows and Jimmy remembered how he and the rest of the estate who had come out to wave him off had wondered just who Lee Won-king's uncle really was.

A BOOK OF FAVOURS

Chapter 3

"Grubs up"
said a screw as he slid a plastic tray through the bars to Jimmy.

"Enjoy"
then he chuckled out loud as he walked away. Jimmy looked at the food which he had no intention of touching for he knew how it worked on the inside. He could see the splinters of glass as they glistened in the sad excuse of mashed potatoes that were smeared over the plate. All that Jimmy had to do was to bide his time as he waited for Joseph to find his book of favours. They had to get the word out onto the street that Detective Inspector Rooney needed to be found. If they could locate the missing cop they would have Jimmy's missing alibi that would be enough to get him pardoned from the life sentence that he had just begun.

Jimmy left the untouched tray of food on the floor for the screw to collect later as he started to rack his brain to try to think where in the world Mike Rooney could be.

The first time that P.C. Mike Rooney had seen Jimmy Mack had been in 1989. Mike had just moved to Manchester from Sheffield and he had been working on an undercover police operation.

The word on the street was that gangs were competing

against each other to take over the doors on the pubs. They already had the clubs in the area and it had fast become big business. Whichever of the gangs held the doors had total control of the drugs that were being sold there. The doormen just needed to sniff out the dealers and order them off the premises then they could pick off their punters one by one. Everyone had to be searched and any illegal substances taken from them would be shared out later by the same ones that had confiscated them. Money from the so called protection that was going on through the doormen and money from the drug dealing made for a very lucrative business. The gorillas on the doors got to keep the spoils that were part of the perks of the job along with getting to bed all of the women that they wanted. The ones that were fickle enough to be turned on by a bit of muscle that is. Mike's undercover job had been quite easy for all he had to do was look and act like a loser and he even had police funds to buy his drinks and play on the machines.

He had been assigned to walk from pub to pub just keeping his eyes and ears open to what was going on and as a new face in town he had gone pretty well undetected. Looking like a loser had come really easy to Mike as he had just split up with his wife after coming home early one day to find her in bed with her driving instructor.

Mike had given the instructor some very good instructions of his own which had included a very sharp three point turn out of the bedroom and right down the stairs.

Then he had gone on to break the instructor's fingers on his left hand which he had known would have given him a painful reminder of that day every time that he tried to change gear. Luckily the injured adulterer had been persuaded at the station not to take any further action against P.C. Rooney as it had been thought that the adverse publicity might have damaged his career. As the instructor had been married with four children and had got three other women on the go he had taken the duty sergeant's advice. Everyone at the station had soon got to hear of Mike's bad luck so when a job became available in Manchester and the Superintendent had suggested that Mike might be the right candidate for the job he had taken it. The Super was a powerful man and it had been wise for Mike to have listened to him. Mike had blown all chances of getting back with his wife when he had assaulted her lover. She had put up with the violence that he had shown towards her when his job had got on top of him which had been one of the reasons for her to play away.

Mike's job had taken precious time away from him that he could have spent with his baby son and although Ben had got to the age of two Mike had never even spent a whole weekend with him.

Mike had not wanted to go back to live with his parents despite his mother pleading with him to do so. He had never felt that his father had wanted him around when he was younger which was why that he had never really felt comfortable or close to him as a loving son should do.

So at the age of twenty six Mike Rooney, the disgraced copper had walked away from his wife and his son and the town that he had lived in all of his life. He had left everything behind him and he had headed for the bright lights of Manchester. Mike had rented a small terraced house in the less dingy part of Levenshulme which was close to his station. It had two tiny bedrooms and a bathroom which had a sickly Avocado coloured suite and a toilet that didn't always flush.

It was sparsely furnished with sixties stuff and he had shared it with a dozen cockroaches that he thought would face eviction from him if they couldn't meet the rent. Mike had been on his first assignment doing the rounds of the pubs when he had first met Jimmy and he had hated him from the moment he had laid his eyes on him. Jimmy had been everything that Mike hadn't been. Both men were of similar ages but Jimmy had all of the success that Mike lacked. He had his own business, a fine looking son about the same age as Mike's own son but who he got to be with and a drop dead gorgeous wife. Mike had not even liked the way that Jimmy looked and he had been envious of his all year round tan and his expensive clothes.

He had not liked his cocky attitude or the huge amounts of gold jewellery that adorned his lean well toned body. In short Mike had been jealous of everything that Jimmy seemed to have. Mike had never been able to understand how Jimmy could have such a fabulous lifestyle by owning just one little pub set in a scruffy suburb of Manchester.

He hadn't understood how he had made his money but he had made his mind up from day one that Jimmy Mack was up to something and he had made it his job to nail him.

Mike had stood at the bar ordering a vodka and a bottle of tonic as he stared down the sexy blonde barmaid's never ending cleavage and wondering, like most of the men who drank in the Crown how on earth he could get down there. Jimmy had sat at the end of the bar and he had watched as Mike had sat and dribbled at the sight of Julie's heaving bosom. He had known that the new guy at the bar was no different from the rest of the guys who sat at the bar when Julie was working. It had never bothered him for he knew that she was totally dedicated to only him. Her tits had cost him over six thousand pounds and after two operations it had been money well spent for the punters came in from miles around just to look at them. Jimmy had watched as the new face at the bar had ordered a drink and had taken it over to the table near the toilets. He had watched with interest as the stranger had tipped his vodka down the back of his seat and Jimmy had sussed right then that the stranger must have been the filth for only a nonce or the filth would waste a glass of vodka the way that he had just done.

It wasn't the done thing to drink and buy tonic water especially in a pub in West Gorton for The Crown was what you might call a man's pub.

Jimmy had wondered what the law had been doing in his pub and he had laughed at the fact that they had thought no-one would suss the goon in the plain clothes.

Apart from meeting a gorgeous well stacked bird behind the bar and a full of himself landlord Mike had not found anything that would interest his mates at the station so he had finished his tonic water and left for the next pub on his beat. Jimmy picked up the phone to warn the landlord of the Honeycomb pub that the new rozzer was doing his rounds. It was a ring round service that all the local landlords used to report on trouble makers, machine bandits and dodgy notes. Jimmy quite liked the guy in the next pub and he knew that he had a lot more on show than he had.

Jimmy might have been the man but he ran the cleanest boozer in the area and even his spirit measures were legitimate. What Jimmy did out of sight was a totally different thing.

The screw returned to find Jimmy's untouched tray on the floor where he had left it and he had found it hard to hide his disappointment.

"I'll get you tomorrow you bastard"

he muttered under his breath just loud enough for Jimmy to hear then he smiled sarcastically and walked away. Jimmy got his head down for an early night for he had some busy times ahead of him. He needed to hear from Joseph that he had located the book of favours before Jimmy was thrown to the lions. He was woken up the next morning by a different screw with an equally perverse sense of humour.

"Shit"

shouted Jimmy as he opened his eyes to find a screw stood above him holding an empty bucket of what once was full of water. The contents of the bucket ran down Jimmy's face

"Sorry, I thought that you had passed out, I was bringing you round"

said the screw sarcastically. Jimmy made a mental note of the screws number and smiled. The screw handed Jimmy a mug of tea which Jimmy tried but then wished that he hadn't. Some clever bastard had thought it was funny to put salt in it instead of sugar but Jimmy swallowed it then took another mouthful just to piss the screw off. It worked, for the look on the screw's puzzled face more than made up for the two mouthfuls of salty tea that Jimmy had just taken.

"That was good" lied Jimmy.

"Don't suppose you have another cup do you"?

"No I haven't but I'm sure we can get you one when I take you to recreation later"

Jimmy was dreading being put with the other inmates. He needed to be put on a rule 32 until things were put right and he hoped that Joseph would soon be on his way over to the Crown to get things sorted for him.

Chapter 4

Joseph Royal was up bright and early the next day. He hadn't slept well and he had a lot of work ahead of him to prove his client's innocence and get him out of prison. The first thing that he did was to arrange a date for Jimmy's appeal then he went into his garage and picked up the items he needed from his tool bag. He grabbed a quick breakfast to set him up for the day making sure he drank several cups of coffee to keep him alert. Then with Jimmy's instructions fresh in his memory he double checked that he had all he needed. He picked up his briefcase and the bag he had packed in the garage then he left for the Crown to do what Jimmy had asked him to. When he reached the pub he was surprised to see old Tommy Proctor already outside picking up the dog ends before he swilled down the pavement. Tommy had worked unofficially for Jimmy for the last few years. He didn't get paid for it but he got drinks put in the book and he got to keep all the dimps that he found. Tommy collected the dog ends to make himself roll ups and he always managed to find enough to keep him in baccy for the week.

"Morning guv, how's Jimmy doing"?

"He's been better Tommy but that is why I am here to pick up a few things that he needs"

"Well Julie ain't here Guv but she'll be back before opening time"

"That's alright Tommy, Jimmy has told me what to get. He said to ask you for the key to the function room"

Tommy knew that the posh lawyer was kosher so he unlocked the front door and he invited him into the pub whilst he got the key that he had asked for. Joseph took the key from Tommy and assured him that he could manage on his own then he told him to get on with his cleaning. He had known that Julie wouldn't be there for Jimmy had told him that he would send her on a useless errand to get her out of the way. Julie would never realise what was going on and it would give Joseph the time alone that he needed to carry out Jimmy's instructions. He climbed the stairs to the first floor and walked down the corridor to the end room that he knew was where his task lay. He opened the door and turned on the lights for it was dark and dingy in the room despite being morning. The room smelt of must and stale smoke and Joseph pulled back a heavy curtain to get to a window. He was going to open a window to let a bit of fresh air in if only whilst he was there to stop himself from feeling sick. The window was firmly nailed down with six inch nails for added security and Joseph wondered how Health & Safety would feel about that. He tried the other two windows in the room to find they were all locked in a similar fashion so he eventually gave up. He closed the curtains and walked over to the gents toilets taking his tool bag with him.

He quietly unlocked the toilet door and walked in and then immediately locked the door behind him. He put his back to the door and started to walk on the tiles counting them as he did so. He counted eight tiles forward then three tiles to the left then he took out a chisel from his bag. He pulled out a pair of surgical rubber gloves and put them on then he started to chisel carefully at the grout that surrounded the tile that he had picked out. He took care not to make too much noise so as not to alert old Tommy and before long the grout was all gone and the tile was loose. Joseph prised the tile up taking great care not to break it and he breathed a sigh of relief as he spotted a brown paper package. The package was below the tile as Jimmy had said it would be and Joseph put the tile to one side and picked up the package. Although he knew the door was locked Joseph looked around him to make sure that he was completely alone. Then convinced that he was alone he started to open the package. Joseph's heart was beating fast as he looked into the bag. There were three books just as Jimmy had said there would be. A red book, a black book and the one he had come to fetch, the purple book. He pulled out the purple book and noticed that it had a small letter F on the front corner, F for favours. Then without even being tempted to look at the other two books Joseph put the package containing them back into the hole beneath the tile. He put the purple book that he had come to find safely in his inside pocket before taking out a tube of ready made grout. Then with surprising skills that Joseph had not even known that he had, he very carefully put some new grout back around the disturbed tile. For a lawyer he made a bloody good handyman and by the time he had cleaned up his mess it was hard to see that anything had ever been removed from the floor. Joseph knew that there would be no functions in Jimmy's absence so by the time there ever was another one the tile in the toilets would be well and truly fixed.

He checked that he had left no clues to his visit there, put away his tools and took off his gloves. Then he locked the doors behind him and took the keys back to Tommy who was busy rolling his days supply of fags.

"Thanks Tommy, tell Julie I will call her later"

"Okay Guv, give Jimmy my best and tell him I know he is

innocent and Charlie was me mate"

Joseph said that he would tell Jimmy then he left the pub before Julie returned. He looked around before getting into his car then he got in and drove twice around the block. Working for Jimmy Mack had made Joseph extra cautious and only when he was sure that he wasn't being followed did he head back to his place of work.

Joseph got back to his office where he instructed his secretary that he was not to be disturbed under any circumstances. He poured himself a black coffee then went into his office locking the door behind him. He took a long swig of coffee then loosened his tie as he sat at his big desk. His hand shook nervously as he took the favours book from out of his pocket and he opened the pages slowly, as if scared to see what he would find.

He knew that he had one very important call to make so he turned very quickly to the section labelled P. Jimmy had a great way of cataloguing, it was alphabetical with a difference and Joseph was amazed at what he was reading. Under the letter P there were papers, politicians, ports and police and the last section was probably the biggest in the book. Joseph was looking for prisons and he found them pretty quickly. Walton was on the list and Joseph picked up the phone and made his first call and within seconds he was speaking to the governor on his direct line. When Joseph was completely sure that he had the right person he said very simply what Jimmy had told him to say.

"I have a message from a friend concerning a favour, he said to say that the time has come"

There was an awkward silence that Joseph interrupted by saying

"Would you like to know the date"? Joseph asked

"No, that is not necessary – tell me what you want"

Joseph smiled as he told the governor that he would like the prisoner known as Jimmy Mack to be kept in solitary confinement until his imminent release.

"It is quite important to our mutual friend that he has your personal assurance that his friend will be well treated and that he will come to no harm whilst he is in your care"

"I will see to it at once, is that all"?

"Yes providing you do what I have just asked you to do then your debt will be written off, forever. Goodbye"
Joseph Royal took out a red pen and put a thick line through the prison governor's name after he had written the date on it.

Governor Atkins gave a long sigh of relief as he picked up the internal telephone to relay the instructions he had just been given. He spoke to the same guard that had poured the cold water over Jimmy that morning and explained to him that the prisoner known as Mackintyre should be treated with the utmost respect right up to his release. He told the guard that under no circumstances should this prisoner come to any harm at all. He was adamant that if anything should befall Jimmy that he would hold anyone on his watch totally and personally responsible. The screw realised from the urgency in the governor's voice that he had made a very silly mistake and he instantly regretted having ever done it. Governor Atkins put down the phone and he poured himself a rather large scotch which he knocked back in one. At last it was over at a lot lower price than he had ever imagined that he would have to pay. Tears filled his eyes as he realised that at long last he could put behind him the terrible events that had taken place at 'The Pink Flamingo'. It felt as though a big weight had just been lifted from his shoulders.

Jeremy Atkins had been the deputy governor at Strangeways prison when he had fallen into debt to a total stranger that he had never even met.

His wife and family were still living down South in a small hamlet in Warwickshire until their house was sold and until Jeremy had moved to his new post in Liverpool. Jeremy was tired for he had worked long hours trying to impress his superiors. He felt like an outsider for most of his colleagues were from the North but more than anything he had been very lonely. Jeremy remembered only too well the night he had been travelling back to Strangeways coming back from a meeting in Stockport. He had been heading back towards town on the A6 when his car had stopped in traffic at a set of lights. He looked out of his window to see a seedy looking shop with cheap pink lights flashing intermittently in the upstairs window that had caught his attention.

He was thinking how cheap and nasty it had looked when he had seen the girl. She had long dark hair and she was wearing the shortest of skirts that complimented her long shapely legs. She wore tight P.V.C thigh length boots that looked like they had been sprayed on and as she moved Jeremy could have sworn that he got a glimpse of her pink panties. Just before the lights turned to green it seemed as though she looked his way and she smiled a beautiful smile at him.

Jeremy could not explain why he did what he had done next for instead of driving straight on he started to indicate and he drove round the block and pulled up at the side of the massage parlour. The girl watched as Jeremy turned the engine off and then realising that she had just turned his engine on she turned to walk in the door and she had beckoned Jeremy to follow her. He stood on the first step and looked up to see the lovely young lady about seven steps above him. From where he stood he could see right up her short skirt and he realised that the pink he had glimpsed was definitely not her panties. He went hard at the sight of her naked private bit and he became very excited at the thought of the immorality of it all. She went through a door at the top of the stairs where she waited for Jeremy to join her as she knew that he would.

She smiled at him as he joined her and he was surprised to see that she looked a lot older than he had first imagined her to be. Jeremy hadn't minded for every inch of her beautiful body exuded sex and Jeremy wanted her desperately. He handed her the fifty pounds that she had asked for and then he followed her submissively into one of the rooms.

The room was dimly lit and it had just a single massage bed against the wall. There was a small wash hand basin and a wicker tray half filled with new condoms next to the bed. The used condoms lay at the bottom of a matching wicker waste basket half covered with paper tissues.

As she started to remove his clothes for him every sense of decency left his body and the next twenty five minutes proved to be the most exciting of Jeremy's full fifty one years on this earth. The girl taught him to enjoy erogenous zones that he never knew had existed. After they had finished the young woman who called herself Charmaine opened the door only to be confronted by her next punter. He was a small time crook called John Docherty who had been released from Strangeways prison only that very morning. The same place that Jeremy had been on his way back to.

John had just finished a six month stretch that he had taken for Mick McCardle and Mick's brother had met John as he had left the prison. He had given him a wad of cash that John had gone straight to the nearest boozer with. Then he had drank all he could afford making sure that he had enough money left for a taxi, a blow job and a good Ruby Murray afterwards. He could barely stand when he reached the Flamingo and almost fell onto Jeremy as he was leaving.

John might have been drunk but not too drunk to not recognise one of the toffs who had kept him banged up for the last six months.

"Well if it ain't the old governor, you dirty bleeder wait till the lads hear about this"

Jeremy's colour left his face. He knew that he could not afford to be caught like this and he made a quick dash for the door. As he did so John made a grab for his collar and Jeremy pushed the drunken man away from him. John had drunk far too much Stella to stay on his feet and could not stop himself from falling. He fell down the whole set of stairs and cracked his head sharply on the wall at the bottom. Jeremy looked on in horror at the still lifeless body that lay at the foot of the stairs and he couldn't move.

"Is he.....dead"?

Charmaine nodded as she put the latch on the front door and turned off the lights. Crystal one of the other girls emerged from the other room where she had just been having a quick wash.

Her last punter had left five minute earlier and she had told the drunk to wait for five minutes whilst she got ready. The crash had caused her to come running out of the room.

"What the fucks going on here"

she said as she looked down to see her next punter lying behind the bottom door.

"Jesus Charmaine, what the fuck have you done"?

Charmaine didn't answer, her instead she went to the phone and called Jimmy Mack hoping that he would know what to do. Jimmy had taken the call on his personal line and he looked at Julie as he picked up the receiver. Julie didn't need to be told she left the room Jimmy's business was just that. Julie had learned a long time ago not to ask questions for what you didn't know, you couldn't tell. Jimmy listened as Charmaine explained to him what had just happened.

"Who is there right now"?

"Just me, Crystal, the stiff and the guy from the nick"

"Right keep the door locked and your mouths shut. I'll send someone round to clean it up and I'll tell the boss what has happened. Now put the punter on the phone that's a good girl, you have done a good job"

Charmaine handed Jeremy the phone and watched as he listened to Jimmy and just nodded.

"Yes I understand, thank-you"

Jeremy handed the phone back to Charmaine who nodded as she took one last instruction from Jimmy before hanging up. Then she led Jeremy down the stairs both making sure that they did not stand on the poor stiff lying at the foot of the stairs. Jeremy tried not to look at the corpse's face as he squeezed past his body to get out into the fresh night air. He walked onto the street and threw up against the wall as he thought of the life he had just taken. It was a sad worthless life that had spent the last six months waiting for freedom only to have it taken from him so cruelly. Jeremy's hands shook as he opened the car door. He quickly got in and drove away slowly taking care not to bring attention to himself. He drove to the Showcase cinema complex and bought himself a ticket for one of the movies that was showing and he went in to watch it just as the voice on the phone had told him to.

Five minutes after Jeremy had left the parlour a white carpet van pulled up outside it and two large Nigerian chaps got out. They rapped on the door which was opened by Charmaine who had been keeping watch as she emptied John Docherty's pockets.

One of them threw a piece of carpet onto the stairs which they then threw the corpse on as though he was a dead dog. Then with very little effort they carried it out between them and threw it roughly into the back of the van. Less than one hour later the van, complete with carpet and corpse had been crushed to nothing at Paddy O'Reilly's scrapyard.

Charmaine and Crystal opened the parlour up again for it was coming up to throwing out time from the pubs and they expected and hoped for a lot more punters. What had just happened there with the stiff had been forgotten and it would never be spoken of to anyone. It had been sorted out and none of them wanted the law sniffing around so it would be forgotten. The whole business had been well and truly brushed under the carpet.

Chapter 5

The screw looked through Jimmy's cell bars to find him sitting up looking anxious. He cleared his throat before speaking.

"Looks like you have friends in high places pal"

"What do you mean"?

"Well put it this way, the party we were going to throw for you will have to be postponed for a while. Looks like you have a guardian angel"

Jimmy knew full well how the party would have gone he had organised so many of them from the outside and he was glad that Joseph had managed to come through for him.

"Oh yeah, the governor will be down to see you in a short while so look smart will you"

Jimmy snarled at the guard for he was able to now and he looked forward to paying him back. He knew that the governor would want to please him and he knew exactly what he would ask him for. His mouth was parched and he still had a nasty taste in his mouth from the horrible tea.

It wasn't long before Jimmy had his wish for the governor arrived about fifteen minutes later when Jimmy had asked for a little more courtesy from the guards, two cups of tea and a shaker of salt.

The governor assured Jimmy he would do all he could to make his stay a pleasant one and he ordered the guard to fetch the teas and the salt.

He was quite curious about the salt but sent for it nonetheless. The screw knew exactly why Jimmy had asked for salt and he watched as Jimmy poured loads of it into one of the cups of tea he had just brought to him. Jimmy picked up one of the cups and gestured to the guard to pick up the other which he reluctantly did. He smiled as he watched the screw pull his face as he swallowed the drink just before he ran to the toilets to spew his ring up. Jimmy raised his own cup up to him as he ran.

"Cheers mate. Always remember what goes around comes around"

Jimmy lay back on his bed and waited contentedly for Joseph to visit and hopefully let him know that Mike Rooney had been found. Once he had his alibi Jimmy knew that he could go home to his lovely Julie. The thought of his beautiful wife made Jimmy suddenly go hard and he shifted it about in his pants until he was comfortable.

Jimmy remembered the very first time that he had ever seen Julie and how he had known then that she was the one for him. She had been playing a game of pool with a girl friend in the Sportsman bar and she had the attention of every guy in the place fixed firmly on her.

She was just nineteen years old and she had a cute little figure that she wasn't afraid of showing to anyone.

She had worn a short denim skirt that allowed everyone at the bar to see her crotch each time she took a shot from their end of the table. Jimmy had never seen so many guys interested in the game before and he had joined them and took in the view himself.

He was even more impressed when she played from the other end which gave him a good look down her cute little yellow vest she wore. Julie had not been a big girl then in the boobs department but she filled a tasty 34b bra. She also had long blonde hair that glistened like gold and the deepest blue eyes that he had ever looked into. Up until that day Jimmy had never really had time for girlfriends for he had been far too busy making money. He had moved back to Gorton and he was living in a small terraced house that he claimed that he rented. In fact Jimmy actually owned the house along with another twelve others on the street. He had invested the monies that he had earned from the scams at school into more expensive stock that he had sold from his lock up. Jimmy had become the youngest loan shark in the country then he had advanced on to drugs which had brought him the even bigger returns. When a man that he knew had suggested that he put his money into property he had done just that and he had snapped up the terraced properties in a run down condition at just three grand each. Jimmy had a guy who worked in the planning department at the town hall who owed big gambling debts to Jimmy. Because of the hold that he had on the guy in planning all of his applications for grants were immediately approved giving him eighty per cent grants to modernise each of them with. Jimmy had a firm of builders that also owed him money from gambling debts so they did all of the works for even less money that he got from the council. Jimmy was not allowed to sell the properties for at least five years but that hadn't bothered him because he had just stuck D.S.S. tenants in the properties and charged them silly rents. With the money that he got from the rents Jimmy sent lads abroad to pick up cheap booze and fags that he sold to the local pubs and before long he had built up quite a substantial patch.

Jimmy bought a case of spirits for fifteen quid and sold them on for thirty making a very nice profit then the sleeves of cigs made him a fiver a go. Jimmy had four good lads driving for him and he was making a turnover of ten grand a week. His overheads including wages came to less than two grand so at the tender age of twenty two he was earning over forty grand a year tax free. Every now and again Jimmy would do one of the rounds with the lads just to make sure that there were no dodgy dealings. He had been on one such round at the Sportsman pub one day when he had first seen the delectable Julie and he was glad that he had chosen the right route. Jimmy made a space for himself at the bar and he continued to watch Julie from behind. The girl she was playing pool with gave Julie the nod that she had an admirer behind her and Julie turned round to check him out.

He could tell by the way she took in his Hugo Boss suit and noticed the sparkling diamond ring that he wore on his little finger that she liked what she saw. She could well have been impressed by Jimmy's dark and mysterious good looks and his sexy physique also. Jimmy was tall, lean and tanned with enough muscles to turn a girl on. He had dark eyes and a stunning smile that was set off by his perfect white teeth. Julie had deliberately leaned across him as she called out to the barman to get her two more bottles of Budweiser then she pulled a fiver from out of her bra to pay for the beers.

Jimmy took the fiver from her that was still warm from being next to her breasts and very gently he shoved it back inside her bra. Jimmy felt the tingles run up his arm as his hand brushed against her soft flesh.

"I'll get those"

"Thanks, I'm Julie Maddox and this is my friend Angel"

"Hi, they call me Jimmy, Jimmy Mack"

The bartender passed two ice cold bottles of Budweiser over the bar to him and he held his hand up to refuse Jimmy's money when it was offered. Julie noticed that, she had never seen the guy before and she didn't know who he was but what she could see was that he was wadded. Julie needed looking after in a way that she thought she deserved to be and she could tell that Jimmy was a guy who could give it to her and keep her happy. All she had to do was make him want her and she wiggled her cute little arse in his direction as she took her next shot. Jimmy watched in admiration as Julie finished off her game of pool, wanting her more and more with every shot that she took.

By the time she had potted the black which had taken an awful lot of stretching over the table Jimmy was so hard that it hurt him. Julie's mother had always tried to give her daughter useful advice on men.

"Don't offer it on a plate Julie and never do it on your first date that way they will always come back for more"

Jimmy grabbed hold of Julie's hand as she put the cue down and he led her out to the car park. He pulled her over to his transit van that was parked outside the door and he opened the back doors on it. Then he climbed up and held out his hand to Julie so he could pull her up too.

He closed the doors behind them then he pushed Julie down onto the blanket that had been covering the crates of booze. He lay above her as he kissed her hard and strong and before long her knickers were off and her well tanned legs were around his shoulders. The crates of bottles clinked hard in the back of the van as Jimmy shagged Julie who cried out loud as they both climaxed together. Jimmy opened a sleeve of Bensons that lay on the floor at the side of him and opened a packet. He took out two cigarettes, lit them both then popped one into Julie's mouth.

"Won't your boss mind you just taking his fags like that"?

"Nah, he's not a bad guy anyway it's one of the perks of the job"

Jimmy was his own boss but he always kept that quiet. As far as everyone was concerned Jimmy worked for a Mr Big and he was well connected. Jimmy finished his fag and then looked at the very expensive watch on his wrist.

"Bleeding hell, I've got to go"

He picked Julie's knickers up from the floor of the van and passed them to her. Then he had kissed her before getting up to go.

"Is that it then"?

said Julie, feeling disappointed and thinking that she should have taken her mother's advice.

"No just one thing don't ever wear a skirt that short to play pool in"

"I thought you liked it"

"I do but I'm not having my girl showing her arse to every man and his dog"

He winked at her and handed her a card with his telephone number on.

"Call me tonight"

Then with those words he helped her out of the van and whistled for his mate who had been stood at the back door keeping an eye on their stock. Then without even a backward glance they drove off out of the car park. Julie went back inside to find Angel chatting happily to a big Afro Caribbean guy at the bar so she left her to it and headed for home. Julie was excited for not only was he good looking but he was a bloody good screw too. He was loaded from the looks of him and he made Julie feel like no guy had ever done before. As soon as Julie got in she looked through her mam's old record collection until she found the one she was looking for. Then she put it on the radiogram and played it over and over again. Julie's mother came home from work to hear the sounds of 'Jimmy Mack' being played at full belt and it brought back a lot of memories for her. It had been one of her favourite songs when she had been going out with Julie's dad and it took her back to some of the good times.

When Julie had been born Keith Maddox had left them

both in order that he could get on with his life claiming that he was too young to be tied down. Sandra Maddox had brought her daughter up on her own and she had worked two or three part time jobs in order to give Julie a good lifestyle.

Julie had never been on free school meals and had always had the latest fashion. Sandra had made sure that her girl would want for nothing. Julie and her mother were more like friends and Julie could tell her about anything so as soon as she got in from work Julie started to tell her about the guy she had met. She told her how smart and good looking he was and how cocky he seemed. In fact she told her about everything but the shag in the back of his van.

"He asked me to call him mam, so how long should I wait"?

"A good few hours at least or maybe even tomorrow"

"Tomorrow! You must be joking what about if I love the guy"

Sandra was shocked to hear her daughter talk about love for she was the one who had always said that she would never fall in love. She had always said that she wanted to travel the world and see a bit of life before settling down to one man. She had said that she would not get married until she was at least forty and here she was suddenly claiming to be in love with someone that she had only just met.

"Well if you think you love him girl perhaps you should call him now"

Julie jumped up quickly and she gave her mother a big hug then she went back into the hall to make the call to Jimmy Mack.

She called the number on the card but got no reply so she continued to call it every ten minutes until the guy she had met at the bar that day eventually answered it. Jimmy smiled as he remembered Julie telling him about this night over and over again.

They used to tell it to D.J. who loved the way that his parents could still seem to be so in love as they had been when they first met. Jimmy loved Julie all the more for telling him how eager she had been to call him on that first night. He remembered coming in from doing his rounds and running to the phone in case he missed her call and he remembered how nice it had been to hear her voice. He had invited Julie round to his house that night and she had stayed just as he had hoped that she would. She stayed the next night and the next and within one week she had moved in completely and they were both madly in love.

It had been a classic whirlwind romance that had got stronger with time. Now eighteen years later Julie was still the most precious thing in Jimmy's life and as he sat alone in his cell Jimmy thought that he needed Julie more than he had ever done before. Thinking of Julie and the good times that they had shared together made Jimmy realise just how much he did love her and the tears started to well up in his eyes. His thoughts travelled from that very first date and the ten minutes that they had spent in the back of the van right up to her tearful face as she watched him being taken from the courts. He remembered how delighted he had been when Julie had told him that she was pregnant and how they had arranged to get married before Julie put too much weight on. Jimmy had idolised Julie and he would have married her whether she had been up the tub or not, the fact that she had been just brought the wedding on a bit earlier.

Probably the best day of their lives had been when their darling baby son had been born. David James Mackintyre had entered the world on 27th May 1987 weighing a grand eight pounds six ounces. D.J. as they had nicknamed him had inherited Jimmy's chiselled chin and Julie's brilliant blue eyes and to Jimmy and Julie he was the most perfect baby in the world. Jimmy felt as though he could touch D.J.'s podgy little fingers as they were on that day and tears filled his eyes as he thought of them.

Joseph Royal turned up at the prison to see Jimmy at just the right time before Jimmy had the chance to start feeling sorry for him-self.

A BOOK OF FAVOURS

Chapter 6

Joseph explained to Jimmy that he had used up about ten favours from the book and that the word was out on the street to look for Mike Rooney.

"If he is out there Jimmy we will find him I can guarantee it"

The date for the appeal was for in ten days time and Joseph was confident that they would have located Mike Rooney before then. The other good news was that he had put a visiting order in for Julie who would be in to see Jimmy the next day. Jimmy cheered up at that news and Joseph took advantage of his good mood to ask him a few more questions.

"Jimmy, think very carefully. I know that we have been through it lots of times before but let us try it one more time. There might just be something that you remember that could help at your appeal"

Jimmy lit up a cigarette that Joseph had brought in for him and thought back to the night of old Charlie Reeds murder.

"Did you see Charlie on the night of his murder"?

"Yes, he came in before he went on his shift he had a pint of Guinness and had a bet on the dogs for the seven thirty. Then he finished his pint and said that he would be in the next day to pick up his winnings and left"

"Who else was in the pub at the time, can you think"?

"Well Julie was behind the bar and Tommy was collecting

pots. There were a couple of young lads playing on the fruit machine and the usual tea time lot were sat at the bar. Old Beryl and her dog were sat by the door and a couple of strangers came in and played a few of games of pool for about half an hour then sat in the corner swapping stories.

Christ Joseph it's hard enough to remember yesterday never mind then"

"Okay so that was the very last time you saw Charlie"

"Yes it was, I promise"

"Right then what about the knife, when did you last have it and how did it end up in the old man's back with your prints all over it"?

Jimmy thought long and hard but he could not remember all he knew was that he hadn't done the murder so it must have been a set up.

He had no idea who would hate him so much to do this to him then he suddenly remembered something.

"It was in the office. I remember it now. D. J. had a tack stuck under his trainer and I took it out with my knife"

"When was that Jimmy, think"

"Probably a couple of days before old Charlie got done in"

"Good, now can you remember what you did with the knife"?

"Yeah I took the tack out then I put the knife back in the drawer and I locked it like I always do"

"So the knife was locked away in your drawer"

Jimmy nodded, he was sure that he would have locked the drawer.

"So who else has a key to your drawer Jimmy"?

"Nobody does that's the trouble, only me"

No matter how hard Jimmy tried he could not remember taking the knife back out of the drawer. Jimmy's sense of security was usually pretty good and he had lots of different hiding places, if anything he was too careful.

"Okay forget the knife for now what about your alibi. What were you doing Jimmy at the time of Charlie's murder"?

"What was the time Joseph"?

"Well it was just after ten in the evening when the station got a call off Charlie. He had heard noises and said that he had a prowler in the yard. By the time a car got there at ten thirty Charlie was dead but still warm"

"I would have been on my way back from New Mills"

"Was there anybody with you or did anybody see you"? Jimmy shook his head he hadn't seen a soul or taken his mobile.

"No-one saw me. I was supposed to meet a guy at the train station but he didn't show"

Jimmy could have kicked himself for being so careful. Mike Rooney had called him earlier that day to arrange a meeting with a guy from the drugs squad. It was a new squad that was operating out of Macclesfield and Mike had told them that they were ready to hit Jimmy's patch in the next couple of weeks. Mike had told him that it was to be a covert operation code named Operation Sandstorm and they intended to take no prisoners. Jimmy had listened to what Mike had to say for he was pretty much in the know since being made up to Detective Inspector and his information usually proved to be useful.

Mike had been the local copper on the beat when he had first moved to Manchester about fourteen years before. Now he was a D.I. and he carried quite a bit of clout. Unfortunately in the last ten months he had also become a coke head and he owed Jimmy more favours than he could ever afford to pay even on a senior officer's wage. Mike had offered Jimmy information on the drugs deal in exchange for a clean sheet and Jimmy had been happy to agree to it. He had known that Mike would have run his slate up just as much again within a month or two for he had a bad drugs habit that he needed to feed.

Jimmy's plan had been much bigger than just getting to know the team who would be watching him. His plan was to watch them and to wait until they did a bust and then take the lot of it from right under their noses. If they were to do several stake-outs and busts Jimmy would let them do it and then take the spoils and the information for himself. It would have been worth wiping Mike's slate clean albeit for a short while. Mike had insisted that Jimmy should go alone for the meeting and that he should tell no-one of his plans not even Julie. Julie had never asked anything about Jimmy's business and she had never even wanted to know and Jimmy preferred it that way.

She would share the spoils with him and she would rub his brow when he was tired but she would never ask where any of the cash they had came from. Jimmy had sat in and watched 'The Bill' on the television with Julie then he had set off for his meeting at New Mills train station. He had got there at nine thirty and had waited patiently for the other car to arrive as planned. The car was to have flashed at Jimmy then when he flashed back the contact was to walk over to Jimmy's car and pass him the list of names and faces. He had waited until five to ten then left for home not telling a soul where he had been. Even at the trial Jimmy had not been able to say where he had been that night for it would have involved Mike Rooney and Jimmy was not a grass. Jimmy couldn't understand what had happened to Mike and he was worried that he had been caught up in something big. If Jimmy would have known that Mike would disappear he could have got another alibi which was why it was important for Mike to be found. He was glad that people were looking for him on the streets.

"Don't worry Jimmy if Mike is still in Manchester we will

locate him in the next twenty four hours, trust me on that"
Jimmy felt a lot better now that he knew that he was safe
inside and he was looking forward to seeing Julie the next
day to re-assure her that he would soon be out by her side
again.

A BOOK OF FAVOURS

Chapter 7

Mike Rooney scratched hard at his itching crotch as he lay cramped on a stinking old armchair in a dirty hovel of a room. He was being put up by someone that he knew who lived in a high rise block of flats in the lovely suburb of Ardwick Green in North Manchester.

His hostess was one-eyed Betty an old Tom that he had probably caught the crabs off that he was currently host to. He got up and walked over to the sink to try to find a cup clean enough to drink out of but he was out of luck. The sink was piled high with dirty pots that looked as if they had been there for weeks. He picked up a mug and wiped out the furry mould with his finger before running it under the tap. He turned the kettle on and went to take a pee in the badly stained bowl of the bog and wondered what the hell he was doing in such a dirty hell hole. Then he remembered that he had no choice for he was in hiding big style. He had done a really bad thing and he had no idea what he should or could do next. His plan had gone terribly wrong for all he had intended to do was to fit Jimmy Mack up on an aggravated burglary charge or at the very worst attempted manslaughter.

Once Jimmy had been banged up Mike could have started to get on with his life again. He could get help with his drug problem and owe no money out to anyone and maybe even settle down. The plan had all gone pear shaped but Mike had not reckoned on the guilt or the nightmares that were tearing him apart. Mike had never wanted to kill old Charlie that is why he had stuck Jimmy's knife into a part of his back that he knew would not be fatal to him. He had even made enough noise feigning a break in so that Charlie could phone the police to make sure that someone could be with him just after Mike had left. Mike felt sick as he remembered the frightened look on old Charlie's face as he had turned to look at his attacker. Over the years Mike had sat and spent time in the pub with Charlie buying him the odd pint of Guinness or two and discussing the horses with him. The old man had been a very good source of information to Mike without actually realising it and the poor old sod had even regarded him as a mate. Jimmy's knife had slid easily into the little guy who had been no more than skin and bones and he had cried out in pain as it had entered his body. Mike could still see the look of questioning on Charlie's face as he had watched the brick coming down to end his life.

Mike had panicked when his plan had gone wrong and he had no alternative but to get rid of the only person who knew what he had done. He had picked up a full size brick that lay by his side on the floor and he had smashed it hard against Charlie's fragile skull. Charlie had cried out one last time before Mike had delivered the final blow on him. He remembered watching his father killing a rabid dog that way and Mike had continued to smash Charlie's skull until his gurgling sounds had finally stopped. Then Mike had left Charlie lying in a pool of his own blood as he calmly peeled off his surgical gloves and headed quickly for home.

Mike had quickened his pace as he went down the back entries that led to his house and all the time he was wondering what his next step would be. He entered his house quickly and quietly then locked the door behind him as he drew his curtains but left the lights off. He took two bin liners from the kitchen cupboard and took them upstairs with him to the bathroom. He cursed as he looked down to see the old man's blood splattered on his shoes and his pants. He undressed quickly as he ran the bath water and he put everything he had been wearing including his watch into the bin liner which he tied up then put into the second bag. Then he took a chair and stood on it as he pushed the black bag into the attic with other bags of Christmas decorations. Mike had climbed down after closing the hatch before getting into the bath where he tried to clean away his sins. But no matter how hard Mike had scrubbed his skin with the loofah he could not get rid of the memory of the despicable deed he had done. Mike thought about the implications of what he had done and realised that he was in a no win situation. If he handed himself in at his own station and explained that it was a set up that had gone wrong he would have been labelled a bent copper and he would have been sent down for Charlie's manslaughter. Mike thought of the many faces that he sent down in his own climb up the promotion ladder and he knew that he wouldn't last a week inside.

Then he thought about Jimmy Mack who had been put away for a murder that he did not commit and he knew that if Jimmy thought for one moment that Mike had set him up that he would be a dead man. All that he could hope for was that he could remain undetected for as long as he could and then he could try to slip out of the country. Once he was dressed Mike started to carry out his plan of action. First he made a call to the station to ask to take three weeks holiday.

He had explained that his mother was not well and that he was going to stay with her for a while. The duty sergeant took the message and had been quite relieved to hear that

Mike was finally taking some time off.

He hadn't been himself for the last few months and the strain of his promotion was starting to take its toll. On top of that they had just had a vicious murder on their patch and the sergeant had thought that D.I. Rooney could do without knowing that especially whilst his mother was ill.

Mike ended the call and then phoned his mother who was pleased to hear from him as usual.

"Hiya mum I'm just phoning to let you know that I am off on holiday. A couple of mates from work have invited me to go to Greece with them for a couple of weeks so I'm all packed and ready to go.

"Oh that will be nice for you son"
said his mother sweetly thinking how nice it was to hear that her son had friends. She had worried so much about him over the years for he had never mentioned friends or girl friends and he very rarely got to see Ben, their grandson. She thought that he had never really got over the split with Patsy despite his insistence that he had.

"Is dad there"?
he asked nervously, he had spent a life time of trying to please his dad but he never felt as though he had.

"No son he is out playing golf but I'll tell him you called. Have you spoken to Ben recently"?

"No mum but I might just give him a call and see how he is doing"
The last time that Mike had spoken to his father the conversation had got very heated and Mike had slammed the phone down on him. He had only spoken to his father that time because his mother had not been in. He didn't like the way that he had criticised him for not seeing his son or how he didn't call his mother as often as he should. Mike didn't know if he would ever see his dad again and he had wanted to make amends.

"Tell dad I am sorry for putting the phone down the way I did"

"I will son and make sure that you have a good holiday. Goodbye son"

"Goodbye mother. I love you"

Mike cradled the phone in his hand long after his mother had gone. He wanted to call her back and tell her what he had done and let her help to make it better like she had always done for him in the past.

One thing that Mike had always known was that his mother had loved him unconditionally even if his father hadn't. Mike had one more call to make before he took off and he slowly pressed the numbers to call his ex wife, Patsy. He needed to ask her about Ben and he needed to make his peace with her. There had been far too many things left unsaid.

"Hello"

answered a young voice that Mike sensed was his teenage son.

"Is your mother there"?

asked Mike in a soft voice hoping that Ben might know who it was.

"Just a minute please, dad there's a man on the phone asking for mum how long will she be"?

Mike put the phone down wondering why he had called in the first place Patsy had a new life and Ben had a new dad and Mike knew that he had no right to intrude into their lives so he had hung up instead He had been out of their lives much too long for that. He took out a pen and a piece of paper and he wrote a letter to his solicitor that he put in a stamped envelope. Before he sealed the envelope he bent down and pulled a letter from under the set of drawers which he put into it. Mike packed himself a small overnight bag and made sure that he had his credit card. He left a note for the milkman to cancel the milk then he locked up his house and left, posting his letter before he got into his car. He drove to Piccadilly train station and parked his car long stay then he jumped on a 211 bus to Ardwick Green to try to find one eyed Betty. Just as he had expected she was sat on a wall next to the Apollo theatre waiting for her drunken punters. Betty was the wrong side of fifty but looked much older. Her missing eye had been gouged out by Dick Sewell or Dick Sewers as he was better known for he was the scum of the earth.

He had been her pimp and she had very foolishly tried to rip him off one night when she had been short of cash and short of punters. Dick had used Betty as a warning to his other girls and he had reduced her to becoming a second class tom. Betty worked the back alleys and the bookies now and she worked for peanuts. She still had her fair share of punters though for when Betty took her teeth out she was said to give the best blow job in Manchester.

"Guvnor, how the hell are you"?
Betty shouted, excited to see a friendly face. Mike shushed her quickly.

"I need a place for a few days Betty"

"Are you in trouble Guv"?

"Only the woman kind Betty, is there any other"?
Betty laughed, of course she would put him up, she would be glad of the company. It was good for her to have her own place but it got pretty lonely at night in her high rise apartment for she had no friends.

She had time a lot of time for Mike Rooney for he had let her off a few times over the years for a bit of useless information when he had been a mere bobby on the beat. She would even throw in a bit of sex if he wanted it, on the house of course. Betty walked with her head held high in contrast to Mike who had followed her sheepishly till they reached her flat. The flat was on the forth floor of a high rise block and was supposed to be for over sixties but Betty's social worker had managed to get her in there. The lift, like the public telephone had been vandalised by yobs so they climbed up three flights of urine soaked stairs. Betty's front door was protected by three sets of locks which made Mike smile for one swift kick would have put the actual wood of the door itself through. They entered the flat to be greeted by the worst smell that Mike had ever known with the exception of that from a three week old corpse that he had found once. The stench in the apartment actually made the earlier stairwell experience seem quite pleasant in comparison. Mike had needed a hide out and he had been so mixed up and confused that after sharing three bottles of White Lightening cider with Betty on that first night he had ended up in her bed.

Only once during his stay had Mike sunk to such low levels and it was the one time that caused him to catch crabs. Mike scratched furiously at his bollocks until they were sore. Betty had promised to bring back lotion for him but all she ever brought back with her was fags and booze. Mike desperately needed a bath for he had felt dirty in more ways than one so he took the pile of dirty washing out of the bathtub and threw it onto the floor. A beetle shot from beneath where the clothes had been and Mike drowned it in the cold water. He scooped it out of his water and flushed it down the loo which was just about flushing then he took a bath whilst Betty was out earning. Throughout the day Betty hung around looking for work at the local bookies because it was warmer than on the streets and she knew who had a few quid and who didn't. She would wait for some old geezer to have a good win on the horses and then she would pounce on him. Betty had no disillusions about herself anymore but she also knew where to hang about. She had never been able to choose her men even when she had two eyes. She knew that she stood a better chance of pulling the punters when they were either pissed or flushed so it was the bookies by day and the boozers by night. She liked having Mike around for the company but he was starting to cost her and half of the tricks she did went towards his keep. Betty didn't know what was troubling Mike but she knew that he was in more trouble than he was letting on. She had listened to him screaming out in the middle of the night and she was concerned at the weight he had lost since she had last seen him. Mike was on coke and Betty had managed to get him a few lines but she earned nowhere near enough money to feed his habit. Betty put her lipstick on, licked her lips then put on her sunglasses to hide her missing eye. Then she put the tenner that she had just earned down her bra and went out to look for her next punter.

"Cheers my love"

shouted out the seventy two year old guy who was sat on the toilet with his pants still hanging around his ankles and a big smile on his face.

Betty sat in the bookies for almost another hour with no luck and she had just been getting ready to leave when the Fitton brothers walked in.

She listened carefully as she heard Mike Rooney's name being mentioned but she had said nothing. Billy Fitton had been just about to ask the old hag in the corner but he had been put off by her scent as he approached her then his brother had given him the nod and they had left together. Betty found a big dimp on the floor and she asked Mike Evans for a light.

"What did that bag of shite want"?

"They were looking for some copper called Mike Rooney and it must be important because it is worth a ton to anyone with information. Mike Evans looked down at the Racing

Post at the page that was open and pointed to one of the runners.

"Look at that for a coincidence Mickey Rooney is running in the five o clock at Chepstow with odds of fifty to one. If I had a ton I know where I'd be putting it"

Betty looked at the paper. Mike Evans wasn't lying for once, the horse was running that afternoon and Betty was sorely tempted by the odds. She wasn't that good at maths but she knew a hundred quid at fifty to one would mean a long time off the streets. Betty didn't like a grass but it was three hours to that race so she decided to go home and see what Mike had to say about it all before handing him in.

Mike lay soaking in the bath contemplating suicide but he didn't have the balls to keep his head under the water for long enough to do it. He knew that he couldn't stay at Betty's place for much longer for it was filthy and he was slowly losing his sanity there.

He needed money to get away and he desperately needed to score. He looked down in disgust at his pubes that were alive with wildlife and he scrubbed so hard with carbolic soap that his dick nearly fell off. He picked up a dirty towel from the filthy floor and he carefully patted himself dry. He needed that lotion to put an end to his itching, he needed a cigarette and a drink but most of all he needed a fix. Betty had been gone for more than three hours and she had promised to bring him something back. Mike was getting agitated and he didn't know if he would be able to wait for her. Mike cursed Jimmy Mack for getting him hooked on the shit in the first place. He hadn't done it openly of course but it had been as a result of Jimmy finally being able to get his claws into him. Jimmy had been a thorn in Mike's side for the previous fourteen years and Mike had grown to hate him over the years,

Mike had been trying to pin something on Jimmy from the

first time that he had ever met him. He had never been able to put a finger on it but Mike knew that Jimmy must be guilty of something.

It was ironic that finally, the only thing that he had been able to actually put him away for, was a crime that he had not committed. Mike had been going into The Crown for about six months when Jimmy had let him know that they knew that he was the filth. They had been enjoying a friendly game of pool as they passed away the afternoon before the racing started.

Jimmy had asked Mike what he actually did for a living and he had kindly stopped Mike from making more of a fool of himself than he needed to by letting him know that he already knew the truth.

"So is being a copper just a part time job then"?
Mike had nearly choked on his tonic water. He'd had no idea they knew.

"We knew from day one mate anyway I don't have a problem with the law. I don't bother them and they don't bother me, savvy"?
Mike had nodded knowing exactly what Jimmy had meant. He had suspected that Jimmy had a few of his own men on his payroll.

"Anyway you can have a proper man's drink now and do me a favour. The draymen are starting to think I'm going soft ordering so much of that girly tonic" Mike had laughed despite feeling stupid at being caught out. He had been getting sick of tonic water that had just made him burp all day and thought that it would be good to get back on the lager. Mike's patch was so rife of petty crime that he had his hands too full to look closely into Jimmy's business but he had always kept a discreet eye on his place and the comings and goings. He had managed to pick up a couple of narks over the year that gave him enough information to earn himself commission but no matter how well he paid for information he could never get a thing on Jimmy. Mike had always thought it strange that The Crown didn't have doormen at the weekends despite the fact that all the other pubs in the area did. There was never any trouble there apart from the odd drunken scuffle that was soon sorted out. Even the prevalent drug scene had not seemed to affect his business and the only problems in the past had been complaints from distant neighbours about glue sniffers using Jimmy's pub car park. Mike had not been able to understand how Jimmy's place could remain so squeaky clean with the kind of people that went in it. He remembered being astonished the day that a face from his past in Sheffield had strolled into the Crown one afternoon in the early days.

Mike had been on undercover duty and he had hidden behind his racing paper when he had heard the familiar voice. Pete Collins ran the Sheffield door scene and he had been trying to muscle in on Manchester. The Beswick crowd were already at war with the Ancoats mob over who ran the protection racket there so Sheffield had stood no chance. Mike had listened as Pete Collins had offered Julie his protection services to her he had also listened as Jimmy had come up from the cellar and told the lads to sling their hooks.

"Let me leave you a card, in case you should change your mind"

Pete Collins slid his card across the bar top towards Jimmy.

"I won't but I've got your number anyway. I'll put it in my book"

Jimmy smiled, he knew that they would be back soon and he had intended to be ready for them. Collins and his monkey crew did all return later that evening where they had started to cause a bit of havoc.

Before Julie had a chance to call for Jimmy they had taken the baseball bats from up their sleeves and started to smash the place up. Julie had screamed out for Jimmy to help her but he was down the cellar.

Collins had jumped over the bar and he had started to smash the bottles that stood behind the bar on optics with the large bat in his hand. Then he had mistakenly turned his attentions to Julie who was trying to stop him smashing up her bar. Jimmy appeared from the cellar armed with a large fire extinguisher which he set off right in Collin's face causing him to scream out loud. Then he had set about the others with it and chased them all out of the pub as they screamed out in pain after being half blinded by the foam.

Mike had arrived just after it had all kicked off but he could tell by the expression on Jimmy's face that he wasn't happy. Tommy Proctor had seen it all and was happy to fill Mike in with all the gory details even mentioning that the lads had left their weapons behind them in the chaos. The police had arrived to get statements but no-one had seen anything, not even the weapons full of fingerprints. Mike had been surprised to hear that until he picked up the newspaper the following day to read the headlines. 'Gangland leader found floating in the canal' Mike had known that Jimmy had been involved somehow but no matter how hard he had tried he could never find the proof. He had tried to find things out about Jimmy and his pub at the station but he had always drawn a blank and once it was even like his Superintendent had warned him off Jimmy. Mike had watched as some of the biggest faces he knew went through Jimmy's back room which was famous for its card games. They started with twenty pound Jacks and went on with no limit to the stakes so it was said. Only once had Mike had joined in when he had managed to lose a whole weeks wages in no time at all. Mike had taken the chance in case he picked up a bit of info but all he had found going on in the card game room was card games. Jimmy had known most of the guys in the back room from schooldays and beyond. They were the boys who had started their careers as shoplifters who had gone on to post offices. They were the petty burglars who had gone on to doing big bank jobs and payroll hits. They were men who would sell their own grandmother if she fetched enough money to get them their next hit. Some of them were the dope dealers off the corners that had eventually moved up to selling crack cocaine. All of the men had earned big money at some time in their careers and all of them had managed to lose it sat round Jimmy's card table. Some of the men who sat in his card games had masterminded some of their biggest jobs there and all of them had had something from Jimmy in one way or another. Jimmy ran a book in his back room and his funds were endless with very good rates for those who could pay up in time. He had access to so much cash that Mike knew he was a bad one but Jimmy got to be the annoying itch that Mike could not scratch.

Mike scratched his crutch as he heard someone at the door and he hoped that it would be Betty back with the lotion but more important with the coke. Betty opened the door and looked at Mike and he had known straight away that something was terribly wrong.

"What have you done Mike, why are people looking for you"?

"What do you mean what people"?

"Don't fuck with me Mike. People are looking for you and you are in my gaff so tell me what the hell have you done"? Mike had bit his lip nervously, his mouth was dry and he desperately needed to score especially now he had heard this news.

"It's nothing Betty I promise just a gambling debt, did you get the gear"?

Betty pulled the thirty quid from down her bra

"No but I'll get it now, stay here"

Betty went back down the stairs but she had no intention of looking for a dealer. She had known that Mike was in much deeper than he had let on. Instead she headed over to the pub across the road from the bookies and asked for the Fitton brothers. The guy behind the bar pointed her in the direction of the brothers who were sat at the table in the corner and she went over to join them.

"I can take you to that copper you are looking for"

"What does he look like old woman"?

"Jesus lads I know the guy from old. He's fortyish with brown hair and a beer belly although at the minute he looks a bit straggly and in need of a few good meals.

The brothers jumped up excitedly knowing that if they could bring the Rooney guy in that they would gain much needed brownie points.

"Money first"

Betty wasn't as daft as she looked not where money was concerned.

Johnny Fitton took the money from his pocket and he handed it to her.

"If you are pissing with us old woman I will poke your other eye out"

Betty grabbed the money from his hand and shoved it down her bra.

"Fuck you arse hole now follow me"

Billy Fitton made a quick phone call before him and his brother followed the old tom out of the pub and across the road to her apartment block. She unlocked the door then she led the boys up the stinking stairwell to her flat. Mike had been listening out for her to return. He had heard her footsteps and he could tell from the other sounds on the landing that she wasn't alone.

He checked that his pistol was in its holster pressed firmly to his ankle and he sat back and waited to be taken. The door opened slowly then Betty stood back as the Fitton brothers entered her flat.

"Whatever you do, don't make a mess in there"

The brothers both held their breath as they entered the dirty hovel wondering how they could possibly make more of a mess than the one that was already there. Mike had offered no resistance and he had stood up and quietly walked out with them.

"Sorry Kiddo, I've got to live"

Betty apologised as Mike was taken past her and led down the stairs.

They brought him out of the block of flats to find a shiny limousine parked outside with blackened windows. Two big black men wearing long dark overcoats stood by the side of the highly polished car. One of them opened the back door of the car as the others approached it whilst the other big guy helped Mike to get into the back seat of it. Billy Fitton felt something being pressed into his hand and he looked down to find an envelope that was crammed full of cash sitting in the palm of his hand.

"Thanks boys"

came a voice from the back of the car then the window went up and the car pulled slowly away.

"Do you know who that was? Fucking Hell bro he just spoke to us!"

The Fitton brothers watched with open mouths as the car pulled away out of the close as they counted the money they had just been rewarded with. Mike was numb he didn't know who had him or where he was going but he had a feeling he was dealing with the Mafiosa. A chloroformed pad covered Mike's face and he thought no more.

Chapter 8

Julie was at the end of a visit with Jimmy when they got the news from Joseph and they both got pretty excited. There was a week to go before the appeal and with Mike Rooney located it meant that Jimmy would have his alibi at last. Both Julie and Jimmy thought of sitting by their pool sipping cocktails in the sunshine and they got quite turned on at the thought. Julie put her tongue into Jimmy's mouth and her hand down the front of his pants. The guard coughed so they would know he was there.

"Fuck off pervert"
was all that the guard heard before Julie bent over and went down on Jimmy. He took the subtle hint and went to the bog to take a slash after masturbating himself. Julie was a good looking woman with a fine pair of jugs that did her justice and seeing her go down like that had been much more than he could take. The guard had thought about her as he shot his load at probably the same time that Jimmy did. By the time that the guard had got back to Jimmy's cell Julie was getting ready to leave for she had a big Welcome Home party to arrange.

She kissed Jimmy one more time before leaving and she winked playfully at the screw as he led her out. Jimmy smiled to himself as he watched her walk away taking in every lovely wobble that her tight little arse made as she moved.

"Tenerife here we come"

Jimmy remembered the first place that they had bought on that perfect sunshine island and he had compared it in his mind to the one that they owned at present. The first one had cost only twenty three grand and it had a shared pool. They had bought it ten years earlier and it was in Las Americas right by the sea. He had told customers that it was time-share as he always played down his assets that way no-one would ever know just how much money Jimmy had. By the time that Jimmy had married Julie he had been a millionaire. He owned over twenty properties in Manchester as well as two bookies and a massage parlour and a newly built carpet warehouse.

Just seven months after their wedding D.J. had been born to them but after a couple of months of motherhood Julie had soon become bored. Jimmy had bought The Crown Hotel for her and it proved to be a very good move for between his businesses he could transfer funds. Before long Jimmy had added another string to his bow and had got into the money laundering business. For every thousand pounds that he took he paid seven hundred and fifty pounds and he just kept the dirty money out of circulation for a while. Then when it was safe he changed it for pesetas and his stock of foreign currency grew and grew. When the Euro was brought in there was a lot of black money that needed shifting pretty quickly. Jimmy had used his pesetas up to buy an exclusive villa up in the hills on the South of the island. It had its own swimming pool, beautiful gardens and a separate apartment in the grounds. It had cost him just over one and a half million pounds when he bought it but within three months of the new currency coming in it was worth over two million pounds. The sudden sales of properties that were bought with black money had turned the property market upside down. As usual everything that

Jimmy invested money in brought him great rewards. He employed a gardener who lived in the apartment and who took care of the house for Jimmy in his absence. Jimmy had been looking forward to retiring there with Julie. Julie's birthday was just two weeks after Jimmy's and he had bought her a brand new four wheeled drive motor that sat up the driveway waiting for her to use it. Their plan had been to wait until D.J. had finished his exams then they would go to Spain for good. D.J. had told them that he did not want to live abroad and they had respected his wishes. Jimmy intended to give the carpet business to D.J. to allow him to grow up earning a good living without ever having to break the law. D.J. had been brought up by his grandma who had been a full time nanny to him from being a baby. They thought the world of each other so when D.J. had asked could he stay with his grandma Jimmy and Julie had agreed knowing that he would be in good hands. They also knew that he would come over for lots of holidays. D.J. would have his own little empire that Jimmy had been able to build up for him but in order for that to mean anything Jimmy had to clear his own name.

Julie headed back to The Crown in a much better mood than when she had left it and she couldn't wait to tell all of the regulars the good news. Tommy Proctor had whooped in delight.

"I always knew that Jimmy was innocent. He hasn't got a bad bone in his body. He is as honest as a piece of string"

Julie had raised her eyes up to the heavens wondering where old Tommy got half of his daft expressions from. She loved the pants off Jimmy and she always would. She had known from the moment that she first saw him that he had money but from the second that he kissed her in the back of his transit van it wouldn't have bothered her if he would have been a tramp. Julie liked the money and all the things it gave her but she would give it all up just to have her Jimmy back by her side.

Julie's mother had brought her up alone and she had worked up to four jobs to give her everything she needed. Julie loved her mother almost as much as she loved Jimmy for she had made her the girl that Jimmy had fallen in love with. At the tender age of twenty one Julie's life had been pretty much complete. She had a wonderful husband who loved her as much as she loved him. She had a beautiful baby son and a mother that she adored who gave her all the support she could ever need. She also had a pub of her very own that Jimmy had bought for her when she had complained about being bored one day. Julie had done bar work from the age of seventeen and she loved to chat to the punters and play pool so when Jimmy had taken her into The Crown one day then handed her the keys she had been over the moon. Jimmy had also paid for Julie's sagging bosom to be uplifted after giving birth to D.J. After the operation she had gone from a pert 34B to a 36C giving her an even better figure. Behind the bar Julie had been the perfect landlady for she was blonde, busty and bubbly and whilst her mother took care of the baby Julie took care of the customers as the bar continued to prosper. The pub did really well with Julie at the helm and Jimmy doing the books and Julie never once asked about Jimmy's other business. Julie was the queen in The Crown and Jimmy used to joke that she was the jewel in his crown. He lavished her with diamonds and beautiful jewellery and continued to spoil her rotten and she loved it. Her wardrobe was full of designer clothes and she owned over sixty pairs of shoes all with matching handbags. Julie's maintenance cost Jimmy about a grand a week which included her hairdresser and nail technician who both came to the pub to see her. It included her St Tropez tan that kept her with an all year round dark tan like Victoria Beckham had and that involved going to the salon at least once a fortnight.

It also included the second lot of plastic surgery that took her from a 36C to a very ample 36DD. Julie had bio face peels twice a year. She had Botex injections put into her lips and eventually as she got older she had liposuction treatment on her thighs. Jimmy had literally made Julie the woman that she was which was a gorgeous but a very expensive one. All Julie wanted was to get Jimmy out of the country so that they could enjoy all the wonderful things that they had worked so hard to get. First though she had to get him out of the prison.

Julie remembered the day after old Charlie's murder when the police had burst in to arrest poor Jimmy. She had been terrified and she had called Joseph as the police were taking him down to the nick. Joseph had picked her up on the way round to the station and he had told her not to worry. She had waited for Joseph to come out of the interview room and remembered the concerned look on his face as he came out of it.

"Well have you sorted it"?

"We've got a problem Jools, and it is a serious one"

"What kind of problem"?

"Charlie Reed was brutally murdered last night"

"Yeah I know, we heard the police and ambulances going past, he had his head smashed in didn't he"?

"Yes, he also had Jimmy's knife stuck in his back full of Jimmy's prints"

"No you must be wrong, they can't have"

Joseph tried to calm Julie down.

"The other thing Julie is that he doesn't have an alibi"

"Yes he does, he was with me"

"What time was he with you Julie"?

"All night Joseph he didn't leave my sight all night"
Joseph admired her loyalty but it was no use for Jimmy had already said that he had been out for a drive on his own.

"There is one person who might be able to vouch for Jimmy and we are looking for them now"

"It's not a woman is it Joseph, please tell me if it is"

"No Julie don't be silly it's not a woman it's an Inspector Rooney"
Julie rushed over to the desk to ask for Mike Rooney only to be told that he was away on leave.

"I've already asked Julie, but don't worry we will get hold of him soon"
Even though Joseph had promised Julie that he would, he hadn't been able to find Mike Rooney. Three weeks later Jimmy had found himself in the dock with lots of incriminating evidence against him backed up by forensics and with no alibi for his movements. Julie had sat in Crown court as she watched the man that she loved get a life sentence. She had seen the way that he had swooned when he realised that he was not going home and she had seen the look of terror on his face as they had taken him away. Julie knew that for all of his scams Jimmy was not a murderer and she would do all that was possible to prove it.

"Dad didn't kill old Charlie did he"?
D.J. had asked as they took him away and Julie had felt her son's manly shoulders shake as he had spoken to her.

"No my darling he didn't and don't you ever think any different"
D.J. walked into the pub to witness the celebrations.

"What's happened, have they let dad out"?

"Not yet they haven't darling but they will soon because they've found that copper, the one who can give him an alibi"
D.J. whooped with joy then he poured his mother a large

Bacardi and coke and he pulled a half of Stella for himself whilst her back was turned. D.J. had always known that his dad was different. He had never been picked on at school like the other boys or had his bike taken off him. He had heard people say that his dad was well connected, but to him his dad was just that, his dad.

The celebrations carried on until late in the night with well wishers coming from miles around to pass on their best wishes to Julie. The only one who didn't show his face was Mike Rooney.

A BOOK OF FAVOURS

Chapter 9

Mike Rooney was doused in ice cold water in an attempt to bring him to. His hands were tied behind his back and he felt as though he was trussed to a chair. He opened one eye very cautiously and looked down on the floor to try and figure out where he had been brought to but he didn't recognise any of it.

"Is he awake"?

"Not quite you must have really knocked him out"

"Well he's got twenty minutes to come to then he should be here"

Mike did not recognise the voices nor did he know who they were talking about. All that he knew was that he had twenty minutes to come up with a good story and which story would depend very much with who he was dealing with. His arms tingled through being tightly bound and his mouth was bone dry and Mike moved his tongue across his gums to try to lubricate them. He needed something to help him cope with the stress that he was under. Mike thought of all the stress that he had faced at work both before and after his promotion. He remembered how it had been all work and no play until he had been introduced to the drugs.

He had finished work one night after a very long shift and he had needed very much to chill. He had sat alone at the bar as he usually had and had started to get bored with his own company so when one of the lads asked if he wanted to play cards he had joined them. Everyone knew that Mike was the law but it didn't matter for in The Crown there was no law apart from Jimmy's. Mark Hilton was the big noisy one and he was keeping everyone happy with his endless supply of jokes and it helped Mike to wind down a bit. Then they had all started on the Glayva which was a sweet sticky drink that was knocked back to avoid the taste. At two quid a shot Mike couldn't really understand why people should pay for something that they didn't want to taste but he had gone along with them. Just the same way that he had gone along with them when they had took a full bottle of the stuff into the back room. Six shots later Mike had felt totally relaxed and he was sharing funny stories about his work. The guys had put up with Mike because Jimmy was footing the bar bill so they had all laughed at his jokes and they had made him feel like one of the lads. By the time the card game had started Mike was half cut and hardly able to stand so he was not really the perfect candidate to get caught up in a serious game of poker. A new pack of cards was opened and shuffled as was always the case with a new game. Mark Hilton won the cut for dealer and he dealt the cards to the six other faces in the game and then to himself. John Ryan started the betting with a twenty pound note that he put on the table which was matched by the large Nigerian who sat to his left. Mike was next and he put twenty of the ninety pounds that he had in his wallet onto the table. He intended to have just one quick game and then he had intended to make his excuses and leave but he found himself being dragged further and further into the game. The drinks had started to go to his head for he was feeling sick and just a little bit the worse for wear. Mike looked down at the cards in his hand. He had two Jacks, two threes and a king. He threw in his king only to pick up a queen but he was still quite happy with his two pairs so he kept up with the bets.

Mike was down to his last thirty pounds when four of the others dropped out leaving just him and Mark left in the game. Mark raised it to thirty leaving Mike with a good hand but with no more cash to bet with. He matched the thirty with the last of his cash and he was relieved when Mark chose to put in his thirty and paid another thirty to see him. Mike turned his cards over slowly to reveal the two pairs and Mark cursed and put his own cards unturned to the bottom of the pile.

No-one but Mark knew that he had thrown a full house in, no-one had been able to see his hand unlike Mike's hand which had been on display to the all through a wall mirror. Mike scooped up the kitty from the table that had amassed to a good few hundred quid so he decided to stay and play for a while longer. Mark had let him take the next few hands which along with the few more Glayvas that they all sank managed to put Mike in a much lighter mood. Then the stakes were raised to fifty pounds and it was game on. Mike put his fifty quid on the table and he picked his cards up one by one. The two of spades was the first card followed by the four of spades then the five of the same suit. Mike started to get excited until he picked up the ten of diamonds for he had been hoping for a flush. Then he turned over his fifth card to find that it was the three of spades. Any spade would do him for a flush or a six or ace would give him a run. He tried to remember where the aces were, he knew that they were due so he threw in his ten of diamonds and asked for just one card change. He looked at the card that big Mark had just dealt to him and he kept a straight face. It wasn't the ace that he had been hoping for but it was the six of spades and it had turned his otherwise poor hand into a running flush.

John Ryan had changed two cards and raised the stakes to a ton so Mike reckoned he must have picked the aces up.

He knew that his hand would beat that so he played on. The atmosphere had suddenly changed and all of a sudden the mood at the table seemed quite serious. There was about fifteen hundred quid on the table and all seven men were still in and it went round again. Chalky rubbed his chin for a few minutes before throwing his cards in. He only had ace high and although he could have bluffed with that he knew that the stakes were ready to hit the roof. As the pile of cash on the table got higher Mike's pile got lower and he did a quick count before it got back round to him. There were still three of them in the game and Mike had one hundred and eighty pounds in front of him. It was twice as much as he had started with but nowhere near enough to keep him in the game. He threw two fifties onto the table and waited to see what Mark would do. Mark matched Mike's money and it passed to John Ryan who thought for a minute or two before doing the same. Mike looked down at the eighty quid in front of him realising that it wasn't enough to keep him in the game with the stakes as they stood. He had shifted nervously in his seat as he wondered what he should do when maybe the Glayva kicked in. He knew that he had a very good chance of taking the pot which stood at over three grand if he stayed in the game but in order to stay in he needed more cash to play with.

"Your shout mate, are you in or out" asked John Ryan.
Mike hated to think about quitting so he did exactly what Jimmy had hoped that he would do one day and he asked for a loan.

"How are you fixed for a loan Mark"?
Mark's pile was almost as low as Mike's pile so he shook his head.

"Jimmy will sort you out a couple of grand if you are short"

Tony spoke as he took out Jimmy's account book. Mike

nodded and Tony put him in the book then he handed Mike the money that he had needed to stay in the game. Mike threw one hundred pounds onto the table then he had raised it two hundred more which put the game out of Mark's reach with the hand that he was holding. John matched the cash that Mike had just put in and he raised it a further two hundred which was more than he could really afford. Mike did the same and the game continued that way until most of Mike's two grand he had borrowed had gone. John put in five hundred pounds and paid another five hundred to see Mike's hand, much to Mike's relief. Mike turned his cards over triumphantly one by one to reveal a running flush. The others at the table looked impressed as Mike started to scoop the money on the table up with his hand. John Ryan reached out and stopped him then he turned his own five cards over to show his royal flush on the run. Mike felt his head go really light and he went weak at the knees.

He could feel the cold beads of sweat drip down his brow and he felt physically sick at the thought of what had just happened. John Ryan was stuffing his winnings into his jacket pockets whilst the others stared at Mike as if waiting for a reaction from him.

"Any more for any more"?

No-one answered. John Ryan had taken most of their money and Mike didn't look like he fancied playing anymore. He counted out the two hundred pounds that he had left and he passed it to Tony.

"Take this off the two grand that I owe Jimmy will you"

Tony took the money and took out the book and he marked off the money that Mike had just handed to him.

"That's a straight two grand that you owe then providing you pay up"

"What do you mean I only borrowed two grand"?

"That's right you did at ten per cent interest so you owe two grand still and if you pay within the week that's all you'll owe otherwise it goes up by ten per cent for each week that it is outstanding"

Mike felt gutted when he realised the enormity of what he had just done. He had, through his own stupidity and greed become one of Jimmy's debtors and he knew that he earned nowhere near enough to be able to pay him back. His head had started to spin as he realised what he had done. As Mike had left the pub and walked out into the dark evening he could still hear the others laughing loudly and he had known that they were all laughing at his expense. Mike had been well and truly had by Jimmy and his men and after years of being the predator Mike had become the prey. It was then that Mike knew that he would have to become a bent copper in order to survive and he started off the very next day at the station. No-one questioned Mike's interest or his visits to the evidence room which was full of a mound of goodies just there for the taking. Mike managed to take over a grand in cash that he put into his inside pocket and he put a couple of bags of smack into his trousers. He paid the money to Tony for although it was loaned by Jimmy Mack through Tony he knew Jimmy would never get involved in the dealings. He went out to try to find one of the low lifes that he had arrested for drug offences in the hope that he could find a buyer for the different drugs he knew he could put his hand to. Jimmy had been driving through the streets when he happened upon the Pink Flamingo. It was a small massage parlour on Stockport Road in Levenshulme that was above a newsagent's shop. Mike knew of the Flamingo, it was one of the many parlours that operated in the area and Mike knew that the girls who worked there sold extras. Mike also knew that Jimmy had an involvement there although like everything else concerning Jimmy he had not been able to prove it. Mike had carried out private surveillance on the place once many years ago and he had been surprised by some of the punters that he had seen calling into the parlour. As a young police constable he had been frightened to see higher ranking officers from his station and others call in. He had been naïve enough to think that they might have been calling in on police business but the length of time they had spent there and the look on their faces as they had left the place had told Mike otherwise.

Mike left his car across the road where he could keep an eye on it and walked over to the Flamingo. It was on a busy road with heavy traffic flying past and no-one really took any notice of Mike entering the shop.

He walked up the stairs and was met by Marcia, a beautiful black girl with masses of long wild hair who looked a little wary of Mike.

"It's alright Marcia I'm not here on police business"

Marcia smiled and let her chiffon top slip to reveal a smooth expanse of flesh as she moved closer to Mike.

"Well if it is pleasure you are here for I'm your woman" she whispered in his ear. Mike could feel his heart beating fast beneath his shirt and he wished that he could afford to pay for her services. He had serviced himself for as many years as he could remember but he desperately needed to be held. The recent change in his fortune had left him vulnerable and after years of being alone Mike very badly needed someone to love him even if it was for money. He didn't have money but he did have something that he thought that Marcia might prefer. He took a bag of smack from his inside pocket and held it up for Marcia to see. He saw her dark eyes light up at the sight of it and he knew that he could afford the love that he required after all. Marcia took the bag of powder from his hand then she took hold of

Mike's tie as she led him slowly into one of the side rooms. Mike had not remembered leaving Marcia or known how he had ever managed to drive home that night for everything had become a distant blur to him.

He woke up the next morning with a nasty taste in his mouth and he ached all over. He looked down to his chest and smiled as he saw the long scratch marks that Marcia had left there the night before. He remembered taking the crack with Marcia and how he had felt as it hit its mark. He remembered forgetting all of his problems if only for a short while and he certainly remembered having the best orgasm that he had ever experienced in his life. Mike had another packet that he had intended to sell but he had promised Marcia he would return and he did many, many times. It hadn't been difficult for Mike to turn to the seedy things in life. In fact with his never ending supplies of drugs that he had started to take from his hits on the streets Mike found himself a whole new lot of buddies. The more drugs that Mike took he found the more he needed and before long he could not get enough of the stuff to satisfy his hunger. He had tried most of the drugs that he had taken from the evidence room until he had hit rock bottom literally. Rocks were pure cocaine that Mike would take through vodka or gin like the expert that he had become. He had caused a security alert at the station where they had realised that lots of evidence had gone missing and he knew that it was being watched. Over the weeks that it had taken Mike to have become addicted he had managed to take out a few grand in cash and enough drugs to give him the taste for them and to get him a great sex life. He had also managed to sneak out a small pistol complete with leather holster and ammunition.

Mike had taken the gun with the intention of selling it on but he had found it difficult for no-one was interested in a piece with history especially when it had come from a copper. Mike wondered how it had ever got so bad, his debt to Jimmy had grown as he had become a slave to his habit and now he was trussed up in a living nightmare. Mike heard someone approaching and he was glad that he had not sold the pistol and that he could still feel it pressing against his ankle. It made him feel safer.

The door burst open and Joseph Royal walked into the room to find Mike Rooney trussed up like a chicken.

"Mike, thank God we have found you. Where the hell have you been"?

Mike heard some-one say his name and the voice sounded quite friendly so he opened his eyes and looked up to find Jimmy Mack's lawyer stood above him.

Joseph ordered the two guys that had been guarding their prisoner out of the room as he started to untie Mike who looked as though he had been to hell and back. As Joseph stood above Mike he had to hold his breath to avoid the stench that Mike was giving out. The last time that Joseph had seen Mike was in a courtroom about six months earlier and he had been a fine figure of a man. He had just been commissioned and he had been a well respected figure in the law courts whereas now he looked like one of the no marks that he usually put away. Joseph could tell by Mike's actions and his appearance that he was addicted to something.

"Jimmy needs you to give him an alibi. He's been set up for the Charlie Reed murder and we've been looking for you for ages"

Mike looked shocked as though he didn't know that Charlie had been killed and Joseph started to fill him in on what had happened.

"I think some-one must have spiked my drink and whoever it was kept me held up somewhere. I managed to get away and that's when your men picked me up. It's the first I've heard about the murder, but of course I'll give Jimmy his alibi. Do you think I could have something to eat first and maybe get a shower and a change of clothes"?

Joseph handed Mike a glass of water then he pulled him up.

"We'll go back to mine and get you cleaned up and then we can sort out this alibi. Don't worry Mike we will have Jimmy out before you know it"

Joseph led Mike out of the room and out to his car and Mike was surprised to see that his prison had been just a normal motel room. He got into Joseph's posh car with leather seats and laid his head back as he thought of what he would say to Jimmy. Joseph drove through the countryside until he reached his home in the stockbroker belt of Alderley Edge. The electronic gates opened as the car approached and they followed the sweeping driveway up to the front door. The door was opened by a young pretty, olive skinned lady who kept house for Joseph and he spoke to her in Spanish.

Within minutes she had made a tray of sandwiches and a pot of coffee that she brought into the lounge to them before leaving to get on with her cleaning duties. Mike ate the sandwiches greedily adding truth to his story of being kidnapped. Joseph asked him about the night that Jimmy had been sent to meet some-one. He wanted Mike to remember all he could that might help his client to get off the charge and he left Mike to try and remember whilst he went upstairs to run him a bath.

Mike had done nothing else but remember things since the night that he had caved poor old Charlie's head in and his body shook as he thought of it.

He had run up so much money with Jimmy with the gambling and the drugs that he knew that he would never be able to pay it all back. His debt had stood at over five grand at the last count and it was growing all the time.

Mike had hoped that he could get hold of Jimmy's red book and destroy it and then it would be Jimmy's word against his. He had called into the pub when he had thought that Jimmy might be out the day before old Charlie's murder in the hope of finding the book. Unfortunately Jimmy had been there so Mike had asked to discuss something with him in private.

Jimmy had taken him into the back room that he used as an office. He remembered sitting opposite Jimmy at his big black desk when D.J. had walked in on them.

"Dad I've got a tack stuck in the bottom of my new trainers"

"Yes D.J. and I've got a meeting so can it wait"?

"Not really dad I'm going out in a minute and they are my best ones"

Jimmy excused the rude interruption and opened a drawer and pulled out a knife. It was small with a five inch blade and it had a white bone handle that Jimmy took hold of as he picked up the trainer. He put the blade underneath the tack which came out with one swift pull. Just at that minute Julie screamed out for Jimmy that two lads were trying to rob the pool table so he and D.J. had run to her assistance. Before he ran out to Julie Jimmy had opened the drawer and popped the knife back but in his haste he had forgotten to lock it. Mike had acted quickly he had pulled out an evidence bag, opened the drawer and carefully put the knife away without getting his own prints on it. Then he had closed the drawer and sat back down to wait for Jimmy who was back within a couple of minutes.

The lads trying to rob the pool table had run away when they had seen Jimmy and D.J. coming at them and the crisis in the pub was over.

"Where's the bloody coppers when you need them"
he had joked and Mike remembered laughing as though all

of the worries of the world had been lifted from his shoulders.

"Sorry about that Mike now what was it you wanted to see me about"?

Mike had gone on to tell Jimmy about a new squad that were working out of Macclesfield and how he could get Jimmy names and dates and faces.

"What is in it for you Mike? What do you get out of this"?

"Hopefully a clean slate and then that's it. I can get you a meeting with the guy who is heading the operation but he will only deal with you. Only you Jimmy and if you breathe so much as a word to anyone else about this then the deal is off. If you like I can set the meeting up for tomorrow. Are you interested or not"?

Jimmy had nodded, of course he was interested. A new squad in the area would mean a lot of drug busts and if Jimmy knew who he was dealing with then he could follow them. Then when the team did carry out a bust and take the haul Jimmy could have some-one take it from them. As far as Mike was concerned Jimmy knew only too well that his clean slate wouldn't last for long. Mike had promised to call Jimmy the next day to arrange the meeting and both men had stood up and shook hands.

A handshake meant a lot to Jimmy for his word was his bond but to Mike it had meant nothing. Mike had known that Jimmy had never trusted him in the past but since he had become a user he had changed. Mike's plan had changed a little once he had Jimmy's knife. His plan had been to use Jimmy's knife in a robbery when he knew that Jimmy had no alibi to back him up because he had been sent on a wild goose chase by him.

The next day Mike had called Jimmy from a payphone giving him a time and a place and strict instructions that he should go alone.

"New Mills train station at nine thirty sharp just park at the bottom under the trees and wait for a car to approach. It will park opposite you and it will flash its lights at you. Flash back and wait for him to come to you"

Jimmy had agreed that he would and he thanked Mike for helping him out.

" Your debt is paid in full Mike and I won't forget what you have done"

Mike remembered Jimmy's words and he dreaded to think what he would do if he ever found out the truth. He would probably have him killed.

Mike had watched as Jimmy had left the pub later that evening then he had walked down to the yard at the bottom of Bents lane. He had sneaked past the hut in the yard and made sure that old Charlie was alone then after he was sure that he was Mike had sneaked back to the gates. He had rattled the gates so that Charlie would call the police who he knew would be out with him within twenty minutes. Then he had hid behind an oil drum and waited for old Charlie to come out. Charlie had heard the noise and had phoned the station as Mike had known that he would do then he had walked over to check the gates. Charlie had been stood at the gate when Mike had crept up behind him and stuck Jimmy's knife into him. He stuck it into a part of his back that wouldn't cause too much damage to Charlie but that would definitely harm Jimmy. That was when Mike's plan had gone horribly wrong and there had been no turning back. Instead of falling to the floor as Mike had thought that he would Charlie had cried out in pain and he had turned to see his attacker.

Mike would never forget the look of terror and confusion on old Charlie's face as he had looked into Mike's eyes. He would never forget that look he had given to him just before he had been forced to take the old man's life. Joseph walked into the room to find Mike trembling and crying and he recognised what he thought to be the symptoms of cold turkey and he helped Mike up.

"Get a nice soak in that bath Mike I've left some clothes out for you. I'll get a message to Jimmy that we have found you and once you have sorted his alibi out I will see if I can find some' snow' for you"

Joseph led Mike upstairs to his luxury bathroom and left him to get on with his soak whilst he went downstairs to get a message to Julie. He knew that she would be waiting for him to take her to the prison and he couldn't wait to tell her the good news.

"Have you spoken to him Jimmy? Has he confirmed Jimmy's alibi"?

"He's in a bad way Julie but he's having a quick bath then we will call in the station. He didn't even know that Charlie was dead. I'll get a message to Jimmy then we will pick you up on the way to the station"

Mike had finished his bath and Joseph turned round to see him enter the room looking a lot smarter than when he had first arrived there.

"Mike is here with me now Julie so we will see you soon. Bye Jools"

Julie said to give you a hug but you don't mind if I pass on that do you"?

Mike had just shrugged, his mind was in turmoil and he didn't feel able to keep up with all the lies and deceit. He knew that he didn't deserve the kindness that Joseph and Julie were showing to him.

"Give me a minute Joseph I think I left something in your bathroom"

Joseph waited as Mike ran back up the stairs and he heard the bathroom door shut to then seconds later he had heard the sound of the gunshot that rang through his house. He screamed out as he ran to the stairs realising what Mike had just done. He got to the bathroom just before Angelica did and he tried to open the door but it wouldn't budge. Mike's lifeless body lay behind the door and Joseph had to use all of his strength to try and push the body out of the way. He made just enough room to be able to squeeze into his bathroom where he had found the body of Detective Inspector Rooney with his brains blown completely out. Bits of which were still sliding down Joseph's Italian marble tiles that they had splattered on. Angelica peeked into the bathroom and she had screamed long and hard at the gruesome sight that lay before her. Joseph had turned her head as he led her away before calling the police then he had called Julie to tell her the bad news.

"Joseph where are you, are you on your way over"?

"No Julie there has been a change of plan"

"What do you mean Joseph am I not coming to the prison with you and Mike"

"Mike isn't coming Julie because he is dead. He has just topped himself"

Julie had sounded so cheerful that Joseph had hated himself for having to tell her the bad news. He heard her cry out and he could say nothing that would comfort her, nothing that could take away her obvious pain.

"What about Jimmy's alibi Joseph and his appeal. This will destroy him Joseph you will have to tell him, I can't"

Joseph had not been able to tell Julie anything other than what had just happened. He had promised to go to Jimmy as soon as the police had finished at his house, to give him the news personally. Joseph had hoped that Jimmy would be strong enough to take the news but first he had to console his cleaner who was having hysterics as she stood by his side.

Julie put down the phone and cried unashamedly as she stood behind the bar. She was still crying when D.J. came home and she had to explain all over again what had happened.

"He'll be alright mam because dad is a survivor so don't cry"

Julie loved their young son's old head and she gave it a playful rub then she poured a large Bacardi and coke for herself and a half of lager for D.J. They sat down and they started to talk about what this terrible news would mean to Jimmy.

"Well Mike was going to be your dads alibi because it was only him who knew where your dad was at the time of Jimmy's murder"

Julie stopped as she realised what she had just said. Jimmy had told her that he was going out on business on the night of Charlie's murder just after he had spoken to someone on the telephone. She remembered the time because they had just watched The Bill on the television.

Jimmy had never ever told Julie any of his business dealings or explained to Julie who somebody was or what they wanted. She had asked him after he had been arrested after his knife full of his fingerprints had been found at the scene of the crime. She loved her husband more than life itself but even she had felt compelled to ask.

All Jimmy had said was to ask her to trust him which she had done but it had been hard for her. She had listened to all of the evidence given against him before the jury had found him guilty.

"Your dad said that it was Mike who had called him on the day of Charlie's murder but Joseph said that Mike has been on holiday and that he hadn't even heard about the murder"

Julie's eyes started to fill as she realised how bad it all would look for Jimmy for even she was starting to have doubts.

"Mike Rooney wasn't on holiday mam I remember because he was sat in dad's office the day those two
scallies tried to rob the pool table"
Julie could remember Mike being there as Jimmy and D.J. had chased the two lads away because he had joked about coppers not being there when you needed them.

"That's it! That was when dad last had his knife, the one that the police found stuck in old Charlie"

"How do you know son, how can you be sure"?

"Because that was why I was in dad's office that day. I was going out and I had a tack stuck under my new trainers. I walked into dad's office and he had been angry with me for just walking in on them.

He took the tack out with his old knife then that was when you shouted that those lads were trying to rob the pool table"

"Think carefully D.J. What did your father do with the knife"?

"I can't remember I think he might have put it in the drawer but I can't be sure. I'm sorry"

"Don't be sorry darling you might just have saved your dads bacon. Think about it. Mike Rooney was one of the last people to see the knife, he was the only person who knew where your dad was that night and he has just blown his brains out. Quick let me get to that telephone"
Julie picked up the phone and she called Joseph who was still at home dealing with the police and she told him what they had just uncovered.
Joseph had listened to Julie's story and wondered why he had never realised earlier that Mike could have been involved. It seemed obvious now but the only trouble was that they still had no evidence and the main suspect was dead. It would be quite difficult to put the blame on a dead man especially when the dead man had been a copper.

Joseph needed to find proof and he needed to find it fast for the appeal was only days away.

He also needed to go to see Jimmy and deliver the bad news to him but Joseph hoped that the latest revelations might help to soften the blow.

Joseph left the forensic team at his home to conclude their investigations. With two witness statements one being from a prominent lawyer and having found the gun next to the body it was obviously a simple open and shut case of suicide so Joseph was more than happy to leave them to it.

He had a lot to do starting with telling his client that the appeal might have to be cancelled and he knew that Jimmy would not be very happy.

Joseph drove over to Longsight and called into the police station to speak to the Superintendent. Luckily he was there but he had been otherwise engaged and Joseph had been shown to his office where he had waited for him to finish his other business. Superintendent Collins had been horrified to learn of the death of one of his senior officers who he had believed to be in Sheffield taking time off to look after his sick mother. It never looked good on paper to show a suicide.as it reflected on the station and the extra workloads that were being imposed due to government cutbacks. He had always had a bad feeling about Mike Rooney yet he could never explain why for he always did his job.

Mike had worked under him for fourteen years and yet he knew so little about him as a person. Mike Rooney had been very much a loner and on reflection Superintendent Collins could not remember a time in all of the years he had known him that he had ever been out with him socially. It upset him to think that any of his coppers were bent but part of his job was to listen to what the lawyer had to say.

He had been appalled when he had heard Joseph's

allegations against Mike Rooney but he was fair minded and he had promised to look into them for Joseph. Feeling satisfied that the police would investigate his findings Joseph sped down the motorway to let Jimmy know both the bad and the good news.

Chapter 10

Jimmy Mack sat waiting in his cell. He was excited at the prospect of Mike Rooney being found and he couldn't wait to see Julie and Joseph. Being inside had given Jimmy a lot of time to reflect on his life and had made him realise just what a lucky man he was. He wondered how D.J. was going on at the warehouse and hoped that he liked being his own boss. Jimmy thought back to when he had first bought the warehouse and of all the interest it had created with the guys around town.

In his first week as the owner Jimmy had been inundated with requests to use it for lots of illicit dealings. During the early days Jimmy had more than recouped the cost of it from local hoods who had used it. It had been used for storage, drops, deals and planning for it had been spacious and quiet enough for people not to be disturbed. Now it was totally kosher and he had handed it over to his son so that he could build his very own empire on the right side of the law. He heard the sound of footsteps approaching his cell and he jumped up excitely.

The disappointment was clear to see on Jimmy's face when he realised that Joseph was alone for he had been looking forward to seeing Julie.

"Sit down Jimmy we need to talk. Julie isn't coming today but she sends her love and she will call you later"

"What is it Joseph? What did Mike tell you"?

"It's only a hunch at this stage Jimmy but we think that Mike knocked Charlie off and that's the good news"

"Are you crazy? Why would Mike want to see Charlie dead it wouldn't make sense. Anyway if that was the good news what is the bad"?

"The bad news Jimmy is that Mike Rooney is dead. He blew his brains out at my house this afternoon"

Jimmy's heart sank, he felt sick and he felt totally dumbfounded. Mike Rooney had been Jimmy's only hope of getting off the murder rap and now that he was dead Jimmy did not know what would happen.

He had known that Mike had been on a downward slippery slope but it made no sense for him to have killed old Charlie. Even if he had wanted to kill him for some reason Jimmy couldn't understand why he had used his knife to do it or how he had got hold of it.

"The bastard set me up" Jimmy shouted out angrily as he realised how he had managed to do it. He told Joseph how Mike had visited him the day before the murder and how he could have taken his knife.

How he had arranged for him to be out of the way and how he had insisted that he told no-one of his plans. Then he had cleverly disappeared leaving Jimmy up the creek without a paddle but Jimmy had no idea what Mike would get from it all. Mike had told Jimmy that he needed to clear his debts but it was a poxy five grand that Jimmy would have paid more than to retain him. Jimmy was mad.

"Sit down Joseph and take out a pen and some paper"

Jimmy looked at the screw who was stood within earshot at the bars.

"Scram and don't come back until you are yelled for"

The screw took Jimmy's advice and Jimmy and Joseph put their heads together.

"Have you got the book"?

Joseph nodded and took it from his inside pocket. He knew how important the book was to Jimmy and he wasn't about to cock up again the way that he had with Mike Rooney. Mike had not been frisked properly and Joseph had not double checked for if he had done he might have found the gun that Mike had strapped to his leg. Joseph felt guilty for that and he was determined to make it up to Jimmy.

"Who have you used so far "?
Joseph pointed to the favours taken and Jimmy looked through the others.

"I don't know how the appeal will go Joseph and I can't take the chance of losing it so I need a back up plan"
Joseph whistled as Jimmy told him of his plan. It was like the 'Great Escape' and the 'Italian Job' rolled into one but ten times greater and it used up almost all of Jimmy's small favours.

Jimmy explained to Joseph how his favours system worked and as he listened to him Joseph couldn't help but be impressed at some of the names in Jimmy's book. Especially the ones written in capital letters that were either very good friends or ones who had owed Jimmy big time. What Jimmy needed to know was whether or not the big boys were available for a particular day and whether or not they were up for it.

"Come back tomorrow Joseph and let me know who is in. Tell them nothing other than I need a big favour and that you will be in touch"
Joseph nodded. He would do as Jimmy had asked him to and he was excited at the very thought of it. Some of the names that Jimmy had asked him to call were the highest of the high from all parts of the community.

They included the Mafia, the Triads, ex I.R.A and some of the biggest nutcases in Manchester.

"Holy Shit, ain't this going to be the daddy of them all"

he had said to himself before yelling to the guard.

Jimmy sat on his bed and racked his photographic memory that stored dates, times and places as accurately as any computer. He had never written down details just dates for it would have been far too dangerous if he had ever put pen to paper. Jimmy needed to know numbers before he could plan the biggest job that had ever gone down in history.

He thought back to his lucky escape from the Millenium diamond scam that had been big but had also been one that he could have got caught at. The diamond robbery had been his baby but it had got too many nannies for Jimmy's liking especially from overseas. Jimmy preferred a close knit group and he had known that the Dome job was doomed from the moment that he had realised that information had been leaked. Jimmy had got out just in time and he had smiled when he had read about it in the newspaper especially when he realised that a double cross had taken place. That was why Jimmy could only trust his most loyal friends or use people who had too much to lose if they crossed him.

He could not afford to ever be banged up the way that he was which was why he needed plan B to get him out. Jimmy thought carefully of the route that the meat wagon had taken when it had transported him from the Crown Court. He knew that the route was varied for obvious reasons so one of his favours to be recalled needed to be in security which he knew he held right at the very top. He needed bodies hundreds of them and he knew that he could use small time gamblers and tinkers for that. One of the important players in Jimmy's plan was the computer guy at Greater Manchester Police who he had saved for such an occasion. He was a very clever man with a very stupid liking for young boys that had caused him to be in Jimmy's book in capitals.

Three of Jimmy's houses were used by rent boys and it had been in one such house that Jimmy had managed to acquire his police computer guy. Jimmy owned a very busy massage parlour on Stockport Road in Levenshulme which he rented out to Maureen for a very high return. On top of the rent that he got from it Jimmy also received a share of each of the girl's money that they received for 'massages'. Any extras that the girls provided and were paid for was money that they kept all for themselves.

On the whole The Pink Flamingo made Jimmy a lot of tax free cash for very little work. Maureen told him one day that she had been asked about providing young boys but she had not been keen about having them mixing with her girls at the parlour. Maureen had few morals but she had told Jimmy her philosophy one day that 'arses were for shitting out of'. However Maureen's life was governed by pound signs and when she realised how much money they each could make she started to warm to the idea. After long talks and a look at Maureen's business plan Jimmy had decided that she could have three of his houses. Maureen was to be totally in charge of the whole operation seeing Jimmy only to hand over monies. Jimmy would have no known association with the business just as he did or didn't with the Flamingo. The three terraced houses that were used by the rent boys were all on Stockport Road within walking distance of the Flamingo and all handy enough for Maureen to keep a close eye on.

The deal that they had with the rent boys was that Jimmy got fifty per cent of all monies taken and Maureen and the boys shared the rest. They had nine boys doing between six and ten punters a night at fifty quid a go which gave Jimmy a very nice two grand a week minimum.

Maureen was a shrewd old bird and had thought of other ways of making money which included making videos which could be sold at a later date. Each boy would set the recorder with each new punter and they would be recorded by discreetly hidden cameras. Each tape was labelled with the date and when given, a name.

Over the two years that the houses had been in operation Maureen had managed to set up a very lucrative mail order business. She had also very cleverly managed to accumulate about sixty favours for Jimmy two of which were biggies.

Peter Parker had been one of Jimmy's biggies. He was a senior systems analyst working for greater Manchester Police at Trafford and he had the access and ability to throw the whole of the police computers in chaos. Jimmy's plan involved putting all of the police computers out at a precise moment and Peter Parker was the exact man to do that for him. Peter's supervisor status gave him access to the main frame and his lust for young boys gave Jimmy the right to control him.

Peter Parker had been one of the first punters caught with his pants down and at the time he had been astride a fifteen year old boy.

The fifteen year old was Justin Wright the brother of one of Maureen's boys called Damian. Justin had been short of cash one night and he had managed to persuade Damian to let him do a few tricks. Peter Parker had been one such trick and he had become completely besotted with Justin so much so that he had told him his real name and even given him one of his business cards. When Maureen saw Justin at the house when she called to pick up the rent she had gone crazy.

"Jesus Damian, who the fuck is the baby face? It's not a bloody crèche"

Damian had known better than to lie to Maureen for she was his means to him feeding his habit so he had told her the truth.

"It's my kid brother Maureen and he's made a regular punter already"

"What do you mean"?

"Well he's got a posh punter that works for the police and he's arranged to meet him next week. The nonce has even given Justin his business card with his telephone number and everything"

Damian waved the card at Maureen who took it off him and read it. She knew at once that Jimmy might want to add this name to his collection for she knew Jimmy quite well and his passion for collecting favours. The line of work that the punter whose card she was holding might prove very useful to Jimmy in the long run. She put the card in her pocket and collected the rent promising to have a word with the boss about letting young Justin work for the odd night or two.

"The rent might have to go up though because we will be taking a risk"

Justin had agreed for Peter paid him twice the normal rate for his services and Justin actually enjoyed the love and attention that Peter gave him. Maureen had called Jimmy on the phone the next day to ask him to call to see her. Jimmy had gone round to Maureen's house and they had sat and watched the video recording of Peter Parker's night of passion. Jimmy had been totally sickened at the sight of the executive and the schoolboy for he was totally heterosexual. However he had realised that Peter Parker would come in very useful so he had agreed that Justin could continue to work and he arranged for Maureen to get him a good selection of videos to threaten him with. Four weeks later he took Peter's number and he had called him from a payphone.

"Can I speak to Mr Parker please"?

"Peter Parker speaking. Can I help you"?

"No but I'm sure that I can help you. I am a friend of Justin Wright"

"I think you must have the wrong person I don't think I know a Justin"

"Well you have called his name out often enough but if you are unsure I can always show you the tape"

Jimmy had known by the gasp then the sudden silence that he had the man on the phone in the palm of his hand.

"How much do you want"?

"I want nothing at the moment. Go out to the telephone box across the road from your office and I will call you there in ten minutes. Bye"

Jimmy put the phone down and stepped outside of the box to have a fag.

Peter Parker had started to sweat. Someone knew about his illicit love-making sessions and he was about to find out who it was. He made an excuse to go out to his car and left the office. One of his young assistants watched him through the window as he went out of the building and over to the public telephone box.

"I told you that old Parker is having an affair. I bet he is ringing her now.

I feel sorry for his poor wife they've only been married a few months and already she is checking up on him. She asked me about that meeting last time she phoned"

"Which meeting"?

"Exactly"

Peter's programmer looked over at the two gossips who were sharing a joke at their boss' expense and he wasn't amused. As far as he was concerned Peter Parker was a bloody genius and what he did out of working hours was no-one else's business. He had been head hunted and had come from working with the Ministry of Defence with impeccable references. The programmer thought of his own wife and he understood why some marriages might need a little spicing up then he got back on with his work and didn't give Peter a second thought.

Peter jumped as the telephone rang then he had picked it up tentatively.

"Is that you Peter"?

"Yes, what do you want of me"?

"Just to let you know that Justin is only fifteen years old Peter. Did you know that"?

Peter hadn't known but he had felt himself go hard at the thought of Justin's tender young flesh. The fact that he was younger than Peter had known made him seem all the more appealing.

"Do you want money for the tapes is that what you want"?

"The tapes are not for sale but don't worry no-one will see them. I will keep them somewhere safe for you until you have earned the right to get them back"

"Thank-you"

"Don't thank me Peter. One day I will call on you for a favour and you will oblige me and only then will I destroy the tapes"

Peter had breathed a huge sigh of relief. He had expected to be blackmailed and he was relieved that he hadn't been. It would have been awkward to explain to his new bride where their money had gone to.

"What about Justin, what will happen to him"?

"Business as usual but he will have to have a rise and I mean a financial one, goodbye"

Jimmy put the phone down and Peter did the same and left the phone box adjusting the contents of his boxer shorts as he did so.

"The dirty bugger, I told you he was on the phone to a bird"

The junior had been watching Peter as he left the phone box

and he had seen the smug expression on his face as he had touched himself.

Peter let himself back into the building and he went up to his office which was the hub of technical activity but his mind had not been fully on the job.

It had been on the beautiful golden haired boy who had become the love of his life. Peter smiled as he thought of the young boy with the laughing eyes and the tender soft skin who had stolen his heart with his first kiss. Peter hadn't known young Justin for long but it had been long enough to let him know that he loved him. Peter was totally besotted with Justin and he wanted to be with him constantly. He was so different to Madeline the childhood friend that he had married to quell rumours of his sexuality. Madeline's parents had been great friends of his family for years so when Peter was railroaded into finding a wife she had been the obvious choice for him. Peter felt mean towards his wife sometimes for he was sure that she knew that he could never love her and yet she never complained. She seemed happy to play the devoted wife to him and at thirty two years of age Peter wondered if she had felt that her biological clock was fast running out.

In the bedroom she could do nothing for Peter and the only way that he could manage to get a hard on with her was when he thought of his young man. Peter worked hard and put in long hours and he was able to blame his lack of sexual motivation on that. Madeline had read something similar in a magazine and she had allowed him a certain amount of space as the magazine had suggested to do. Although sometimes when they did make love she couldn't help but think that his mind was elsewhere.

Jimmy knew exactly what part Peter would play in his plan for it was Peter the puff that would put the spoke into the wheel of police communications. Jimmy had done a bit of gay bashing when he was younger along with tramp bashing and other bashings that you couldn't mention anymore. It had been part of the youth culture on the estate but he had grown up and now so long as the gays didn't bother him he wouldn't bother them. Big artillery would be a bit of a problem because since the 9/11 incident in New York security had been tightened up in England. Jimmy had to think of an alternative to hardware and he came up with sheer numbers. There could be eight cops on bikes flanking his wagon but a mob of two or three hundred could easily overpower them. Jimmy knew that he could rely on the tinkers for there were bloody hundreds of the buggers who would do anything for a tenner never mind a brand new set of clothes. He had a guy with a clothing warehouse with major gambling debts who he knew could supply him with up to four hundred sets of identical clothing which would cover the money he had lost playing blackjack at the casino.

Jimmy chuckled as he thought about the police putting out a description of the escaped prisoner only to find that everyone in the area was wearing the exact same clothing. It was a brilliant idea.

Then Jimmy needed a couple of head cases with shooters to cause a bit of pandemonium on the streets. He would choose proper nut cases that would get looked after by the 'do gooders' when they got caught.

He also knew that if he had the men all in different directions that it would use up the armed response units in the area and keep them occupied. Jimmy needed an ambulance that would block the road just prior to his break out that needed to be seen to be attending a road traffic accident. The ambulance was easy for he had a doctor at a local private clinic who was earmarked for providing that for him. A top surgeon at the clinic had been stealing drugs for years to placate his wife's addiction. He had written out false prescriptions for ages before getting caught but Jimmy had sorted it for him and had put him in touch with a supplier. Providing an ambulance would be the least that the doctor could do for him so Jimmy included a bit of an ambulance chase down the motorway for good measure. He knew that once he got out of the wagon that the helicopter would be out looking for him and that it would do no harm to send the police on a wild goose chase.

Jimmy got excited as he could see his plan falling into place but he was also getting tired so when the screw brought his dinner he stopped making his plan. Jimmy smiled at the screw who had brought him the extra portion of pie that he had asked for. He was getting used to the food and even to the screws who now all treated him with respect but in two days he knew that he would be a free man again and he just couldn't wait.

Joseph called into the Crown when he got back to Manchester to let Julie know how Jimmy had taken the news of Mike Rooney's death. She was anxious to know that he was okay but she was even more concerned at Joseph's next piece of news, that Jimmy didn't want her at the appeal.

"But why doesn't he want me there, he needs me"?

"Yes he does Julie and this is what he wants you to do" Joseph made sure no-one was around as he told her that Jimmy had a plan and when he told her the bit that concerned her Julie's face lit up. He had told Joseph to ask Julie to arrange cover for the pub.

She had to get hold of the Scottish couple who had looked after the Crown the last time that they had gone on holiday and ask them if they could do relief for her.

Joseph had told her that Jimmy said not to forget the sunscreen and that was a private joke that Julie understood only too well. It meant that she must pack a bag, take their passports and book two tickets to Tenerife. It also meant that she was going to be with her Jimmy sooner than she had imagined and she couldn't wait. Julie thanked Joseph who needed to get home to chase up the favours then she got on the phone. She called the Scottish couple who promised to come down the following day. She called her mobile hairdresser and nail technician and arranged for appointments with them for the next morning. She called the travel agents to arrange the flights and she called her mother to ask her to look after D.J. for her. She had been on the phone to the travel agents when D.J. had walked in.

"We're not going away are we mam because if you are don't include me in your plans, I'm far too busy with work"

"I'm going babes but I know that you are a big boy now and I wouldn't dream of making plans for you other than for you to stay at your gran's"

"Brilliant, send me a card won't you"

Julie said that she would. She knew that D.J. loved to be with his grandma just as much as she loved to be with him. She had looked after him from him being a baby and sometimes Julie could not help but be envious of the loving relationship that they had between them.

Julie knew that D.J. loved her too and she knew that it would give her and Jimmy time to catch up on the time that they had spent apart so she would forfeit her son to her mother. There were only three things that Julie had treasured in her lifetime and they were her mother, her husband and her son and she was grateful that she still had all three. So many of her school friends had been married two or three times and they had still ended up alone with a handful of kids. Others had ended up with arseholes of husbands who used them as punch bags. Julie counted her blessings then went to pack a small suitcase for part of the fun of going away on the last minute was buying the clothes that they needed after getting off the plane.

D.J. was busy packing at the same time that his mother was. He loved to go to stay at his grandma's house. His dad had bought her a large detached house in the nice village of Cheadle where she lived with her two big dogs Jack and Vera. The dogs were Rhodesian Ridgeback dogs that stood almost as high as two small ponies and D.J. loved to take them out for long walks. His grandma lived in the country compared to where he lived and he loved his time outdoors. He had lots of things that he wanted to talk to his grandma about. He wanted to tell her about his new role as manager in the carpet warehouse but most of all he wanted to tell her about his theory on Mike Rooney and how it would prove that his dad was innocent. He also wanted her to store the birthday present that he had bought for his dad's birthday. It was a couple of months off but it was to be a big one so D.J. had bought him a jet ski that he could use on holiday when he got out of prison. Once D.J. had asked his grandma whether or not his dad was a criminal and she had told him very diplomatically that she didn't think that he was but that he certainly knew a lot of people that were. D.J. had known in school that his dad was special. He remembered going out with his dad when he had been little and of some of the remote places that he had visited with him. Everyone had shown respect to his dad just as they had with him and D.J. felt proud of him which was why it was so important to prove his innocence. One night a couple of years earlier he had walked in on his parents to find them counting a mountain of pesetas that had covered most of the front room carpet.

He had asked where it had all come from to be told that it was their holiday fund so he had asked no more questions and he had helped them to count it only to find it came to over one million pounds.

D.J. knew that money like that had not grown on trees but just like his mother he had no intention of ever asking where it had come from. D.J. kissed his mother then left to go to his grandma's house for a couple of weeks.

"Give dad my love won't you and I'll give yours to grandma"

"Tell grandma to look after you and tell her that I will call her soon"

D.J. gave his mother a big hug and a kiss that spoke volumes and she knew that she would miss him loads. She would have loved for him to want to go to live in Tenerife with them but she knew that he wouldn't. They had always taught D.J. to be his own man so they couldn't object when he stuck to his own beliefs. Julie kissed her son who was growing up to be a handsome young man then she gave him one last hug then waved him off as he left.

Chapter 11

Joseph had got back to his house to find that it was dark and empty. Not only had the police team gone but so had his cleaner. Poor little Angelica had left her country to come to England to find a new culture only to find that it was just as evil as the one she had left behind. The gruesome suicide in the bathroom had been more than Angelica could take so she had left a sweet note thanking Joseph for 'tanking her on'. Joseph knew that he could easily get a replacement from the agency but he had decided to do without any help until he had sorted out Jimmy's problem. He loosened his tie then made himself a pot of fresh coffee and a big club sandwich then he had sat down to make his calls.

The first call he made was to Lee Won-king and Joseph was surprised to get through so quickly when he heard the Chinese voice on the phone.

"I've been instructed to call you to ask for a favour"

Lee had smiled to himself for he had waited many years to be able to repay Jimmy for the wonderful thing that he had done for him and now it seemed that the time had come.

Lee remembered when he had first arrived in this country that had become his home all of those years ago. He had been a frightened little kid running from danger from a country he had only known as home.

Jimmy had been a complete stranger and yet he had not

only saved Lee's life on that first day at school but he had also given him new clothes to go home in. Lee had been a scraggy little Chinese kid in a strange country and Jimmy had helped him. He had become a very good friend to him for no reason other than the fact that he liked him and Lee would never forget that. Lee was no longer a weak little boy for now he was one of the most powerful men in the country. He headed the Triad movement in the North and he owned and ruled more than half of Chinatown. He was seen as an Eastern God not to be messed with and was almost untouchable. He had gone to live with his uncle twenty three years ago, the uncle who had taught Lee everything that he knew. His uncle had headed the families for many years but he was now nearing seventy and he had passed all responsibility on to his nephew. Lee was head of a big organisation and he had the power to be able to grant Jimmy whatever favour it was that he wanted. All he had to do was ask.

Lee had been sad when he had first been sent to live with his uncle but over the years he began to realise just why his mother had insisted that he must not live with her. For six months after him moving away there had been an explosion in the back of the chip shop that had taken his poor mother's life. If Lee had been there with her then he would have been killed as well but he hadn't, for he had been safe with his uncle. The same uncle that his mother had entrusted him to for that very reason. The same uncle that had taught him how to get revenge, the same uncle that had shown him how easy it was to kill when your heart is full of hate. That was what Lee had done when he had found the ones that had killed his mother. He had been just eighteen years old and he had been able to capture the two men responsible and tie them up. He had been able to cut off their testicles with a filleting knife and deep fat fry their body parts as the men had screamed as they watched. Then as they had both slowly bled to death he had been able to shove their own deep fried bollocks into their mouths and he had managed to stop their screams. Jimmy had been there for Lee at his mother's funeral just as Lee had been there at Jimmy's wedding by which time they had both become big men in their own rights. Lee had become a Master of Tai Kwan Do and his body had grown into the body of a strong powerful man. His skin had become a canvas for the beautiful Chinese signs that adorned it and even back then he had been recognised as a leader. He had thick shiny hair and big prominent eyebrows above his diamond black eyes.

Jimmy had never mentioned to anyone what he had done for Lee and he had recognised the humility in that. 'There is no need to say what is obvious' was an old Chinese proverb that Lee very much believed in.

Lee's power and might unfortunately came with a high price. It had made him a target for other gangs that were fighting for control and he had to keep a highly protected lifestyle. The last time that he had seen Jimmy had been only a couple of years earlier when Jimmy and his family had gone into one of Lee's restaurants in Chinatown for a meal to celebrate their wedding anniversary. Lee had been fighting for control of Chinatown at the time and he had known that his life was in danger so he had not shown his face. Instead he had watched his old friend Jimmy and his family through the two way mirror on the wall.

A message had been sent to their table saying that the management hoped that they had enjoyed their meal.

The waiter also told them that their meal was on the house. Lee had watched Jimmy looking around as if he had known of Lee's presence but Lee had been nowhere to have been seen. Lee had not been able to resist teasing Jimmy and he had sent over a tray of fortune cookies at the end of their meal. Jimmy had opened the one closest to him and he had read his fortune out loud 'An unasked favour is the greatest favour of all' He had smiled as he stood up and he had walked over to the large mirror that hung on the wall concealing his pal who was stood on the other side of it. Jimmy had stared hard into the mirror knowing that somehow Lee would know that he knew he was there.

Lee spoke to Joseph who had been waiting for a response to his question.

"I am ready to do whatever he asks me whenever he wants me to do it"

"I will tell him and I will call again tomorrow, thank-you. Goodbye."

Joseph was extremely pleased with his first result. He poured himself a drink and sat back down to make his next call.

Before he did he thought about how little he and Jimmy actually knew each other. Despite having worked for him for many years there were names in the book that Joseph had heard of but of who he had no idea how they were known to Jimmy. Joseph had not thought twice about helping Jimmy when he had been asked to even after he had been told that it could prove to be very dangerous. Maybe it was because that Jimmy had put so much trust in him that Joseph was determined to put everything that he could into the plan for him. Joseph had never done anything dangerous in his life apart from on the ski slopes and he was starting to enjoy the excitement that came with the danger.

Chapter 12

Alberto Vincente was enjoying a large vintage brandy with his beautiful wife Maria when his private phone rang out. He got up to answer it and Maria made herself scarce as she always did when her husband talked business. It was Joseph on the phone asking the very same thing as he had just done with Lee Won-king.

"Of course I will do anything that I can for my very good friend"

"Can I call tomorrow with the details"?

"Certainly my friend, I will await your call"

Alberta walked over to where his darling wife sat sipping her cognac and he kissed her tenderly on the top of her head.

"The time has come my darling, to repay the favour"

Maria put down her drink and took hold of Alberto's hand and smiled.

"Be careful my darling"

It was Alberto's turn to smile for Jimmy had given them back the most precious thing in their lives and no favour would be too much. Alberto would give his life for Jimmy if it was necessary.

"Let's go upstairs and check that the birthday girl is still sleeping"

Alberto took hold of Maria's hand and he led her up the sweeping staircase that led to Violleta Sophia Vincente's bedroom suite.

The Vincentes lived in a splendid Manor house in the country that looked more like a prestigious hotel than a home. Young Violleta had what would be looked on as the presidential suite in the home. Violleta's vigilant nanny sat outside her ward's bedroom door for since the night of the kidnap she had sworn never to let her out of her sight again. Margarita had been a first class nanny who had been devoted to her charge yet she had not been able to prevent Gaz Mutch's lot from getting their hands on her darling baby. Margarita still had nightmares when she remembered the snatch and how it had happened on that terrible night. The chauffeur com bodyguard had taken Mr and Mrs Vincente out to their weekly bridge game and Margarita had been in the house with only the baby Violleta for company. It was the week that the pool man was away on holiday and it was also the night that the gardener had decided to take his wife out to the theatre so it was quieter than usual. Margarita had bathed and fed baby Violleta who was sleeping soundly in her crib. Margarita was sitting by her side in an armchair reading a book when she thought that she could hear a dog barking loudly. It sounded as though it was just outside the window and Margarita peered out to see a loose Pit Bull Terrier running wild in the courtyard. The house was secure so Margarita had assumed that the dog had got through a hole in the shrubbery and that it had come in from the road. The dog looked quite vicious as it ran around in circles barking loudly below the window. Margarita feared that the dog's constant barking might wake the baby up so she had been quite relieved when she had spotted a man climbing over the front gate. The man held a dog lead in his hand that he was waving about wildly as he shouted to the noisy creature to shut up. The alarm had sounded and the man was clearly visible on one of the many monitors that guarded the home. Margarita turned the alarm off before it could transfer itself to the police station for she could see the reason that had caused it to go off. The man got down from the gate and walked towards the dog that ran towards him as he called it. Margarita was pleased that the owner had come to claim his escaped dog before it had managed to wake baby Violleta up. The man walked towards the gate then he had turned to gesture to Margarita for her to open it so he could get out with the dog and Margarita had pressed the button to activate the automatic gates.

The large wrought iron gates slowly opened as the man and the dog approached towards them then suddenly for no reason the man fell to the ground and the dog ran off into the road. The man jerked as he lay on the driveway as though he was having some kind of epileptic fit and Margarita did not stop to think before she ran out to help him. As she ran to his side a big white van screeched into the driveway and stopped outside the front door that she had left open in her haste to help the man. The chap on the floor jumped up and grabbed Margarita before she had chance to get back to the house and he trundled her to the front door and pushed her inside. Despite her struggles she was overpowered and soon Margarita found herself being taped to a chair and she looked over to where baby Violleta still lay sleeping in her crib.

"Please don't hurt the baby she is the daughter of Alberto V……"
Before she could finish speaking her mouth was taped completely shut.

Two of the men carried the crib complete with sleeping baby out to the van and put it into the back of it then the driver walked back into the house and picked up some baby food from the kitchen and a white fluffy bunny rabbit. One of the other two men came in and started to rifle through the drawers only to be shouted at by the big Scotsman.

"We have got what we came for, let's go"

Then he loosened the tape from Margarita's mouth just enough for her to be able to breathe so that she wouldn't die before passing the message on.

"Tell Vincente to be at the restaurant at ten o clock sharp. Tell him that if he calls the police he will never see his daughter alive again"

The kidnapper walked into a old Roman vase that stood in the large hallway causing it to crash onto the marble floor where it broke into a hundred small pieces. He rushed out and jumped in the passenger seat of the van which started to move away taking baby Violetta with it. The driver reached out to press a button that opened the gates enabling them to pass through. Once the van was out of the driveway on the road the gates closed behind them leaving a very distraught Margarita tied up inside. Margarita struggled to get her hands free but they were tied far too tightly. She bit at the piece of tape that the man had loosened around her mouth to allow her to breath. Some of it was stuck firmly to her lip and she could taste her own blood as it pulled off her skin as it came away and she cried out in pain. Then very slowly she chewed away until she was able to shout for help but the house was so isolated that no-one could hear her. She looked on the floor and she saw her handbag that lay where the crib had been. She thought that if she could reach the bag then she might be able to get to her mobile phone and use it to try to get help. With no thought for her own safety she started to rock the chair backwards and forwards until eventually it fell to the ground. Margarita cried out as her head banged hard against the carpet then she slowly shifted herself closer to her bag with the chair still attached to her body. She then, very cleverly for a woman of her size, managed to get her foot through the handle of the bag. Then she kicked it with all of her might causing the bag to go into the air and she watched as all of its contents flew out. The mobile phone ended up somewhere near her head so Margarita had to shuffle up to get as close to it as she could. Luckily the phone was switched on and she had fast dial on it. Alberto had bought the phone for her for her last birthday and he had installed all the numbers that she needed so that she could reach them in an emergency. At the time she had thought it was too new technology for a lady of her years to use but now she had been glad that he had got it for her. Summoning all of her strength she managed to hit the number one key with her chin and miraculously she found that she had managed to get through for she could hear it ringing out..

Alberto's mobile phone rang out just as he was about to declare his hand of cards so he took it from his pocket and answered it. As he did so he had turned on the loud speaker so everyone listened in horror to the loud screams of the nanny.

"HELP ME PLEASE, THEY HAVE THE BABY"

Alberto jumped up and signalled to Alphonso who ran out to get the car then he and Alberto sped off into the night. Maria sat in a state of shock as her host went to get his car to take Maria and follow the men to their home. As Alphonso drove the car home Alberto was screaming down the phone to let Margarita know that they were on their way to rescue her. Margarita could faintly hear somebody on the phone but she continued to cry for help until they arrived by which time she was hysterical and hoarse. The gates opened to allow the car in and it raced up the drive and screeched to a halt at the front door. Alberto ran in the house to find his nanny tied to a chair lying on the floor next to where the crib and his baby had been.

"Violleta my darling bambino" he cried as he ripped the tape from his nanny's mouth.

"Sir I am so sorry but I couldn't stop them"

Margarita was crying but she stopped when she saw her employer pick up at the phone.

"Don't call the police Sir they said if you did that they would kill her"

Alberto froze as the anger flowed through his bloodstream.

"They said that you must be at the restaurant at ten"

Alberto looked at his watch. It was ten minutes to nine which meant that he had just over one hour so he picked up the phone and called the one person that he thought might know who was involved.

Alphonso had untied Margarita who was holding onto Maria who had just arrived there and who was crying hysterically herself.

"Jimmy, it is Alberto Vincente here. They have taken my baby Jimmy some bastard has got my princess. What shall I do"?

Jimmy told him to find out all he could about the gang involved and he had promised to meet him at the restaurant in thirty minutes.

"Chiaou" finished Alberto then he turned to comfort his distraught wife.

"My darling, please do not cry this way. We will get her back I can promise you that"

Alberto made three more phone calls before leaving for the restaurant for he could see that the ladies were deeply distressed.

He called the doctor to ask him to come over and prescribe something for Maria and Margarita. He called for someone to come and sit with the ladies then he called for some of his top men to meet him.

As soon as the doctor had arrived Alphonso drove his boss

to their meeting place. They drove into the car park to find seven Mercedes cars already parked there in a straight line. Alphonso parked up next to the straight line of polished vehicles then him and his boss went in through the back door. The other of his men were briefed on what was going down so they all listened intently before they all took their places.

Two of them manned the back door, eight of them sat at four window tables as if waiting to take a meal and the others listened to the rest of Alberto's orders. Jimmy drove into the dimly lit car park to find it half taken up by Alberto's people's cars. He parked up his car then he walked round to the back door where he was grabbed by one of Alberto's henchmen and he was frogmarched into the kitchen with a gun held to his head.

"Christ Alberto I'm on your bloody side"

The gorilla loosened his grip on Jimmy and he put his gun away as Alberto took hold of Jimmy and kissed him on two cheeks as was his custom. Then they sat down and Alberto told Jimmy all that he knew. Jimmy took stock of the fact that there was a white Mercedes van, a pitbull terrier dog and a big man with a Scottish accent and he already had a good idea of who might be involved. He ordered four of Alberto's men to get in their cars and to take up strategic positions on the main road. One in the Co-op car park one in the side street next to where the road forked and the other two on either side of the road in readiness to follow whatever might turn up. None of them knew what to expect but when some-one did turn up it had been nothing like any of them had thought it would be. At ten o clock on the dot a pizza delivery boy drove into the car park on a 50cc scooter and he stopped outside of the front door.

The delivery boy got off his scooter and he was just untying the pizza boxes from the back of his bike when he found him-self being whisked off his feet and taken roughly to the back of the building. It all happened so fast that none of the diners eating there that evening were aware that anything was going on as they sat enjoying their meals. The delivery boy had no idea what was happening to him and he started to cry as he was thrown across the kitchen from one man to another. It was only his second day on the job and he had been warned of people trying to rip him off for the odd pizza or two.

No-one had told him about what was happening to him right then. Alberto pushed his men to one side and looked directly at the boy.

"What is the message boy"?

"Nnine ninety nine Sir but it doesn't matter you can have it for nowt"

The boy stuttered nervously he didn't care about the money or the job they could stick their job even though he did like riding the scooter.

Alberto grabbed hold of the two pizza boxes and he opened the top one to find Violleta's soft pink cashmere cardigan inside it and the very sight of it brought tears to his eyes. He opened the second box to find a note that read:

FIVE MILLION POUNDS IN CASH BY 9.OOA.M. Leave it in a bag in the bottle bin on the car park.

He glared at the young boy who was cowering in the corner with pee trickling down his leg onto the floor.

"Who gave you the boxes boy"?

"I don't know who it was, just some bloke said it was a joke and that you would think it was really funny and laugh your head off"

Alberto had never felt less like laughing. He turned back to the boy.

"Who was it, if you want to live son you had better tell me"
The boy looked really scared and he had started to cry

helplessly.

Jimmy held the boy by the shoulders and spoke to him softly.

"Listen son you could be in big trouble here but I like you because I think that you have been set up so you tell me all you know and I will try and make sure that you don't get hurt, okay"

The boy nodded and he started to tell Jimmy all that he knew. A man had given him twenty quid just to do a delivery for him at a certain time.

"Did the man have a Scottish accent"?

The boy nodded. Jimmy needed to know one more thing to confirm to him it was who he thought it was.

"Tell me son did he have a scar on his face"?

The boy laughed nervously because the man did have a scar on his face, one that went down his cheek and across his mouth. He told Jimmy this.

Jimmy smiled he knew exactly who they were dealing with. He led the boy to the back door and shoved a ten pound note in his top pocket.

"Go home boy and forget everything that has just happened. If you mention this to anyone we will have to come looking for you. Comprende!"

The poor lad ran round to his scooter which he frantically tried to kick start. It took about six fumbling efforts before the scooter actually started up and he went speeding out of the car park as he headed to the pizza shop to hand in his notice.

"Ali Campbell is the monkey we are looking for and Jason Mutch is the organ grinder"

"Where can we find him Jimmy"?

"You can't. Leave it to me I have a score to settle with him from many years ago. You get the cash together just in case we need it. Can you get your hands on that much at this short notice"?

Alberto nodded to Jimmy. It would be difficult but a few phone calls should do it. Jimmy left to round up a few of his own men and he headed to where he knew they would all be. There was a stripper on at the Pineapple with bazookas the size of melons that she had been just about to get out for the lads as Jimmy had entered the pub. He tapped each of the boys on their shoulders and gestured for them to follow him out of the pub. The crew moved reluctantly from their front row seats as they left their drinks and the delectable Delilah with her delicious melons delightfully on show. Jimmy waited on the car park for them then making sure that there was no-one in earshot he began to question them.

"Ali Campbell where can we find him"?

"Well he usually hangs out at the 'Star' piped up Tall Robbie.

"Why? What do you want him for"?

"They have snatched a baby, Alberto Vincente's baby to be exact"

"Fucking Hell have they got a death wish or what"?

Jimmy looked at his watch it was twenty past eleven and he had just over eight and a half hours to get things sorted.

"Is Ali still Jason Mutch's number one"? "Yeah"

"If they snatched a baby where do you think they would they take it to?"

"Well Jason has a gaff on Princess Road and he does a lot of dealings at his video shop in Cheadle"

"Anywhere else we might find him"?

"He has about eighty young runners that live in the flats at Brinnie but it's too open there someone might see them"

"Okay Robbie you and Pete go to the Star. If Ali is in there watch his every move and follow him when he leaves"

"Sammy do you know which is Jason's gaff on Princess

Road"?

Sammy nodded, he was hungry for action especially with the likes of Jason Mutch and his cronies and it showed.

"You take Sonny with you and wait outside. Call me the minute you see anything suspicious and I mean anything"

"Right boss"

"Tony you come with me, we'll take the video shop"

Alberto Vincente had headed home to try to get the cash together. He had about two million in his safes and he had a good idea where he could get the rest from. It wasn't the amount of the ransom that they had demanded for Alberto was worth fifty times that amount but it was the timescale that was a problem for him. Alberto had a Picasso in his private study that he had acquired in the eighties. It was one that he couldn't put out on display because it had come with a big haul from the Tate Art Gallery unofficially.

His dear friend and confidante Carlos had asked on many occasions to buy the painting from him but Alberto had always refused. Now was a good time to sell and if it gave Alberto his precious baby daughter back he would happily forfeit it.

He called Carlos who had promised to send his man over early the next morning with the cash for Alberto and to collect the painting for him. Once the money was sorted Alberto used all of his time and his strength to comfort his poor wife who was still totally beside herself.

Alberto had known Jimmy for many years. He knew of his reputation that spoke only good of him. He was a powerful man with many connections but more than that he was an honourable man who could be trusted. Alberto hoped that he could trust Jimmy in this matter. He tried to call him but his line was permanently busy so he left a message instead.

"Call me when you know anything. I will be waiting. Chiaou"

Tall Robbie and Pete had found Ali in the Star. He was stood at the bar knocking back the McCallum whiskies in doubles. He was on his own which was strange and he kept looking at his watch. He ordered another drink

"I'll just have the one that I came for then I'll be off"
He said in a broad Scottish accent. The girl behind the bar handed him the drink as she joked with him.

"Ooo on a promise are we? It's not like you to be going this early"

"Sort of, see you tomorrow"
Then he had knocked the rest of his drink down and left the pub.

Pete and Tall Robbie were just a few minutes behind him leaving the girl behind the bar sniffing at her armpits as she wondered what she had done that had caused her to lose all her punters at once.

Robbie and Pete got into the car just as Ali's car left the car park and they followed him cautiously down the main road. Ali stopped his car outside an Indian take away leaving the boys trailing him to park a little further down the road. There was a queue at the Indian so the boys waited patiently in the car watching carefully in the wing mirrors so they didn't lose him.

Sammy and Sonny had been sat opposite the house on Princess Road for ages but they had not seen or heard a thing. They called in to Jimmy who had told them that it was quiet at his end too so for them to stay there for a while longer much to their disappointment.

Ali had left the pub and he was on the road somewhere and there was a chance that he might happen to go there so the boys were instructed to wait there for a while longer. Jimmy was just starting to think that they were all wasting time sat around when the door to the video shop slowly opened. A young woman dressed in white came out of the shop and she looked around cautiously then locked the shop door behind her.

She started to walk down the road and it looked as though she was heading towards the twenty four hour garage on the opposite side. Tony got out of the car and walked quite quickly so he would get to the garage before her and he took out a fiver and asked for twenty Bensons.

The attendant gave him the cigarettes and his change then he asked if he could help the young lady who was next in the queue. Tony took the cellophane wrapper from around his cigarette packet as he stood just enough in earshot of the woman to hear her ask for nappies.

He ran back to the car to give Jimmy the good news.

"This is the one Jimmy, she has just asked for nappies"

Jimmy called the boys in. Tall Robbie and Pete were following Ali who seemed to be heading in Jimmy's direction anyway and Sonny and Sammy were just glad to be relieved of their boring house watch.

The young woman walked back to the shop carrying the packet of nappies that she had just bought from the garage, under her arm.

She looked behind her before opening the door then when she was sure that she was not being followed she entered the shop. Tony got up as though to follow her but Jimmy stopped him.

"Ali is on his way over let's wait for him to turn up and we can go in with him"

The baby was crying loudly when the woman returned with the nappies and she was worried to see Crazy Harry holding the baby over his big shoulders. She took the baby from him and lay her down to change her only to find that the poor baby's nappy was soaked through.

"Poor little bugger no wonder she was crying so"

"Just shut it up Milly and don't go getting sentimental on

125

me, you had all your kids put into care didn't you"?

Milly nodded but that didn't stop her liking the poor little mite that lay before her. Harry was getting restless and the crying had done his head in.

"Where the fucks Ali and Danny they should have been here ages ago"?

"Ali rang before he is on his way back and Danny has gone with Jason to sort a bit of business out"

"Well they had better hurry up because I am not cut out for babysitting"

"What's going to happen to the baby Harry"?

"Well her parents are rolling in money so they will give it us and we can piss off to the Costa del Crime with loads of money"

"Where"? Julie was not a bright girl and she had never been further than Heaton Park so she had thought that the Costa del Crime was a real place.

"Forget it just shut that kid up before I do"

Ali pulled up at the side of the video shop and he sat in the car whilst he gobbled his curry and rice up. He didn't like sharing his food so he just pigged it down till he felt sick. He got out of the car and he threw the screwed up piece of paper carelessly onto the floor.

"You should put that paper in a bin mate"

came a voice from behind and Ali turned round to see who had dared to say that to him only to feel a good right hand jab to his jaw that caused him to fall backwards. Before he hit the floor he felt a heavy blow to the stomach that managed to dislodge the food that he had just swallowed and he started to bring it all back.

Tony put his hand up over Ali's mouth and he felt the warm vomit spill through his fingers. He picked the paper up from the floor and stuffed it hard inside Ali's mouth as Ali's eyes almost bulged out of his head. Then he taped his mouth closed and he threw Ali onto the floor where he left him to choke quietly on his own vomit.

"Told you not to drop litter" he said cheekily as he went through his pockets looking for the key to the shop. Ali's face turned red as he tried to struggle but it was no use for the vomit trapped in his windpipe fought with the air that tried to circulate and the vomit finally won.

Jimmy and Tony used the key to open the door and they started to creep up the stairs. As they neared the top they could hear someone singing a lullaby which at least meant that the baby was still alive. They took out their guns and had them ready as they listened at the door to check out the numbers in there. They could only hear one other voice other than the woman singing and it sounded like crazy Harry.

"I'm going to call Ali, he said that he would be back in an hour, I think that he is taking the piss now"

Jimmy kicked the door open and with Tony he rushed in taking Harry and the girl both by surprise.

"Ali can't hear you Harry because he is dead"

Harry went for his gun but Tony got to him first as he whacked him in the face with the butt of his revolver. Harry fell to the ground and the young woman held the baby out to Jimmy which he carefully took from her. She had no intentions of getting into more trouble than she had to. The baby looked none the worst for her ordeal as she smiled up at Jimmy and he could not wait to phone her father and give him the good news.

Tony was busy taping Harry and Milly back to back on a pair of chairs as Jimmy spoke to Alberto on his mobile.

"Jimmy anything to tell, have you found anything yet"?

"Only a gorgeous baby girl that is looking for her papa"

"Mama Mia, they've found our baby. Where are you Jimmy"?

"We will be with you in thirty minutes just put your money back under the mattress"

"Thank you my friend, I owe you"

Robbie and Pete had watched as Ali was taken care of and they had waited until he was well and truly dead before they threw his lifeless body into the boot of his own car. When they were sure that Jimmy and Tony were alright Pete got into Ali's car and drove away with Robbie following closely behind. They drove up to the reservoir where Pete took Ali's car to the top of a slope. Then he took off the handbrake and jumped out of the moving car as it headed for the water at the bottom. The car sank complete with Ali's lifeless body in the boot to join the rest of the rubbish that lay there.

Sammy and Sonny got to the video shop just as Jimmy was locking up. There was a notice in the window that read CLOSED DUE TO BEREAVEMENT that was totally accurate.

"Jeez boss how come we miss out on all of the action have we done something to offend you"?

"No Sammy you haven't done anything wrong call me at eleven, take the Merc and make sure that you are tooled up"

"Thanks boss I'll call you in the morning. Come on Sonny let's go"

Sammy dropped Sonny off at a club then he went home with the intention of getting a right good shag from his missus for there was nothing like one before a big hit.

Alberto and Maria Vincente were waiting at home looking anxiously out of the window and they opened the gates when they saw Jimmy's headlights approaching. They ran out onto the courtyard eager to see their precious baby daughter return home safely. Tony was sat in the back seat carefully cradling the most precious cargo he would ever be likely to handle again. Jimmy stopped the car and the doors were quickly opened by a very expectant father. Tony passed the sleeping princess to her doting papa who showered her sleeping face with a million kisses. Maria Vincente was soon by his side and the two of them cooed over the little bundle of joy that they had never expected to see again so soon.

"We owe you Jimmy big time. I can't thank you enough but what about the captors"?

"Sorted but listen to the one o clock news tomorrow"
They all had a couple of celebratory drinks then Tony and Jimmy left to sort out a little unfinished business that they had"
They got outside then Jimmy called Jason on Ali's mobile.

"What the fucks going on I can't get an answer from anyone"
shouted a very irate Jason.

"Ali speak to me you Scottish twat"

"Ali can't come to the phone right now because he is what you might call a little indisposed"

"Who the fuck is that"?

"Just someone wondering who the fuck you think that you are and someone who has the baby. It's my shout now but I'm willing to cut you in so meet me tomorrow at twelve thirty sharp at the Roman Lakes"

"How will I know who you are, do I know you"?

"Not yet but you will pretty soon. I'll come to you but I'll call you on Ali's phone first"
Jason looked both puzzled and angry as he turned to look at Danny.

"Looks like Ali's let us down again. Some goon has just told me that he is moving in on us and that he is taking the lion's share. He's got the kid so he holds the trump card, for now anyway. He wants to meet tomorrow"

"What about the money boss"?

"Fuck the money for now what about Ali, Harry and Milly. If he's got Ali's phone and the baby he must have my people too and I want them back and then I want his guts for garters"

Jason would have to wait until the next day to find out what had happened to Ali and it was only the bottle of Jack Daniels that him and Danny had just polished off that had helped him to accept it as he did.

Sammy called Jimmy right on cue the next morning and he had listened carefully as he was given his orders. He picked Sonny up and he filled him in on the plan then he had let him take the wheel for the rest of the journey for Sammy had far more important matters to deal with. He glanced at his watch to see that it was thirteen minutes past twelve and almost time. He took his pistol from his pocket and cocked it in readiness..

It was twelve fifteen when Jason's car stopped at the traffic lights near the Roman lakes. His mobile rang and he answered it hoping to get a clue as to who he was messing with.

"Are you smiling"?

asked Jimmy strangely as if about to take a photograph of him.

" I am always smiling mate" were the last words that Jason spoke.

It was a hot day and the windows to the car were down. The lights were just about to change as another Mercedes car pulled up alongside them. Sammy let down his window and he had looked Jason directly in the eye before he had pulled the trigger on his piece and blew Jason away. Jason smiled no more but Jimmy did as he heard the shot come down Ali's mobile. He had dropped Ali's cell phone down the nearest sewer then he had rushed home to listen to the lunchtime news.

Alberto and Maria Vincente had been celebrating the return of their baby daughter all morning with friends when Alberto noticed the time. It was almost one o' clock so he switched on the radio just in time to catch the bit of the news headlines that he had been waiting for

'A man was shot down in cold blood as he sat waiting at traffic lights earlier today. It is suspected that he was a gang member and that the incident was drug related'

There was a loud cheer that ran through the Vincente household as they all raised their glasses and toasted.

"To Jimmy"

Alberto and Maria remembered that day as if it was only yesterday. They looked down at their beautiful little daughter who was sleeping peacefully and they took it in turns to bend down and kiss her gently on her forehead. She opened her beautiful violet coloured eyes to see her father's face above her own and she gave him an angelic smile that melted his heart.

"Thank-you papa for a wonderful birthday party. I love you so much"

"Thank-you princess for making our lives complete. We love you too"

Then making sure that she had fallen back to sleep they tiptoed out of her bedroom past an ever vigilant Margarita who sat in the corridor.

Maria never spoke of Alberto's business but where Jimmy was concerned she felt that she had to for they owed him so much.

"Whatever he wants Alberto. You must do for him"

The criminal world had been thrown into turmoil at the news of Jason's sudden death and no-one could figure out who had been responsible. Jason had made so many enemies over the years that it could have been one of a hundred people. The police were only too happy to have finally put Jason to bed for he had been a thorn in their side for a long time.

They had been unable to ever pin anything on him for he had always managed to find a fall guy to take the rap for him. Lots of people had grassed on him but none would ever take the stand against him as he had started to become a law unto himself. His death had also left a hole in the market with at least six other gangs fighting over control of his patch which had become very much up for grabs. Jason Mutch had not always been bad he had just turned out that way gradually.

He had started out as an only child who had managed to get into grammar school where he had behaved for the first couple of years. As he had got older he was like any teenage hood that smoked a bit of weed and got drunk and had the odd fight at the weekend. He was a fit lad with a good body that he started to improve when he joined the gym. It started off as a hobby but it had turned into an obsession with him and soon he was taking the steroids that he bought from a guy at the gym.

Jason realised that there was a big market for the steroids so he decided to cut out the middle man. He also began to find his own customers and before long he found himself trading big time. Then his portfolio increased with demand and soon he was selling any drug that he was asked for. His clientele had got so big that he had to employ others to run for him until he ended up with a small army of youngsters working for him.

Jason had three pit bull terrier dogs that became his trademark. He used the dogs to punish any of the young lads or girls that tried to double cross or steal from him by throwing the kid into the back of his van with the dogs. Jason used to take the offenders to a remote location where their screams would not be heard. Even the odd dog walker that sometimes did hear something never passed it any further for Jason's reputation was growing and he was known as bad to evil. Jason usually recruited his new followers from outside school playgrounds. He would start his recruitment by giving away free samples to kids that he knew did not have a mind of their own then when they were hooked on the drugs he would swoop.

He gave the kids goods for services and once they were with him he reckoned that he would have them for life however short that might prove to be. At the time of Jason's death he had over eighty young runners working for him who depended on him on a daily basis, he also owed a lot of money out. The blackmail attempt would have been Jason's only way of getting straight and paying up for an assignment that had already been spent. Jason left a lot of enemies behind when he had died as well as leaving his own gang in turmoil and the local police confused. There was so much confusion in the end that four different people went down on conspiracy charges for the crime whilst Sammy walked free. It was surprising how many other parties actually took responsibility for the murder because for many months after he had died every pub in the land had at least one person that had rid the world of Jason Mutch.

Even the big boys from the 'old days' had smiled at the news of Jason's death for he had even stepped on their toes on his way to the top. It had been cause for many celebrations in their nightclubs that they had retired to for several weeks after his untimely death.

Jimmy wanted none of Jason's territory or his scams for he had been happy just to settle an old score and help a good friend along the way. It had been Jason that had got Jimmy's sister hooked on heroin causing him and his mother years of heartache and at last Jimmy had paid him back.

Susie was a girl that could have had everything courtesy of her brother but instead she had thought that she could handle everything and anyone that crossed her path. She had been quite taken with Jason when she had met him at a club one night and before too long he had her in his clutches with all the other poor sods that he dealt to. Jimmy sold the stuff but he never touched it himself nor would he ever have let his sister take it. Susie had got fed up of walking in her big brother's shadow and she had rebelled big style. She had taken the drugs that Jason had introduced her to and she had turned to prostitution like so many had done before her to pay for the drugs. She had got pregnant so many times and each time she just paid for an abortion until she was told that she would never be able to have children at all. Jimmy had been robbed of the chance of ever becoming an uncle and he had all but lost his sister. Her behaviour had turned her mother into a nervous wreck and given her father even more of an excuse to drink himself into an early grave. Jimmy would never have forgiven Jason for what he had done to his family and he had vowed to get him back. Alberto Vincente's own crisis had given him the perfect opportunity and Jimmy knew that he would enjoy handing out the punishment that Jason deserved and he had.

Chapter 13

Jimmy sat in his cell with his mind racing as he put the final touches to his plan that would get him out of prison. He was excited, for as long as he had enough man power he knew that he could carry it off. It would take almost all of the favours that he had accumulated over the years but it would be worth it for him to taste freedom again. Jimmy knew that his plan would take him out of the country as well as making a laughing stock of the law but best of all it would make a shit load of money for some very dear buddies of his at the same time. Jimmy knew that Julie would love for him to retire and this would be the ideal time for him to do it but before he did hang his boots up he needed to plan this one last job. Jimmy's plan was going to be the biggest he had ever contrived and if he succeeded it would go down as one of the biggest jobs in history. The first part of Jimmy's plan involved him breaking out and that would happen on the way back to Walton prison when the meat wagon he was in would be ambushed.

Jimmy intended to use sheer numbers to overcome his police escort and then as they freed him from his cuffs he would put on his new clothes courtesy of a clothing manufacturer that owed him. The clothes that Jimmy would wear for the first part of his journey would be identical to those that his rescuers would be wearing, all three hundred of them. It would all be very black and white literally. Jimmy smiled to himself as he imagined the chaos as police officers looked for a white male wearing black pants and a white tee shirt as hundreds of them ran riot through the surrounding streets. Jimmy would use three lots of getaway cars with the first one being a van so that he could change into his holiday gear. Then one of the two others would eventually take him to where he had arranged to meet Julie and to his passport and ticket to the sunshine. Hopefully if the plan went to order under the concisely timed orders from Joseph at exactly the same time as Jimmy made his escape there would be four big foreign banks being cleared out. All police communications would be put out of action courtesy of the computer supervisor at police headquarters. The same person would sabotage some of the traffic lights in the middle of Manchester at exactly the same time as the communications system went on the blink.

Liam Docherty would phone in two bogus bomb scares using authentic codes known to the police. These would be at locations in opposite directions of the bank jobs stretching the police force out to the limit. There would also be a number of real armed robberies to keep the armed response units busy and there would be hundreds and hundreds of bogus calls. If Jimmy's plan went well he would be on a plane to Tenerife not long after the time that the biggest haul in history was having a police escort taking it to its secret location. The goods would travel in the guise of radio active material that would be locked away in lead containers and taken away to a government fortress. All people handling the booty after it had been packed away would be sworn in to the Official Secrets Act not to disclose its contents or its location to anyone. Not one of them would ever know what they had actually carried nor would they know for whom. Only four great leaders and their most trusted men and Jimmy and Joseph knew of the plan.

Under Jimmy's orders they would wait patiently for one year before they even looked at what they had stolen between them. Then and only then at Jimmy's say so would they meet up and unlock their treasures which would be shared out equally five ways.

In order that not one of the men involved could betray another Jimmy had arranged for a very special security door to have four new locks fitted. Each of the leaders from each of the gangs that had carried out the robberies would be given their own key ensuring that they would all need to be present to open the door. All four main men were good friends to Jimmy who he knew that he could rely on. They each felt that they owed Jimmy a big favour but Jimmy knew that they were loyal enough to carry out the jobs based on friendship alone. The two outsider men owed Jimmy big favours that they would never be able to truly repay but Jimmy intended to use them anyway. All of the other players in the plan were people who were returning a favour to Jimmy or repaying an outstanding debt. It would almost wipe Jimmy's favours book clean but if it worked it would set him up for life. There were even people involved who would join in for the sheer fun of it. Mickey Mee was one such fellow and he was king of the tinkers with probably the largest army of them all if he ever called them all in. Mickey's guys covered almost all of the country but if Mickey ever put the word out that he was in trouble he could round his men up in less than twenty four hours.

Jimmy smiled as he thought of Mickey's men for it would be them that would be what he would describe as ground cover. All they had to do was to be there wearing the new clothes that they had all been given. The simplicity of it all tickled Jimmy and he couldn't understand why no-one had ever thought of it before. The screw heard Jimmy laughing to himself and he walked over to check on him.

"Give us a cig will you"

The screw took a cigarette from his packet, lit it and passed it through the bars to Jimmy who got on with his plan. He wanted to hit four big banks at the same time but he wasn't sure which ones to do so he made up a compass plan. He pictured Manchester City centre in his mind and pinpointed what he thought to be the centre of it then he racked his brains to what he thought of as compass points. Jimmy knew his banks as all good criminals did so staying as close as he could to the four points he chose his sites and allocated them to each gang accordingly. The obvious choice for the Eastern point had to be his good friend from the Orient which was Lee Won-king. Liam Docherty would take the North whilst Alberto Vincente would be ideal candidate for the South.

The Wild West could be taken by another dear friend of Jimmy's which would be Fred 'Nutty' Nuttall a man with no fear and no morals. Fred was a take out merchant. If anyone wanted someone taken out of circulation then Fred was the man to see. Jimmy had known Fred since junior school and he had been just as crazy then. Fred had been seven years old when he was moved to Jimmy's primary school. He was big for his age but he was a bit backward and as a result he was put down a year. He was an ugly bugger with scruffy red hair and green eyes and he couldn't read or write. Jimmy remembered fondly of the day that Mrs Corbett had introduced Fred to the rest of the class.

"I'd like to introduce you all to the new boy this is Fred Nuttall"

Over half of the kids in the class had laughed at his name for even in 1970 it was a bit of an old fashioned name. At the first play time the new boy had gone over and punched everyone who he had seen laughing at him in the classroom including one girl. He had managed to bloody five noses and at least nine of the children had been sent to see the nurse when the break was over. Fred belted the kids one by one then he had gone and sat down in a corner as if waiting to be thrown out.

He had been excluded from his last school for similar persistent behaviour and he had no expectations from his new school. Jimmy had walked over to Fred and offered him one of his wine gums. Fred had looked up at him with a sad expression on his face as he took two wine gums from Jimmy's packet.

"It's not fair I hate being called Fred and I'm sick of people making fun of it. My dad is called Fred and my granddad was called Fred too but I hate it. It's a stupid name"

"It's not a bad name. I've got a frog called Fred, I like it" Fred got excited because he had a thing about frogs.

"Can I come and see it one day"?

"Course you can but you have got to stop hitting people or they will make you go away"

Fred didn't want to be sent away he had never had a friend and he kind of liked Jimmy with the frog. Mrs Corbett opened the door to find a line of children in tears with bloody noses and she quickly sent them to see the nurse. She had expected to get some trouble with the new boy who had been described by his social worker as dysfunctional but she had not expected him to hit half of her class on his very first morning there. The headmaster had sent for Fred and he had been given a warning. He had tried to contact Fred's parents but he had got no answer when he had phoned them.

"They must be out" Walter Sims had told Mrs Corbett.

He had been right. Mr Nuttall had been out at the pub and his wife had been out of her skull so much so that she had been unable to get to the phone. Jimmy got to like Fred the more he found out about him and they became good pals.

He could even understand why Fred had turned out the way that he had from the way that he had been treated at home. Fred had three brothers who along with his mother and father used to knock Fred around for fun. Violence was the only language that Fred knew and he grew up speaking it fluently. Within one week of being at the school Fred Nuttall had become cock of it and even the older boys were scared of him. Fred enjoyed taking part in anything that was dangerous. He used to jump down a whole flight of stairs to see if he could do it without breaking his legs so needless to say he always had something in plaster. One of Fred's pastimes totally repulsed Jimmy for he liked to blow frogs up. He used to stick a straw up their backsides and blow really hard until the frog was so full of wind that it exploded. The first time that Jimmy witnessed one such killing he had run home as fast as he could to wash off the slimy bits that had stuck to his face in the blast off. Jimmy had got quite worried when his own frog had gone missing on a day that Fred had been round to see him. He had even plucked up the courage to ask Fred whether or not he had anything to do with it. Of course Fred had denied all knowledge of it but Fred the frog was seen no more. Fred was the kind of lad that pulled the legs off daddy long legs just for the hell of it. He used to tie fireworks to cat's tails and he loved to put lit bangers through old ladies doors.

At the age of eleven he had become known as Fred the Dead because of his obsession with dead things. When his rabbit had died in the cold weather Fred hadn't buried it instead he had left it stiff in its cage and he used to go home at dinner time and take it out of its cage and stroke it. Even when the maggots came he kept it to look at. It was only when they had eventually devoured it and all that remained was its bones that he had finally let it go. It was then that Fred started to collect bones as a hobby that remained with him still. When Jimmy went on to the comprehensive school at the age of eleven Fred was sent to a special school for children that had learning difficulties.

It was where all the retards went but no-one would dare to say that when Fred was around. Although Jimmy didn't see Fred through the week he still saw him at weekends and on school holidays and Fred was Jimmy's insurance that no-one would ever mess with him. Fred's older brother was seventeen and he was always being brought home by the law for nicking cars. He probably invented the term joy riding for he took a car each time he left the house. He used to do it to impress the chicks but one day he became terribly unstuck. It had been a sunny day and Jack had actually paid two hundred pounds for a car off a guy in Hyde. Of course Jack had no tax or insurance and he hadn't passed his driving test so when the police had started to follow him he had been forced to race them. Jack and Andy had picked up a couple of fifteen years old and Jack had been trying to impress them with his new motor not realising that he had just bought a death trap. The police had been ordered not to give chase in built up areas but when they had seen Jack Nuttall behind the wheel of a car they had not been able to resist chasing him.

Jack had driven into the estate in an attempt to lose the police but they were still with him right up to the last bend. Jack had tried to brake sharply in an attempt to turn the car around but the engine had seized up causing the car to go crashing into a front garden. A group of young children were playing happily in the sunshine when Jack's car ran into them. Jack had heard their screams and he had seen the look of terror on the young girls face just before he ploughed into her. The four young people got out of the car and they had run off in different directions leaving the distraught parents with the carnage and irreparable damage that they had just caused. The word soon spread around the estate and soon everyone was out looking for Jack who was hiding on a stairwell. He had been scared and hungry and hadn't known what to do until eventually as it got darker he had ventured out and called his cousin. His cousin had heard about the terrible accident and managed to persuade Jack to hand himself into the police so Jack had sneaked off the estate. He had walked down to Stalybridge police station and he had sat on the steps crying as he had waited for it to open. Jack was arrested and charged with causing death by dangerous driving and he was given six years for his crime. Just like the poor girls innocent parents Jack Nuttall had given himself a life sentence for he never managed to get the young girl's face out of his nightmares. It was the nightmares and the way the other inmates treated him that eventually made him go loopy. He spent the first part of his sentence in a Young Offenders Institute outside Stoke where he was doped up on medication for most of the day. Then when he was old enough he was moved to Strangeways with the big boys where he eventually went mad. Jimmy sometimes went to visit Jack with Fred and Fred's dad and it gave him his first insight into the prison service at an early age. It was on their first visit to the Young Offenders Centre that Jimmy and Fred had been recruited to take drugs inside. All they had to do was stick some draw that was wrapped in cling film down their socks and hand it over to someone in the toilets. Jimmy made a pound for his part in it which was probably the first illegal earnings that he ever made. Fred missed his brother Jack although he didn't miss the beatings that he used to get from him. The good thing was that with Jack out of the way it meant that Fred got to have his own bedroom. Three years later one of Fred's other brothers, Paul, got his own flat on the estate and he became a regular porn king of Hattersley. He used to make his own porn movies using Steve Smith of Copley as his male star.

Steve wasn't a tall boy but his nickname was codshead and he was reputed to have the biggest dick in Stalybridge so he got to fill in the main part literally. Girls were ten a penny and Paul's flat was always filled with young would be actresses more than willing to audition for him. Although Steve Smith got to play the part in the movies Paul had to try the girls out to see if they were any good. Fred and Jimmy were paid by Paul to keep watch outside the flat as the movies were being made. All they had to do was make sure that Paul and his stars were not disturbed and for that they got a pound each but as a bonus they got to watch the movies as well. Fred used to charge other boys a pound a go to watch each film and he used to give Jimmy a twenty per cent cut. By the time that Fred was sixteen he had a thriving empire in sex drugs and violence. When he was sixteen he used to charge thirty quid to break arms or legs on someone and by the time Fred was eighteen he would kill someone for seventy five quid with no questions asked. Fred had a cracking right hand that he put to good use in the boxing club that started up on the estate which got him the hero status that he had always craved. His boxing skills were good and they had managed to get him into the army for a short while despite his academic failings. Once in there as well as learning a hundred ways to kill a guy Fred also became the regiment's boxing champion. Unfortunately Fred had never been much good at taking orders and he was discharged from the army within a year of joining it. Knocking his sergeant out cold in front of all the other men did nothing to help his career although it had made him very popular with the rest of his regiment as the sergeant had hit the floor. He had been thrown out of organisations since he had been knee high so he had just bought himself a Kawasaki motor bike and joined a chapter of Hells Angels where he had been able to put his evil to good uses. By the year two thousand Fred had changed his name to Satan and he had become the biggest hit man in the North. Jimmy knew that he could rely on the muscle that Satan otherwise known as Fred could provide. He also knew that his old friend was totally fearless and that he would probably love every minute of his part in the plan. Fred had a lot of problems that not a lot of people knew about and he deserved a break. Jimmy knew that if the jobs all went to plan that Fred would get to make all of his dreams to come true. That is all of them but the one about getting his dream lady into his bedroom. Fred was big and dopey but where some things were concerned he had a heart of gold

Fern Britton off Good Morning Television was one of Fred's weaknesses for he was madly in love with her. He made a point of setting his alarm clock through the week to make sure that he was up at ten thirty so he wouldn't miss one moment of her morning show. Jimmy had listened as Fred had told him all about her beautiful face and her nutty sense of humour which Jimmy had to admit made him laugh too. Fred's idea of heaven would be to live in a big house with lots of land with Fern and with his young nephew Tyson. If nothing else Fred was a dreamer!

Jimmy looked at the time and he knew that Joseph would be back with him in a couple of hours. Then he would know if he had the support that he needed and if he did he could complete his compass plan. Jimmy was happy with his choices that he knew he could trust one hundred per cent. There was only one weak link in Jimmy's chain and that was his Irish connection. Liam was a great guy with brilliant connections and nerves of steel. He was also the most experienced explosives guy that Jimmy had ever known. His Achilles heel was the demon drink that he turned to in his hours of need. Liam couldn't take just one drink like any normal person could for once he got the taste for it he had to drink himself into oblivion. Just like his other friend Fred, Liam had a lot of problems that he had shared with Jimmy over the years and no-one could stop him from hurting the way that he did. The only answer to Liam's problems lay at the bottom of a bottle or a can. Jimmy needed Liam to stay off it for twenty four hours even if it meant that Joseph had to sleep with him for that to happen. Jimmy hadn't mentioned that part of the plan to his trusty lawyer. He wasn't too sure of how he would take it when he did.

A BOOK OF FAVOURS

Chapter 14

Superintendent Collins picked up the phone to call Detective Inspector Mike Rooney's parents to tell them of his death. An officer from the local Sheffield station would have already called round to see them personally but he needed to speak to them on another matter. It was the part of the job that he most hated having to do, to speak to the relatives of the deceased. This one was more difficult because there had been a serious allegation made against Mike Rooney that had to be followed up. Peter Collins knew that he would have to handle this one with care so he decided to make very discreet enquiries in order not to hurt Mr and Mrs Rooney any more than was absolutely necessary. The phone rang out once before it was answered by Mrs Rooney who sounded from the tone of her voice as though she had already been given the sad news.

"Mrs Rooney, this is Superintendent Collins from Mill Street police station. I am just calling to pass on my condolences to you and your husband and I wondered if there was anything that I could do for you"

Mrs Rooney tried to hide her grief as she listened to the kind officer who was on the line. They had been informed of Mike's death only thirty minutes earlier and she was still in shock over it but she was amazed at the compassion that she was being shown by such a senior officer.

"We are travelling to Manchester later today to sort out

Mike's personal belongings. I wonder if we could call in to see you to find out what really happened"

Peter Collins wasn't looking forward to their visit but he used it to help his cause. He needed to have an officer look round D.I.Rooney's home without arousing anyone's suspicions.

"I will look forward to seeing both you and your husband later and I would be grateful if you would let one of my officers pick up some papers that Mike had been working on at home"

Mrs Collins did not appear suspicious at his request and she gave him a time that they would be at the house from. She thanked him for calling and turned to her husband who was shaking his head. Even in death Mike was causing his mother heartache just as he had done for most of his adult life and Sid couldn't help but hate him for it.

"Shall we call Patsy and let her know about Mike"?

"Why, she never cared for him when he was alive did she"?

Mr and Mrs Rooney set off for Manchester without calling Mike's ex wife. They needed to know themselves exactly how he had died before telling his son for although he hadn't seen much of his dad they knew that Ben had cared for his dad. Patsy had been very bitter when they had split up and she had blamed Mike for everything that had happened. She had hated Mike and she had done her best to poison Ben's mind about him. Ben had never understood why his father had let him down so many times or why his mum would never talk about him. He had pretended that he hadn't needed Mike but his grandmother had known a very different side to him and despite his hard exterior she knew that the news of his father's death would devastate him.

Superintendent Collins sat in his office trying to decide just how he was going to explain Mike's suicide to his parents.

He also knew that they would want to arrange Mike's funeral and he wasn't sure whether or not he would be able to offer the kind of service that they would want for him. It all depended very much on whether or not Joseph's allegations were unfounded because if they were true they could well be burying a murderer and they couldn't do that with honours. His gut instinct told him that there could very well be some truth in Joseph's accusations for good coppers did not just top themselves the way that Mike had. Adding fuel to that fire was the fact that Mike had killed himself with a gun that had been stolen from the evidence room along with a lot of other stuff that had gone missing.

Mr and Mrs Rooney arrived in Manchester a few hours after the Superintendent had spoken to them and they sat and listened as he told them exactly how their only son had died. He had tried to soften the blow as much as he could by telling them that he had been under a lot of strain but he did not mention the signs of drug abuse that the coroner had found on his body. They were obviously distraught at hearing the news but acted as graciously as they could under the circumstances. They left for Mike's house taking one of Peter's officers with them and thanking Peter Collins for his time. He took Mrs Rooney's hand thinking how much older she looked than the last time he had seen her at Mike's last promotion party. He also hoped that his officer would not find anything untoward at Mike's house.

Mr Rooney was just opening his late son's front door when his next door neighbour suddenly appeared making enquiries out of nosiness rather than niceness.

"Is everything alright love"?

"Mike is dead"

"I am so sorry to hear that I was just telling my Arthur that I hadn't seen him since he cancelled his milk. I told those other people that came looking for him too. He wasn't that old either. Do you think that you might be renting his house out because if you do my Lucy is looking for somewhere now she is up the spout"

Mrs Collins smiled politely at the nosey neighbour before going into her dead son's home. She had loved her son so very much for all of his life yet there was still so much about him that she did not know.

She had never understood the reason that he had left his wife and small son the way that he had or why he had moved away to Manchester. Even though it had been Patsy's affair he had never told his mother about it.

She could never forgive her son for the way that he had let his own son down for she had thought that even if his relationship with his wife had been over he could have made an effort to keep in touch with Ben. She did understand how he felt unable to show affection to Ben for it was something that her husband had never shown to him and it was something that she had always blamed herself for. Anne Rooney had foolishly slept with a colleague at a Christmas party nine months before Mike was born. She had never admitted it to anyone but she was sure that Sid had known especially when Mike was born showing absolutely no resemblance to her husband's side of the family. Maybe if she had explained it to Mike he might have understood the reason that his father showed him no affection. He might have accepted why it was that it seemed that his father had never loved him the way he had desperately wanted him to. The room felt cold and damp so she opened the curtains to let in some light. She had been told that her son had committed suicide but there was no note to be found and that worried her. Sid had always said that Mike was nothing but trouble and Anne was starting to think that there might have been some truth in that. Mike's death had devastated her but she couldn't help but wish that it had been an accident. That way she could have told her grandson that his dad had been killed serving his country and he could have remembered him as a hero. It would be hard for Ben to accept that his dad thought that he had nothing to live for and Mrs Rooney knew exactly how that felt.

Sergeant Murray had a good look round the house but he was unable to find anything that he could report back with. The knife and the brick had been found by old Charlie's body but if Mike had been involved in the murder there should have been something to point the finger at him. The bathroom had been spotlessly clean and there were no dirty clothes in the washing machine to implicate Mike in the murder. The sergeant thanked Mike's parents for their assistance as he went to go back to the station.

"Did you find the papers that you were looking for son"?

"No perhaps the papers are in his desk at work. I'll look there. Goodbye"

He left the Rooneys alone to grieve whilst he went back to the station with nothing to report. The Superintendent was relieved but he still had his doubts as he thanked the sergeant for his help and for his discretion.

Then he called Joseph who was not at home and left a message for him when he returned. There was nothing to report but Peter Collins felt obliged to let the solicitor know that he was looking into his allegations.

Back at Mike's house his parents were still looking through his things.

"Look, here is Mike's passport so he couldn't have gone to Greece like he said. Why did he phone to tell me that he was going away"?

"He was never going on holiday Anne and he didn't have any friends. He was in trouble and he took the cowards way out just like he always did"

Anne hated her husband to talk that away especially now

Mike was no longer around. Even in his death he could not say a good word on him. She looked at her son's picture on his passport and thought how sweet he still looked. It was a photograph that had been taken about eight years earlier before the job had completely destroyed his life. It was the way that she wanted to remember him for his coffin had been sealed due to the horrific injuries that he had inflicted on himself.

Sid Rooney saw the tears slide down his wife's sad face and he reached out and took her into his arms. He held her tightly to him as he felt her heartache and pain for although he didn't hurt over the loss of Mike he hurt for his wife. Perhaps now that Mike was gone he could find a way to forgive his wife's infidelity from all of those years ago.

Julie Mack was busy checking that she had everything for their journey. The word sunscreen was Jimmy's code for passports and tickets and she had those safely tucked away in her handbag. She had packed very lightly knowing that she could buy whatever they needed when they got there. She touched her newly done hairdo and glanced down at her elegantly painted nails and hoped that Jimmy would appreciate her effort. The Scottish relief couple were settling in nicely behind the bar and Julie watched them on the television screen. They were both having the crack with some of the regulars at the bar who seemed quite taken with them and it pleased her to see that they fitted in as well as they did. Julie realised that they might not be coming back to the Crown and she was happy to see that if they didn't return at least the customers would have the next best thing to replace them. She looked at the familiar faces that sat around her bar and she knew that she would miss some of them despite all of their moans and groans. She had spent so many hours listening to their problems and laughing at their jokes that some of them seemed just like family. As much as she thought of some of her regulars she thought a million more times of Jimmy and if he couldn't come back then she would be prepared to stay out of the country too. They had more money than they could ever spend in one lifetime and Julie knew that she could not bear to be kept apart from him for any length of time. His imprisonment had been totally unexpected and if Jimmy did get free as they hoped he would Julie would never let him be taken from her again. The last few weeks had been a nightmare that they had never expected to happen. If Jimmy managed to get away they would start a new life free from crime. Julie knew that Jimmy earned his money rather dubiously and that his contacts left a lot to be desired but whatever Jimmy had done in his lifetime Julie would stand by him.

She was sure that she had everything that they needed for their journey so she drove over to her mother's house to say her goodbyes to her and to D.J. Julie could not be sure when if at all they would be coming back to Manchester so she went to say her goodbyes just in case. D.J. was glad to see his mum but he was a growing teenager and he couldn't be the little boy that his mother wanted him to stay. He was really grateful that his dad had trusted him enough to run the carpet business for him but he felt that his mother smothered him a bit too much for his liking. By her going away for a while it would give him the chance to grow up without being nagged. He didn't mind being with his grandma for she treated him like an equal so when his mum popped round to say goodbye D.J. had felt quite relieved.

"Big hugs and kisses for your best mother"
Julie had done what D.J. had expected her to but there was none of his friends around to see him so he put his arms around her and gave her a big hug then bent down and

kissed her on her forehead.

"Take care mum and don't worry it will go okay tomorrow"

For one terrible moment Julie thought that D.J. had somehow found out about their plan then she realised that he was talking about his dad's appeal.

"I know it will darling. Take care and I'll call you tomorrow. Bye babes"

She tousled his dark hair that was so much like his father's and kissed him one last time before leaving

Chapter 15

Joseph was going strong with the favours and he had not had one rejection so far. Jimmy had mentioned his concerns over Liam Docherty who was the Irishman that Joseph was about to call next. He knew that he would have to word Jimmy's concerns very carefully when he spoke to him. He called the number that he had for him in the book and was surprised when it was answered by a woman.

"Yeah, What do you want"?

"Is Liam there please I need to speak to him"

"What about? I am his private secretary you can tell me anything"

Joseph had been just about to hang up when he heard an almighty bang.

It was the sound of the woman who had answered Liam's phone falling on the floor when Liam had slapped her for sticking her nose in his business.

"Yeah. What do you want"?

Then Joseph listened as he heard him shouting in a broad Northern Irish accent to the woman who was still crying in the background.

"Stop your fucking whinging you stupid bitch before I give you a real good hiding. Now get the fuck out of my sight"

Joseph heard the door slam shut and suddenly the crying was no more.

"Yeah, who is it"?

"My name is Joseph and I am a lawyer"

"I don't know a Joseph and I don't need a fucking lawyer. How did you get this number"?

"Jimmy asked me to call you. He has a problem and he needs a favour"

Liam was suddenly interested and he knew exactly who Jimmy was. Only certain people had access to his private number and Jimmy from The Crown was one of them. Liam smiled as he thought of Jimmy and the kindness he had shown him when he first arrived in England. It had been ten years ago that he had been forced to leave the country that he had loved and fought for and the one that his wife had died for.

Liam had been Sinn Fein through and through. He had grown up in a country that had been taken over by British troops and he had grown up despising them. Liam had worn the green as soon as he had been old enough to and he had served the cause to the very best of his ability. He had risen in the ranks and he had become one of if not the best explosives man in the organisation. Then ten years ago the movement desperately needed money because donations from America had started to dwindle. Liam had been put in charge of a massive drugs operation which had a street value of twelve million pounds. It was money that the organisation had been desperately in need of. Only the men at the top, Liam and his man on the boat had been aware of the cargo and it had been in touching distance when the Customs officers had boarded the boat. Liam had watched through binoculars just in time to see the officers go straight to his man Mick Murphy. He had noticed how Mick had not tried to struggle and he had known then that Mick had sold them out. Liam had been gutted and felt betrayed and he had headed to the hills where he knew he would find a contact to report what had happened to their haul. He walked into the derelict farmhouse where he was grabbed from behind and thrown to the floor in front of one of his Captains. It was obvious that they already knew of the loss and they were not at all pleased.

"What happened today Liam? Why did it go wrong"?
Liam had shook his head and had wished that he could have given them an answer.

"Do you know what you have cost us"?

"I'm sorry Sir. It was out of my hands"

"No Liam it was in your hands when it went wrong so it is your mistake so now you must pay. You know the rules so what do you think your punishment should be"?
Niall didn't answer for it would have served no purpose. They had been wronged and someone had to pay and unfortunately it would be him.

Mick Murphy would have been whisked away to a safe place and Liam knew that if they were talking punishment then he would have to take it.

"You have three days to bring me the traitor if you don't then you must take his punishment for him"
The leader spoke harshly to Liam with no recognition of how much that he had done for them despite thirty years loyal service. Liam had vowed to give his life to the cause that he had served for most of his life.

He had killed hundreds of people for them over the years and he felt disappointed that all of his hard work and loyalty amounted to nothing with them. He knew that if he didn't find Mick Murphy in the next couple of days that he might as well be dead and he went home to give his wife the bad news. His wife Christine was seven months pregnant with their first child and Liam could not bear to think how upset she would be when he told her the bad news. Liam wiped away the tears that fell down his face.

Before going home he had called to Mick Murphy's home

only to be told by a neighbour that the whole family had left in a taxi early that morning. He had known right then that he had been set up. He had gone home and told Christine who had burst into tears as he told her.

"Let's go Liam we can be out of the country before they know we are gone. We can start a new life and they will never find us"

"It I no use Christine for they will always find us. They have eyes in every street and ears in every port. I will go to see them tomorrow and beg for my life. Don't forget that we have a little one to think about now"

Liams eyes had filled with tears as he remembered patting Christine's swollen tummy and feeling his son kicking strongly inside her. He went to talk to them the next day but his pleas had just fallen on deaf ears.

"You know the way it is Liam and there are no exceptions"

Liam waited until they had left before going home and he took a detour through the pub first. Things didn't seem so bad after a few pints of Guinness and a couple of games of darts and Liam had tried to forget what the next couple of days might bring to him.

Christine had heard someone at the door and she had gone to answer it thinking that it was Liam coming home. As she started to open the door she found herself being pushed backwards into the hallway as six masked men pushed past her. They were all dressed in black and wore masks to cover their faces and they all carried weapons.

"He's not here he's gone away"?

"Then we will sit and wait for him to come back"

"He has left the country he phoned just before his plane took off"

Christine did her best to convince them that Liam was not coming back but they knew Liam too well to think that he would ever desert his wife.

Christine took a seat by the window so that she could warn Liam when he turned up. She saw him turn onto the street and she had jumped up and ran to the door shouting for him to run away.

Liam had seen Christine's swollen figure standing in the doorway as she screamed at him to get away and he had seen the masked men stood behind her. He had not run instead he had walked to the door to take his punishment. He knew that it was him that they had come for and that they would not harm his wife so suddenly he was not afraid. Christine had looked at him questioningly as if to ask why he hadn't run away.

"It would have done no good my darling for this is the way"

he had looked at each of the six hooded men who had entered his home and although they were masked he knew the identity of every one of them. Some he had grown up with and the others he had worked with on many different occasions over the years.

"Can I at least settle my wife down"?

All six men nodded and he took hold of Christine's hand and led her upstairs to the front bedroom.

"I love you so very much my darling and I need you to be brave for me"

Liam had kissed her tear stained face as he held her close to him.

"Promise me that you will wait in this room until it is all over"

Christine had nodded then she had kissed him lovingly before he pulled away from her. Liam had stroked her big tummy gently as he told her how much he loved her and their baby then he had left her crying on the bed as he went down to face his persecutors.

Liam had known what his punishment was to be when he

saw the kind of weapons that they carried. There were six of them which meant that he was to get the triple cripple. He had done it so many times to traitors who had let the cause down. He knew that they would tie his hands together behind his back and that they would cover his head with sackcloth before taking him outside to the garden. He held his hands out behind him and stood still as they put the sack over his head then he had waited as they tied the string round the bottom of the sack. Liam thought that he had felt one of the men kiss the side of his head apologetically and he knew that the men had no choice in the task they had been ordered to carry out. He was led outside and pushed to the floor with his legs apart as he waited for the ritual to begin.

He heard the sound of the six guns being cocked as the chambers filled and his heart filled with terror. He lost control of all of his bodily functions and he shit himself as his body jerked off the ground.

Fear ran through every part of Liam's trembling body for he knew exactly what was to come. He had dished out the same punishment on real traitors so many times before. He had listened to the men screaming out as they begged for mercy and he had ignored their cries.

Liam had seen himself as a soldier fighting for a worthy cause and the men awaiting their punishment were the enemy in the war he fought. Apart from a single bullet through the head or being blown apart with explosives tied to the body the triple cripple was one of the worst punishments that they dished out. The cruel thing in Liam's case was that he did not deserve the punishment and that hurt Liam more than he could explain. He had often wondered how his victims must have felt as they lay on the ground waiting for something to happen and as Liam lay in his own shit on the ground he suddenly got to find out.

Suddenly with precision accuracy the six men took aim and fired their bullets into him. Each man aimed for a particular spot and each man hit his target. Liam felt the first bullet enter his body as he felt the excruciating pain run through him. He heard the other shots but his body had gone numb with fear and it had gone into spasms. Curtains had twitched but no-one had dared to come out until the men had gone. Christine had heard the gunshots and despite her promise to Liam she came out of the room and she ran downstairs to be with him. She had screamed at the sight of her husband who lay bleeding on the ground and she grabbed hold of the last of the six men to leave and tried to pull off his mask.

"Show your face you cowardly bastard let me see who you are"

All Christine had seen was the barrel of his gun as the masked man had pointed it at her face before he had pulled the trigger.

All Liam had heard through his own pain was the sound of his wife screaming out loud just before the seventh bullet was fired, then it all went quiet. Liam had managed to roll over to where he had heard his wife's screams. He was still tied and hooded but he managed to push his head against her body until his hood loosened itself and he was able to see her. Liam would never forget the sight of his beautiful wife lying in a pool of blood with half of her face blown off.

Nor would he ever be able to forgive the ones who had done that terrible thing to her. He rested his head on her big still stomach before passing out.

Someone had called for an ambulance which had arrived at Liam's home a short while after the shooting. Liam had been taken to the hospital but his wife and unborn child were taken directly to the morgue. There was barely room for the living at the hospital with the recent spate of bombings there are had been. Liam had been kept under an armed military guard as he attempted to get well. He was in the hospital for five weeks which gave him a lot of time to think. It broke his heart to remember what had happened to Christine and their baby son and no matter how much medication they doped him up with they could not erase the memories of that awful day.

Although it went against everything that Liam had held dear to him he had decided to give just one piece of information to the Home Office. In exchange for the information they would give him a passage to England and a brand new life. He could have given mounds of information that would have destroyed the cause but despite his own anger he had not done that. He had made a promise to be true to the cause and it hurt him to have to break it just a little as he had done. He gave away the location of arms that were old and that they didn't have the ammunition for which was enough to get him out of the country. There had been nothing to keep him there for his family were gone and the fire in his blood had been extinguished. Liam had sent a package to be stored in a safe deposit box and a letter to a solicitor to only be opened in the event of his death under suspicious circumstances. He had hoped that it would never have to be opened but he knew that it was his insurance to help him stay alive. There was a certain code of honour in the cause and Liam knew that the murder of his wife would have most certainly caused heads to roll. He had hoped that he would be left alone to live the rest of his life without having to look over his shoulder and he put it all in his letter to the General. Although he had left the hospital his treatment had been far from over. He had one leg that was a few inches shorter than the other. It was the right leg that had swung right over his shoulder when it had taken the first bullet. The bones in that leg had been shattered so badly that they could not be repaired leaving Liam disabled. To make his legs the same size he would have to wear a built up shoe for the rest of his life.

Christine's body had been cremated and Liam had thrown her ashes into the Irish Sea on his passage over to England where they had blown freely in the wind. He had said a silent prayer for her as her ashes left the urn and he had said his last goodbye to her. The Home Office had given Liam keys and an address of a house in Manchester. They had paid for Liam's ticket on the ferry and they had given him just two hundred pounds in cash. They had also promised that he would not be bothered by the English police and that his identity would be safe with them. Liam had not cared about anything as he had travelled to England for he had experienced Hell and nothing that could happen to him in his life could ever equal the horror of that. From the ferry he had taken the train to Piccadilly Station which he knew quite well from his work there over the years. As he hobbled out of the station he stood his crutches up against a wall as he stopped and pretended to fasten his shoe lace only to confirm his suspicions. He had been far too clever to have not noticed that he was being followed and he was far too clever not to have lost them. A number 211 bus was ready to leave its stop as Liam hurried towards it. The driver had been in a hurry but he had felt sorry for the chap on crutches and he had opened the doors to let him get on before he left. The O'Grady brothers had cursed as they watched their target get further and further away from them. They hopped onto the next bus that stopped only minutes after the previous one failing to notice that it was a limited stop. Liam had got off the bus just before Belle Vue and had nipped into a small pub on the main road called

The Crown. Tim O'Grady thought that he had spotted him sat at the bar with a drink in his hand as their bus careered past it. They had shouted for the driver to stop but he had refused and took them to the next official stop at Debdale Park a good few ordinary stops down the road. Furiously the O'Grady brothers had stood at the side of the road trying to flag down a taxi but they found it a lot more difficult to do than it was in Belfast. By the time that they had managed to get one Liam was on his third pint of Guinness unaware that they had seen him get off the bus. There was a screech of brakes on the opposite side of the road to the pub as a taxi pulled to a sudden halt. Liam looked around to see that there was only one door for him to get out of and it was the same one that they would use to come in. He picked up his hold-hall and quickly threw himself complete with bag and crutches onto the floor behind the bar. He was at Jimmy's feet and at Jimmy's mercy and he put a finger to his lips as the two burly Irish men stormed into the pub.

"Where is he"?

one of the men yelled at Jimmy at the top of his voice.

"If you mean the monkey on the crutches you have just missed him and if you are friends of his you can pick up his bar bill that he just pissed off without paying"

Tim O'Grady went to look in the toilets as Johnny stood at the bar not realising that Liam was only about two feet away from him.

"If you hurry you might just get him at the airport but you will have to be quick because his flight goes out at 8.35. I can even tell you where he is going if you like"

Johnny nodded and listened as Jimmy told him that he was catching a Monarch flight to Malaga and that he was going from Terminal One.

The brothers looked at the clock to see that it was just

turned seven so they ran out to try to catch the taxi that had just brought them there. It had gone but there was another one dropping off on the other side of the road so they dashed over and got into that one instead.

Once Jimmy was sure that it had gone he gave Liam the all clear and he bent down to help him up from the floor.

"Thank you Sir would you take a drink with me"?

Jimmy accepted and he pulled another two pints of Guinness.

"It's not a bad pint that you pull although not as good as home"

"Where's home"?

"Well it used to be Ireland but perhaps you can tell me where it is now"

He took a piece of paper from out of his pocket and he handed it to Jimmy. He read it to find that the Irish chap had left one hell hole to come to another. The flats that he was looking for left a lot to be desired.

"It's not that far but you might as well get a taxi. It won't cost you more than a couple of quid"

Liam liked the guy behind the bar, he had never asked anything about what had happened earlier and he had managed to put the O'Grady brothers off his scent quite cleverly. He was obviously a player of a high standard and a very quick thinker.

"How come you made up a story like that about the flight to Malaga and the time and everything. Did you make it all up"?

"Did I hell. I've had a fella sat at the bar nearly all afternoon and all he went on about was his bloody holiday until I was sick of hearing it. Anyway I knew that if those friends of yours checked with the taxi firms that they would confirm taking a guy from the pub to the airport"

Liam admired Jimmy more by the minute but he needed to

get off to find out what his new home was like. He had ordered a taxi that was due to arrive any minute so he bought ten cans of cider as a take out and shook Jimmy's hand.

"Thank-you my friend for all you have done. You will be seeing a lot more of me from now on"

Liam's taxi turned up so he picked up his bag and his beer and limped out on his crutches and got in it.

"Bellamy Court, Abbey Hey mate"

The taxi driver chatted away for about ten minutes before pulling up at a block of two storey flats he got out and opened the door for Liam.

"Yours will be up there mate. Sorry I can't help you but if I leave my cab down here on its own it will end up with no wheels"

Liam smiled thinking how it was just like home from home.

The taxi pulled away leaving Liam with his crutches and his luggage staring at a set of stairs he had to master. He looked up to the flats on his floor most of which were boarded up which meant at least that he didn't have to bother about nosey neighbours. A young lad aged about thirteen came up to him and offered to help.

"If you are going up there I'll give you a hand if you give us a quid"

Liam had no choice if he wanted to make it up the stairs and he had ten cans of cider with his name on them so he agreed and the lad picked up the hold-hall. Liam kept behind the boy in case he tried to do a runner which had been pointless for there were two ways in and out of the flats. The boy stopped a flat that he knew was waiting for a new tenant for it had been painted recently. The council had been round to remove the shutters earlier that evening. He put the bag on the floor as Liam walked towards him.

"Give us a fiver mister and I won't leg it with your bag"

Liam put his hand in his jacket pocket as he watched the cheeky kid pick his bag off the floor and he pulled out his gun.

"Tell you what kid. You put my bag back on the floor and get out of my sight and I won't blow your fucking head off your shoulders"

The frightened boy put the bag down and he slowly backed away. He had very wrongly thought that the cripple would be an easy target. Liam had been a target one too many times and he wasn't a guy to be messed with. He let the boy go because he knew that he would put the word round and that he would not be bothered again. He opened the door to his new home and he turned on the light to see that it was small but clean. There was a small three piece suite and a coffee table with a portable television on top of it in the lounge. The kitchen had been painted bright yellow to cheer it up and it contained just a cooker and a fridge. Liam wasn't arsed at what the flat was like for all he was interested in at that moment was the cans of cider that sat in his bag. He hadn't eaten all day and he was very thirsty.

The O'Grady brothers had arrived at the airport but had not caught sight of Liam who they presumed to have got through passport control.

They were too tooled up to pass through security and had just been about to head back to the pub they had seen him in when Tim's phone rang.

"Yeah, yeah, yeah alright see you later then"

Tim had turned to his brother with a puzzled look on his face.

"The hunt is off we are needed back at home"

Liam's letter must have reached its destination and made its point. It seemed as though Liam was finally going to be left alone.

The O'Grady brothers headed for home disappointed they had not got to Liam before they got the call for he had been one of the favoured members before his fall from grace.

Liam had always vowed to be there for Jimmy as he had been for him so he was only too pleased to do whatever Jimmy asked of him.

"Can you give me an idea of what Jimmy wants"?

"Not until tomorrow all he needs to know is whether you are in or not

If you are in I will call tomorrow. Oh I will need a place to stay as well"

"No problem I can put you up if you don't mind slumming it"

Joseph had done what Jimmy had asked him and he had even got an invite to stay at Liam's place which meant that he could keep an eye on his drinking. All he had to do was make one more phone call and if that went well he would have a lot of good news for Jimmy. Joseph could not help but feel excited about Jimmy's big plan and the fact that he was going to play a big part in it.

He knew that he was in possession of far too much information that could cost him his life if he allowed it to get into the wrong hands. He had become the priest in Jimmy's confessional box and he was honoured to take that role.

"Shut the fuck up before I take my belt off to you girl"

Liam was furious with Tulip for answering his phone and he was sick and tired of listening to her constant crying.

He opened the kitchen door to find her cowering on the floor in the corner. Her tears had mingled with the blood from her swollen mouth and she looked a right mess.

"Clean yourself up and get down to the off licence for

some cider"

Tulip jumped up quickly and wiped her face with a tea towel leaving streaks of mascara under her eyes. She took a twenty pound note from the drawer and slipped past Liam as fast as she could as though she half expected another slap. Liam pushed her out of the door and watched as she scurried down the stairs to go for his drinks supply. He knew that she was scared of him and she had good reason to be for since losing his wife and child Liam had become a very cruel man.

Six months after moving to Manchester he had been able to walk without his crutches. His physical wounds had healed a lot quicker than the hospital had thought they would but his mental scars would weep forever. His right leg that had shot over his shoulder with the impact of the first bullet had been so badly injured that the bone could not be repaired and as a consequence he was left with one leg shorter than the other and a very obvious limp. The hospital had given him shoes that were made especially for him with one that was so built up that it reminded him of spastic shoes. Liam hated the looks that people gave to him and he would literally kill anyone who ever dared to make fun of him. The hospital had done all that they could do with the exception of the counselling sessions that they offered to him that he decided not to take.

Liam's memories and thoughts of what happened on that fateful night were his and his alone. It was his loss and his pain not to be shared with anyone. His shattered legs were a constant reminder of what had happened to him and the pain in his heart was what had kept Christine so very much alive. Liam needed drink to help him cope with his thoughts of that time, a drink to help him to remember, before helping him to forget. After a couple he allowed himself to remember all of the wonderful times they had shared together and after a few litres of strong cider the bad thoughts could be wiped away for a short time at least. Only when he was sober could the pain get to him, then or in the middle of his sleep when they would show themselves in the way of nightmares.

The measly two hundred pounds that the Home Office had set him up with had gone within a couple of days. His disability allowance gave him a pittance to get by on so Liam had set himself up in somebody else's business. On his first full day in his new home he had just sat and watched from his window. He had seen the dealing of drugs that went on below his own flat and he had waited until he knew that the young lad dealing had sold most of his wraps. Then he had limped down the stairs carrying only his trusty gun with him. Despite his bad leg he was still able to move quietly and the lad was shocked to find him stood behind him and even more shocked to find his gun stuck in his ribs.

Liam had taken his money and the name of his contacts within two minutes of introducing himself. Within weeks he had taken control of the whole operation and he kindly allowed them to work on his patch. Within six months he was controlling most of the area and he had about twenty of his own country men working under him. In Belfast he had been a very small fish in a large pond but in Abbey Hey he had the chance of changing all of that which was exactly what he had done. Within the first year Liam had recruited enough men to run a small army. There were people that had fled from Ireland and others who had been thrown out but all of them supported the same cause and spoke with the same accent making Liam feel very much at home. The empty flats that had surrounded him became home to a lot of his men and by the time that they had secured the whole block of flats they had made them impenetrable. The one gun that he had arrived in the country with had multiplied a hundred times over until after twelve months when he had a small arsenal of weapons. Liam was an arms expert and soon he had become the biggest supplier in the North. He offered a good discreet service for a decent price. His years working for the cause enabled him to provide clean pieces that were hidden at locations known only to two people, him and the buyer.

They would also be stripped cleaned and disposed of within one hour of them being used with absolutely no risk or comeback to the user. Liam's vast experience of disposing of evidence helped him to provide a top class service to his punters.

Liam also provided a cheaper service where the same guns after being stripped of all evidence were taken to houses in Moss Side where they fetched a much lower price and got lost in the system. His forte was in explosives where he was known to be the best in the world and he had admirers around the world and had been offered a king's ransom for his services. Liam was never short of work and he earned himself a nice packet doing something that he knew that he was good at. His one flat that he had been given expanded into the whole of the block in which he had bullet proof windows and doors installed for his own security. Most of his weapons were on or about his apartments where he knew that they would be safe because of his immunity status. The last remaining tenants in the block had been frightened off but Liam allowed them to come back once a fortnight to pick up their giros in return for doing a bit of running for him. By 1996 Liam had over one hundred 'soldiers' under him half of which lived in earshot he also had Tulip living with him although there were many times that he wished that he didn't.

He had sort of rescued Tulip one afternoon that he had gone out shopping and he had brought her back with him as child might bring home a stray dog. Tulip had been very grateful to Liam who she saw as her new meal ticket and she had remained with him from that day despite the fact that he treated her so cruelly.

Tulip looked like a hooker on a bad day. She wore cheap tacky clothes that allowed everyone good views of her body. She had bleached blonde hair that she coloured herself using different products causing her to have about ten different shades on her head. When she wore her hair up showing her roots it even looked as though she had dark hair. Tulip had been a kiter come shoplifter who had been working and almost caught when Liam had come to her aid. What she didn't get on the cards she would steal from the shops on what had been a brilliant scam courtesy of her stooge partner and best friend Melissa. The pair of them would go on a shopping spree although Melissa would enter the store or shop involved about ten minutes after her partner had gone in. Tulip would choose three expensive tops or dresses that had been pre ordered and take them into the changing rooms where she would carefully cut out the security tags. She would either wear two of the items or put them in her bag and then wait for Melissa to come into the changing rooms to join her.

Melissa would choose where possible the same items and she would take them into the changing rooms where she would pass two of them to Tulip. Then as Melissa pretended to try the garments on Tulip would walk out of the changing rooms and hand all three items back to the assistant. Then she would walk out of the store very calmly then leg it to her car where she would drop off her goods and wait for Melissa to catch her up. Melissa was a sweet looking half cast girl who wore very little clothing and a very obvious hearing aid. If she was asked about her missing garments she would either act dumb or say that another lady had asked to try them on. No matter what the assistant might have suspected they could not accuse Melissa of anything without the evidence that they never had. Melissa purposely didn't carry a bag and very rarely wore a coat so there was nowhere to hide any stolen goods on her. Tulip had been just about to leave the store as Liam had been entering it and unlike her, he had noticed the two store detectives that very obviously had her in their sights. She had just walked out of the door with one of the detectives close behind her when Liam had screamed out at the top of his voice

"There's a bomb in the basement everybody get the fuck out of here"

His warning caused instant chaos in the store and shoppers and assistants alike ran out of the store onto the street. The detectives were too busy trying to regain order in the store to bother about Tulip who made a quick getaway up Market Street. Liam followed her towards Piccadilly Station and watched as she opened a car door by which time he was stood right behind her. He touched her shoulder to let her know that he was there and she turned round expecting to find the security guard.

"Leave me alone or I'll use this on you"

Tulip brandished a small penknife at Liam that he took from her.

"I'll not harm you girl I was just checking that you were alright"

Tulip looked at the guy that stood before her he wasn't the law or a store detective and he had nice blue eyes so she calmed down.

"Sorry I didn't know who you were. I was in a store and there was a bomb scare so I ran away"

"There was no bomb scare I'm just very convincing"

Tulip smiled making her look twice as nice as she had

looked before just as Melissa turned into the car park only
to see that Tulip was chatting with a man.

Melissa jumped in the back of the car and Liam got in the
front seat.

"Fucking Hell girl that was a close shave"

"What"?

said Melissa as she took out her hearing aid and they all
laughed. Liam peeled the parking ticket off the window.

"We got her just in time by the look of it. Another five
minutes and you would have got a parking ticket"

"I wouldn't get a parking ticket because it's not my fucking
car"

then she had revved the car up and headed out of the car
park down Hyde Road until they got to Gorton Market,
laughing all the way. They dumped the Astra car on some
rough ground for which ever scallies got to it first and
knowing that it wouldn't be long before it was burnt out.

"Where do you live, are you from round here"?

"Not really and I don't suppose I live anywhere now.

I was supposed to bring in about five hundred quid's worth
today to cover the rent and all I've got is a couple of dresses
worth about a hundred and twenty quid that'll get me about
forty quid for the two"

Tulip went on to explain that they lived with a guy that did
the markets and that they got most of his gear for his stall in
return for bed and board.

"If I take him two dresses he'll just throw them and us right
out of the window. I might as well go back on the game
again"

"Then why not come home with me. Have a dress each
and I'll put you up for a while but I won't have you on the
game"

Tulip looked at Melissa then she looked Liam up and down.

"No funny business mind"

174

"No"

Tulip and Melissa both went back with Liam where they stayed until Melissa got herself knocked up by one of Liam's men who she consequently went to live with. It took a full twelve months and a really good drinking session before Tulip eventually wormed her way into Liam's bed. Liam had sworn that he would never want another woman but he was only flesh and blood and he had been so off his face that he had eventually, given in to Tulip's sexual advances. Liam had been angry with himself the next day but once he got used to the idea he decided that it was better the devil you know. For a woman Tulip made a pretty good drinking companion and Liam had to admit that it beat having a wank. Liam let Tulip share his bed but that was all for as much as she wanted a full time relationship, he didn't.

They were sat sharing a bottle of cider one night when Tulip over stepped the mark by prying a little too much into his private life.

"Wouldn't you like to have a family one day Liam? I bet that you would make a great dad"

"What the fuck do you know you silly bitch"

Tulip could tell by the sudden anger in his voice that she had hit a nerve and she made it her business to find out why. She had waited until Liam was sleeping before she went through his wallet where she was surprised to find a picture of a beautiful raven haired woman. There was nothing to indicate who it was but Tulip guessed that the woman in the picture must be the reason for Liam's sudden mood swing. She decided to ask Liam about it when he was in a better mood but unfortunately when she did confront him it came out all wrong. They had just finished off a bottle of White Lightening cider when Liam told Tulip to fetch another one quick.

"What did your last slave die of or is that why you don't

have a woman"?

"You know nothing about what I had and you never will" Liam started to cry as he thought about his beautiful Christine and the horrible way in which she had been killed along with their baby.

Tulip felt sorry for she had not expected to see Liam so sad.

"Is it the woman on the photograph in your wallet. Is she the one"?

The blow from Liam's clenched fist sent Tulip flying over the coffee table and she spat a tooth that had been knocked loose out onto the carpet.

"How dare you look in my wallet what were you doing was you going to roll me as well. Is that what you are a fucking thief as well as a slag"?

Tulip cried out loud as she started to protest against his accusations but it was too late to stop him for Liam was like a mad man that had lost control. He kicked out at Tulip's broken body as she lay on the floor.

He kicked her like she was a scabby dog and he continued to kick her until she was still. Liam didn't know if she was dead or just unconscious and he didn't care. He stepped over her body as he went into the kitchen to get himself another bottle of cider. Then he sat down with his bottle as he tried to drink himself into oblivion. Tulip had opened an old wound that Liam normally didn't have to deal with until the middle of the night where it could be disguised as a nightmare. She had caused him to feel unnecessary pain and Liam had been forced to punish her for it. He was sat there just staring at the bottom of the bottle when Tulip started to stir.

She opened her eyes but backed away in fear when she saw Liam sat there. She had taken hundreds of beatings over the years starting when she was only ten years old but never in all of her vile relationships had she been beaten so callously as she had been this time. Her mouth was swollen and she had lost at least two of her teeth.

Her nose felt as if it was broken as did most of her ribs and she badly needed a drink to help ease the pain. Liam recognised the look of need on her face and he passed the bottle of cider to her which was almost empty. Tulip took the bottle and swallowed the one mouthful that was left as Liam went to get another bottle from the fridge. He felt sorry now that he had calmed down and he regretted hurting her that much but he still couldn't forgive her for trespassing into his private world. Tulip was more like a piece of furniture that Liam didn't particularly want but he was comfortable with her around him. She did the washing and cleaned up of sorts and she went out and did the shopping or anything else that Liam told her to do. She was a bit like a mate and Liam didn't have many of them. He was a bit of a loner despite all his men that surrounded him and Tulip was probably the nearest thing to family that he had.

He regretted hurting her but she should have left the past alone. He picked up a new bottle and two glasses and he handed one to Tulip who took it from him.

"Bloody bastard"

she said as he raised his glass to hers.

"Stay out of my past and you will be alright. No hard feelings"?

"Not tonight there had better not be, have you seen the state of my gob"?

Tulip pointed to her swollen lip and the spaces where her teeth had been.

By the end of the last bottle of cider the fall out had been forgotten and a big lesson had been learned.

Tulip knew that there was a lot more to Liam than he was letting on about and despite her beatings she was determined to find out but she would do it discreetly. Over the next few years Tulip could never really be sure where she stood with Liam for one moment he would be nice to her then the next she would get a good beating from him for no reason that she knew of. Tulip took the beatings from Liam that she accepted came with the territory that also gave her a lifestyle that she knew she would not get anywhere else. She had the respect of being seen as Liam's woman and all the money that she needed to spend on what she wanted. There was always booze in the house and she could have whatever drugs took her fancy. As Tulip's beatings progressively got more and more cruel she eventually feared for her life so she made a plan to learn all that she could about Liam's business. Tulip started to listen more and more to what was going on around her. She made notes of meetings and faces and where possible of jobs going down. If Tulip ever had to flee for her life she would make sure that she took information with her that she knew that someone would be interested in whether that would be other gangs or at the worst, the cops.

One night in bed Tulip got to find out more about Liam's secret woman and she couldn't help but feel sorry for him. He had screamed out in his sleep once whilst he was still half asleep.

"No, kill me but please don't touch my wife or babbi, No, No"

This time Tulip had not pried instead she had just stroked Liam's head and sung him back to sleep. Another time when they were both really pissed Tulip had started singing 'Danny Boy' and Liam had burst into tears.

"That was what we were going to call him"

"Who"?

"Our wee babbi. It was a boy because we saw him on the scan but he was murdered along with his marmee"

"I'm so sorry Liam. I don't know what else to say"

"They shot her in the head when she was seven months pregnant and they killed my wife and my wee baby boy on the same day"

"Is that what happened to your legs. Is that how you got your scars"?

Liam cringed for he didn't like anyone to see his wasted legs and apart from those at the hospital Tulip was the only one to have ever seen them. He sat down as he told Tulip about everything that had happened on that awful day and in a way it made it easier to share his pain with someone. By the time that he had finished Tulip could understand more why he had locked away his emotions the way that he had and why he cried out in the night. She felt more close to him as he had let her come just a little further into his very private world.

A BOOK OF FAVOURS

Chapter 16

Joseph had one more phone call to make before reporting back to Jimmy. It was to a man called Fred but then next to his name was Satan in brackets. Joseph made the call which was answered right away by someone with a rough Manchester accent. Joseph spoke softly.

"Is that Fred"?

"Who the fuck is asking and what the fuck do you want"?

"I'm calling for Jimmy. He needs your help"

"Where is he, has something happened to him inside"?

"He's okay but he wants to know if you are available tomorrow"

"I am available anytime for Jimmy and if anyone has hurt him I will kill them. Do you understand"?

Joseph had been told that Fred would be the most loyal of the four men and that he would ask the least questions and he had been right. He had also told him not to be put off by his rough exterior for Fred or Satan as he now liked to be known as had a really soft centre. Joseph found that hard to believe as he listened to the voice that was booming down the phone.

"I'll call you tomorrow and he said to say that he needs you mob handed"

"No problems there mate. I'll be waiting for your call"

Fred or Satan put the phone down and he felt quite excited. In all of the years that he had known Jimmy he had never been asked for a favour. Jimmy had done so much for him and had been his only real friend. He had never made fun of him and he had liked him because he wanted to and not because he was scared of him like the rest of his so called friends. The man had said mob handed so it had to be big and if he was really lucky he might even get to kill somebody. Fred couldn't wait for Joseph to call him and he went off to polish his best pieces just in case.

Joseph felt satisfied with his days work and he couldn't wait to get to Jimmy to let him know that it was all systems go as far as his friends were concerned. He jumped into his car and headed for the prison to see Jimmy for what he hoped would be the last time in there. As he drove down the motorway he marvelled at how together he seemed to be under the circumstances. It had taken a lot of studying and hard work for him to get where he had and he realised that he would be risking everything by going along with Jimmy's plan. Despite the danger Joseph felt a high that he had never come close to experiencing before and just like the others who had pledged their allegiance to Jimmy, Joseph was ready to pledge his all.

Jimmy jumped up when he heard Joseph's voice and he sent the screw off to fetch two prison teas then he sat at the table as he finalised his plan. He was confident once Joseph told him that he had the manpower he needed and he went over the whole of the plan in detail with Joseph listening in amazement. Everything had to be precision timed for it all to go perfectly to plan and Joseph would have to keep in touch with each of them as each part of the plan fell into place. It would have to be one step at a time to ensure that not one person knew more than they had to. Only after doing their own job would the successful ones get to know the final resting place which hopefully would be all of them. No-one would know the final destination until the last possible minute for security reasons. At the exact moment of Jimmy's break out there would be total chaos in the centre of Manchester that would be created by the police computers going down. There would also be major problems with traffic lights in the town centre causing even more mayhem. Liam would phone in two bomb scares at either side of the town centre which would be taken deadly serious due to him knowing the correct codes. There would be over three hundred men on foot all wearing identical clothing who would all show themselves when they overpowered the police escort that would be escorting Jimmy's transport. The men would rush out at the exact time that the transport would be forced to stop at a road block across the road caused by a so called accident with an ambulance in attendance.

Jimmy's break would be made easy with different get away vehicles that he could choose as he pleased. There would be over one hundred hoax calls given to the police who would be so overstretched that they would have to call into neighbouring counties to enlist what help that they could. There would be at least four idiots wielding guns in different nearby areas all of which would take up the time of the armed response units and the police helicopter. But best of all would be the four big foreign banks that would all be being turned over at exactly the same time.

As well as the billions of pounds in cash that they would steal from the banks there would be lots and lots of big fat juicy safe deposit boxes containing riches beyond belief. If all went to plan the total of the hauls would run into billions and billions of pounds.

"Fucking Hell Jimmy it sounds brilliant but what the hell would you do with such a fucking big haul. I mean where the hell could you put it"?

"That my friend, is where my last two big favours come in.

All we need to make it work is a Defence Minister and an army Major"

"Oh and you think that we can just get them on less than twenty four hours notice do you? I mean a Minister of Defence is a pretty big fish"

"Yes it is and he owes us a bloody big favour so I have no doubt whatsoever about him. Just as I have no doubt about the Major, all you must do Joseph is to call them tonight and pass on my orders word for word. Tell each of them to prepare for us and tell them to await your instructions and make sure that the Major informs his men that they are dealing with top secret radio active materials"

Jimmy thought it only fair to tell Joseph exactly why these men owed him such big favours because if anything went wrong during Jimmy's breakout someone would need to know the truth so as they finished their tea Jimmy filled him in on the whole sordid affairs.

Jimmy told Joseph how Pete had managed to land a big contract fixing expensive alarm systems down South. Pete had been fitting alarms after starting his own company called 'Active Alarms' which he did with his brother Dave. Between them they had fitted over three hundred alarms on brand new properties half of which they had revisited after six months to rob. Consequently the company had folded after only twelve months but Dave had got a taste for doing it so he had answered an advertisement in the Times which led to them getting the contract work in London. Dave's wife Susan worked for the council in the Town Hall and she was able to provide him with excellent references that got him the contract work. It took them out of the area into a world that was so very different from their own that showed the true reality of the North/South divide. One of the first alarms that they had installed had cost almost as much as Dave had bought his terraced house in Manchester for.

It was on one of two luxury apartments in Belgrade that cost upwards of one and a half million pounds and in which even members of the royal family resided albeit quite minor ones. The luxury apartments were protected by large electronic gates and monitored by twenty four hour CCTV systems. They were also linked up directly to the police station. Each apartment had its own individual security which included having sensors on every single door and window. It was a very expensive state of the art system that included built in wall safes that were hidden behind portrait paintings.

Dave and Pete had made a wonderful job fitting the alarms and they made sure that they left full instructions and codes with the owners. They also made sure that they took copies with them for their own good, along with names and telephone numbers. One of the apartments was owned by a prominent Minister who was involved in defence and whose movements were widely recorded. It was about twelve months after they had fitted the alarm system that Pete had read in the newspaper that the man in question would be attending a meeting in Brighton that would take him out of his apartment for all of the weekend.

Knowing that the apartment in Belgrade would be empty for the weekend was the perfect excuse for the lads to take a drive out. So Pete had hired a transit van for a few days and he had taken three other lads with him for a bit of antique hunting.

They had all gone in wearing disguises with a combination of wigs and false moustaches along with overalls and alarm manuals just in case they were stopped by anyone. As it was they had not been stopped as they entered the building which appeared to be ghostly quiet.

Before entering the apartment they had rung the doorbell in case the guy had left a house-sitter in his absence. There was no answer so they had let themselves in to find a room that looked as if it had just been picked out of a top class magazine. There was so much stuff that they could have filled three vans and still have come back for more. Pete went straight to the wall safe hidden behind a painting of 'The Laughing Cavalier'

He took the painting down from the wall only to find that the owner had changed the code which Pete had given him the option to do. He had anticipated that and he had come well equipped so he opened his tool box and took out a chisel then started to remove the safe as a whole. The lads moved around the place in awe of the expensive knick knacks that surrounded them. There was so much stuff for the taking that the boys were spoilt for choice. Pete suggested that they took the electrical goods and things that wouldn't break in transit which they started to stack up by the door. Gazza picked up the corner of an expensive looking Chinese rug made from white silk that was in the centre of the room.

"I bet this is worth a few quid"

Pete looked over to see what Gazza was talking about as he held a corner of the rug up. He caught a glimpse of something that didn't look right on the floor beneath the rug so he got down from the stool he was standing on to investigate it. Gazza had just put the rug down as Pete said.

"Pick it up Gazza and pull it out of the way quickly"

Gazza wasn't sure if Pete wanted them to take the rug which was very nice but which weighed a ton but he moved it all the same. The floor was made up of expensive parquet tiles that were so highly polished that they acted almost as mirrors. It had puzzled Pete as to why someone would want to deface them by cutting out a trapdoor in the floor which was exactly what he had spotted there.

He bent down and pulled on the small inset brass handle only to find that the trapdoor was locked firmly. He put his chisel into the crack and then using the whole of his body weight he pressed down with all of his might. The door broke open leaving a secret compartment in full view of them all and Pete saw a brown paper package hidden in there.

He reached in with his hand and pulled the package out half expecting to find official government papers. He opened it to find a video which he suspected from the way that it had been carefully hidden that it would be full of major porn.

"Put the video player back Ian it's time for a break"

Ian put the telly and video back and reconnected them then all four men poured themselves a large expensive brandy each in rich crystal glasses and then they took their seats ready to watch a bit of porn. As soon as the film came on they all felt exactly the same, sick to the pits of their stomachs. Young Ian who had a brother about the same age as some of the kids in the video was physically sick all over the expensive leather furniture.

The video they had expected to see should have been full of sexy young ladies taking their clothes off and having sex but the one that came on had only very young boys. The children were being used for sex in the most repulsive ways imaginable and Ian jumped up to turn the television off. Pete had stopped him before he could do it. Not because he wanted to watch what was going on but because he had recognised the surroundings and the furniture for it was where they were all sitting.

As the man in the video turned to face the camera they were all horrified to see that it was the man whose apartment they were sat in. Pete rewound the video tape and he had got straight on the phone to Jimmy to let him know what they had just uncovered. The others started to look for anything else that might be hidden away in the apartment until eventually they found a lap top computer. It was hidden away in the bottom of a wardrobe along with other discs and videos. Pete and Ian made up the flat pack boxes that they had brought with them and they started to load them up with goodies from the flat. Pete told Gazza and Robbie to take the haul and go back to Jimmy. The way that it was packed in a large box it looked like a return and Pete wanted to make sure that Jimmy got the tape so that he could put it in a safe place. Pete and Ian had decided to stay at the apartment to wait for the Minister to return, who they needed to have a chat with. They stayed the night in the luxurious yet now very seedy apartment not knowing what the next day would bring. The sick video had spoilt what should have been a pleasant day out for them and they had the Minister to thank for that.   They knew that he would not be back until early evening so they had a lie in until lunch time then got up and had a full English breakfast. After breakfast they finished off the bottle of vintage brandy and sat and waited for the pervert to return. It was just after six in the evening when they heard someone at the door. Ian stood behind the door as Pete remained sat on the leather sofa. The pervert opened the door surprised to find that the alarm was not on. He was even more surprised to see Pete sitting on his sofa and he turned to hit the panic button only to be whacked in the face with a cast iron wok. He fell to the floor almost unconscious and was dragged by his hair to his feet only to be kneed hard in the balls.

"Don't make a fucking sound you dirty bastard because if the police come I know which of us is going to be in the most trouble"

The Minister looked down to the floor and saw that the

rug had been moved and he looked up to the two guys that stood above him.

"I am a rich man I can give you enough money to set you up for life"

"You are a dirty fucking sicko who should have his dick cut off"

The man looked in terror just as the phone rang out. Pete passed him the phone and told him to answer it hoping that it would be Jimmy, which it was. The pervert nodded as Jimmy told him what he wanted from him.

"What about the tape, what will happen to it"? he asked the man on the phone who had just explained to him what he owed.

"The tape will remain with me until such a time that I require your services. Until then it will be safe but when I call on you to repay the favour you must do exactly what I ask of you. Is that clear"?

The Minister had agreed to Jimmy's terms as he had no choice. He knew that if the tape became public knowledge that his career would be at an end as well as his reputation as a gentleman.

"Give my friends your car keys and do as they say. They will make it look like a burglary and someone will call the police in a while"

The Minister told Pete where he could find his beloved car and he handed him the car keys before he was stripped naked and left tied to a chair. He had almost passed out when Ian came out of the kitchen brandishing a carving knife and he felt his bollocks retracting at the thought of the danger that lay ahead. Pete convinced Ian to put the knife away for he knew that Jimmy would want this guy alive but he did let him knock ten tons of shit out of him before they left. Ian rubbed salt into his wounds literally after he had smashed almost all of the pervert's expensive ornaments across his head and face. By the time they left him he was barely conscious and his sad face was cut to shreds. He had lost so much blood from his wounds that he slumped forward and stayed that way until he was found early the next morning by his cleaning lady. He awoke to the sounds of her screams as she found him naked and tied up as she entered his apartment.

The police were called in and the Minister made the headlines which read that he had been victim to a most vicious attack they had ever seen. It also said that it had happened so quickly that the victim had been unable to give the police a description of any kind. His Rolls Royce car was found in Birmingham minus its leather seats and walnut console and various other parts. It was thought that it had been an opportunist robbery and despite police investigations no-one was ever convicted or charged with it.

Jimmy had put the video away in a safe place and he had put another name in his favours book. There had been a couple of thousand pounds and a few letters in the safe that they had taken from the wall along with an e mail address. Jimmy gave the boys the money to share between themselves and he gave the computer and the e mail address to young Mike Collins who came up with another paedophile who happened to be a prominent Major in her Majesty's army. It seemed that they both shared the same interests which included very young boys and illicit sex and Jimmy called the Major to let him know that he was in his book. The Major had been expecting the call for he had read about the Minister who he could no longer contact via his website. He too had everything to lose and would do anything to keep his name out of the papers.

"So my friend these are the last two men that you must contact when you leave here. They have no choice but to do what I say so tell them everything that I will tell to you now. Then contact my four friends and tell them a time and what they will need. Each of them will be able to come up with what we need them to but just tell them what they need to know for now. If they question anything tell them to have faith in me, that is all I can say. Have you got all of that Joseph"?

Joseph nodded then set off to finalise Jimmy's plan and to call to Liam's place where he wasn't looking forward to spending the night. Joseph's four bed-roomed house in the stockbroker belt had been furnished to the highest of standards and he enjoyed his creature comforts. He had thought that Liam had sounded quite rough when he had spoken to him on the telephone but Liam's telephone voice had been ten times better that the block of flats that Joseph was driving to, where he was expected to spend the night.

A BOOK OF FAVOURS

Chapter 17

Anne and Sid Rooney were tired out. They had been sorting out their son's personal effects and it had been a lot harder than they had imagined it would be. They had emptied his wardrobe and simply put all of his clothes into black bin liners and they had done the same with his shoes. Annee had phoned the Help The Aged charity shop who were to send a van round the next morning to pick up the clothes and some bits of furniture to sell in their town centre shop. Two local estate agents had been round to value Mike's terraced house and both of them had put similar prices on it. One had said it would go for fifty thousand pounds and the other had said forty six thousand. Sid Rooney had put it on the market with the one with the lower price which was a lot more than he had expected anyway.

Both of the agents had promised a quick sale which is what they wanted but Sid had liked the manneer of the second agent who hadn't been quite as up himself as the first one. Mike owed twenty three thousand on the house due to him taking out a re-mortgage on it a couple of years earlier and there was a charge on the property from a loan company for another three thousand.

After paying the agent's and solicitor's fees there would be about seventeen thousand pounds left over from the sale of the house which they intended to put into a trust for Ben for when he reached eighteen.

If Mike hadn't committed suicide there would have been a lot more money from the insurance company but the fact that he took his own life had invalidated his insurance. They weren't sure about Mike's pension which they had decided to ask the kind Superintendent about when they called in to see him to discuss the funeral arrangements. Anne had found a big stack of pornographic magazines stored under Mike's bed that she had thrown into the bin without looking at them for the pictures on the front covers had been enough to put her off them. As she had been clearing out under the bed Sid had been clearing the wardrobe out and he had pulled out an old shoebox tied with string.

"Well I'll be blowed"

Anne turned round to see Sid looking through old photographs that he had found in the shoebox and she went to his side to look at them with him. She filled with tears as she looked at them for they were probably the only ones that had been taken with them as a family.

On every one of the photos Mike was looking proudly at his dad who was always stood a couple of feet away from him. His mother's arms were always wrapped around him protectively but his father always looked stern. Despite that Mike had kept the pictures hidden away for all of those years. There were lots and lots of photos of Ben as a baby and a beautiful one of Mike holding Ben with such a proud and caring look on his face. Anne had put her hand to her mouth to try to stop herself from crying out loud as she thought of how much Mike must have missed his son. She and Sid had called Mike for not bothering with him but she realised that they didn't know the half of it. They found Ben's Christening cards and a lock of his hair cellotaped to a piece of coloured paper and they even found a Father's day card with a bit of scribble on that Ben must have done for him just before he had walked out on them. Other bits in the box were things from Mike's childhood including a Blue Peter badge that he had won for a creative design that he had sent in. Anne put all of the contents back into the shoe box and she tied it up with the string. She knew that Sid didn't like to see her grieving so she thought she would save it for when she was alone when he had gone out to play golf. All she had left of her precious son was a heart full of memories and a cardboard box which wasn't a lot to show for forty years of a life.

They were just about to retire to bed when Sid thought about the attic.

"We'd better make sure that there is no hidden treasure up here before we go. Pass us a stool love and I'll climb up and take a look"

Anne passed him a stool that she got from the bathroom and Sid climbed up on it and removed the hatch to the attic. He peered into the dark void that looked as if it held only four black dustbin liners and he cautiously reached in his hand and pulled one of the bags out.

The bag was a bit dusty so Sid blew on it before handing it down to Anne who took it from him and put it down on the floor by the stool. There was a big piece of Silver tinsel sticking out of the bag and the green bristles of a Christmas tree that Mike had taken with him when he had left home. Anne had smiled and reached up to take the other bags from Sid that she presumed to contain the same. Sid got down from the stool then took the four bin bags and left them in the hallway with the rest of the things that they had sorted out and put to one side for the Charity Shop.

"Let us leave this lot for the shop to sort out. I doubt that there will be anything of value, do you"?

Anne had shook her head as she picked up the shoe box and

held it closely to her chest for it contained all the hidden treasures that she would ever need. Then she went up to bed where she quietly cried herself to sleep.

At exactly the same time that Anne Rooney was falling asleep Joseph's Jaguar XK8 was pulling into Bellamy Court. Before he had turned his lights off there were four men surrounding his car. He had opened his window nervously as he spoke to the closest of the men.

"Liam is expecting me"

The big guy opened the car door and let Joseph out.

"Don't worry your motor will be fine parked here"

Joseph had been concerned but on noticing the security that Liam had in place he felt much easier and he locked the car and left it under the watchful eye of the four bruisers that had just welcomed him.

He walked up to the first floor where he was met by another two big guys that frisked him before he was allowed to enter into Liam's flat.

Liam and Tulip were halfway through their second bottle of cider when Joseph made his entrance. The first thing that he did was to take the cider bottle into the bathroom and empty it into the sink much to Tulip's dismay. Then he had gestured to Tulip to make herself scarce for a while. Tulip had taken herself into the bedroom where she tried hard to listen to what was being said. She had no idea who the guy in the track suit was but she knew that he was powerful enough to pour Liam's drink away and that impressed her. Joseph knew that Tulip would be eavesdropping at the door so he said very little about their mission. All he did was to give Liam his new mobile phone complete with twenty pounds worth of credit. The phone would be thrown away when they had completed their mission so twenty quid would be more than enough air time for them to use up.

Joseph had strict instructions to keep them all in the dark until the next morning so he chose an armchair that faced Liam's and he started to doze off. Tulip got fed up of listening to nothing so she came out of the bedroom to try to entice Liam to join her but he declined her offer. She knew that she had no chance of finding anything out from Liam so she gave up.

It was just like the old days for Liam and although he had no idea of what the next twenty four hours would hold he was sure that he would need all of his wits about him. He had no idea what would be asked of him but it didn't matter for he could work on five minutes notice. He had access to whatever weapons were needed for the job and he had unlimited manpower on standby. He remembered the old days and the buzz of satisfaction that he used to get when he completed a successful job and he could taste that same kind of fear and excitement again. He could never forget what had happened to Christine and he could never forgive the man that had pulled the trigger and taken her life so cruelly. Many a time he had been tempted to travel back to his home town to hunt down the killer and to punish him but he knew that he mustn't. For despite all the bad that had happened he had made a promise to leave and to take his secrets with him, in return for being left alone. He knew that if he was spotted in Belfast that it would be seen as an act of defiance and despite what had happened he still had respect for the cause. He could not say that he was truly happy in his new life but he had survived until now when he suddenly had the chance to be needed again.

The favour that he was about to repay to Jimmy for saving him from the O'Grady brothers all of those years ago could be all Liam needed to make him feel alive again. All he had to do was to get through the night without taking a drink and without having a nightmare if that was at all possible.

Liam could not see it happening for the drink was the only thing that knocked him to sleep and he was dreading what terrifying images would force them-selves into his broken mind. Even after all of the years that had passed by since he had lost all that was dear to him he knew that the images that tried to destroy him would be crystal clear, just as though it was only yesterday. Liam Docherty feared no man but himself for at night in the darkness of his own mind he became his worst enemy.

Chapter 18

The 10th of September 2003 started off like any other day at that time of the year. Everywhere suddenly seemed a lot quieter since the children had all gone back to school after the long summer break and people were starting to talk about Christmas time. Most people had finished taking their summer holidays and what hot weather the summer had actually brought earlier in the year the start of autumn was about to take away again. There was still the odd sunny day but not many of them.

Joseph woke up slightly earlier than he did at home after a broken night's sleep that had been disturbed more than once by Liam's nightmares. Three times during the night he had been woken by Liam's pleas and cries for help and three times he had got up and tried to placate him. Liam had not woken during his nightmares which had caused him to break out in a terrible sweat each time. Joseph had no idea of what could be troubling the poor man so much as he wiped his brow for him as a caring father might do. He had put it down to some of the horrors that he may have witnessed during troubled times in his old country which was partly true but more personal than he could have guessed.

Joseph could have never fully comprehended the true horror just as no-one other than Liam ever would. Joseph stood up quietly and looked over to his sleeping partner who was still fast asleep. He moved quietly in an attempt so as not to disturb Liam who obviously still needed the rest. He tried to straighten the track suit that he had chosen to sleep in which thankfully was crease proof and he was glad that he had chosen to wear it. He had his suit in the car that he would wear at Jimmy's appeal but he had not wanted to look too out of place for his stay with Liam. He was unaccustomed to sleeping in an armchair in strange surroundings and he had thought it safer to keep his clothes on particularly with Liam's girlfriend hanging around. Girls like Tulip scared the hell out of Joseph who was a good practising Catholic boy. He got up and walked to the kitchen where he put the kettle on so that he could enjoy a nice strong mug of coffee and he put the radio on but made sure that it wasn't too loud. He was stirring his coffee when Tulip walked in wearing only a skimpy see through black top with a matching thong. Joseph coughed as he nodded politely then quickly turned his face away in embarrassment. Tulip recognised the embarrassment and played on it. She bent over provocatively into the fridge and leant down to reach the milk.

"Would you like a bit of this Joseph"?

Joseph took the milk from her and poured it into his coffee then made a quick getaway from Tulip. She laughed and turned the music up loud and started to dance around as she put the kettle back on for herself. The loud music woke Liam up who took the cup of coffee from Joseph before he had even taken one sip of it himself.

"Cheers mate that's just what I needed. What's the weather like"?

Joseph didn't know so he went to look outside and as he opened the door he was met by one of Liam's henchmen who it seemed had stood watch all night as he always did.

"Worried about your car was you, well it's alright I kept

my eye on it"

"No I was just wondering what the weather was like actually"

"It's not too bad but it will rain later on I can feel it in my water"

Joseph thanked him and went back to tell Jimmy what the weatherman at the door had told him and to make himself another cup of coffee.

Liam slapped Tulip hard on her backside as he pushed her to the bedroom door and told her to get ready. Tulip had not argued and she emerged ten minutes later ready but still not wearing much in the way of clothing. She smiled smugly at Joseph as she spoke to her fellow.

"What are we doing today babes, anything special"?

" I've got a big game of poker lined up for which I need some peace and quiet and before you start moaning I need you to do a bit of shopping for me and while you are there you might as well do a bit for yourself as well. Tulip squealed with pleasure as she took a large wad of notes from Liam that he had just taken out of his wallet.

"Cheers babe. Have I got time to get my hair done as well"?

Liam took another fifty pound note out of his wallet and passed it to her. It would suit him for her to be out all day whatever the cost.

"Now piss off and find me a nice leather jacket, I've got a tear in my old one and I don't want to see you before seven o clock"

Tulip didn't hang around, she put on her jacket and picked up the car keys to go out for a legal drive and a legal shop then she was gone.

Joseph sat down with his coffee and filled Liam in on his part of the job. He explained to him that Jimmy wanted him to rob the Bank of South Africa in the heart of Manchester at approximately eleven thirty that morning. He told him that he would call him on the mobile that he had given him the night before and he handed him a stop watch.

"Time is of the essence. I will call you to confirm the exact time for you to act. All you need to know is that this is to be a joint operation with very big rewards for all parties concerned.

"Who are the others do I know of them"?

"Jimmy knows them and that should be enough for you to know. He has put all of his trust in you all and he has made arrangements for you all to have a safe passage. Call me when you are loading the goods up and I will give you your next lot of instructions. You can carry the operation out in any fashion that you choose but you must not tell anyone else any of the plan as it starts to unfold. There is something else that only you can do for him he needs you to phone in a couple of bomb scares"

"Only scares? I'll blow the buggers up for Jimmy if he wants me to"

Joseph smiled for he knew that the brown haired rogue that stood before him was not joking.

"Merseyway Stockport and Oldham Road Chadderton should be far enough away to keep them out of the way for a while"

Liam was intrigued but excited at the thought of the unknown. Jimmy had put his trust in him and Liam was quite happy to do the same. He knew Manchester like the back of his hand and he knew the bank in question. He looked at his watch and synchronised it with the time on Joseph's watch which was showing twelve minutes past seven

"I will need to get going if I'm to be successful, is there anything I need to know before you go Joseph"

"No. Just wait to be contacted, make sure that you have a

full tank of diesel and when it is loaded it must be you that takes it to its next destination"

"Fucking hell Joseph what about my back up"?

Joseph knew that Liam would need someone to bring him back after he had torched the truck, also someone to watch his back.

"You can let your number two follow in a car but he must remain at least one hundred and fifty yards away from you at all times. Any problems you must call me straight away and I will do the same with you"

"That's fine by me. Here's to whatever we are up to"

Joseph asked if he could take a shower before leaving as he needed to be at the Appeal Court for nine thirty and he had a few errands to run and phone calls to make before he left. Liam assured him that he would be okay and that Mickey would watch his car until he was ready to leave.

"Goodbye and Good Luck!"

Liam left to round up the men that he needed to work with him. He knew exactly what he had to do and it required the use of a road digger. He went to where he kept all of his working gear and dug out some Telecom overalls. Then a quick phone call to Simon Collier at British Telecom secured him an official vehicle and all the equipment that he would need to take out the bank's alarm system. Simon or Psycho as he was known to his friends didn't actually owe a favour to anyone. He had worked for British Telecom from leaving school and thirteen years later he knew all he needed to about communications, he also liked a challenge. He had the know how and he could access all of the equipment that Liam would need to take out the communication system. He was Liam's outside man on the inside. He also had the need for excitement and the balls to have a go at anything. When Liam had approached him he had been honoured and all he had asked for in return had been for Liam to pass on some of his explosives knowledge to him. In return Psycho Collier had agreed to provide the stuff that Liam had needed and to take out the rest of the traffic lights and cameras in the centre of town by simply snipping the right cables. Liam had liked young Simon who was like the son that he never had and he had been more than happy to pass on his expertise to him. After arranging to have the phone lines put out Liam made sure that all of his men were tooled up and ready to go as he explained to them that they were on a no questions asked mission. Then he put his own piece away out of sight and he stuffed a few sticks of dynamite down his overalls for good measure. By quarter to nine the 'workmen' had started to dig up the road directly outside of the South African bank. Safety barriers had been put in place and adequate warning signs had been administered giving the job the authenticity it required to make it look like a legitimate job.

The manager of the bank arrived for work shortly after the 'workmen' had set up and he had pulled his face in disgust and tutted out loud at them. He was obviously angry to see the sight of the work hut that was so close to his precious bank. The last time the roads had been up outside of his bank it had lasted for three weeks and his beautiful marble tiled floors had been covered in tarmac resulting in him having to put in a claim for damage to the council. The rates on the bank were ridiculously high due to its location and he made a mental note that he must put in a letter of complaint to the telephone company. He went to his office where he checked out the latest foreign currency rates and he updated his records accordingly before opening of business. Despite the double glazing that he had installed he could still hear the sound of the workmen outside and he dictated a nasty letter of complaint to his secretary before taking a couple of headache tablets. Mr Arends had hosted a dinner party the previous evening and he had felt quite delicate when he had left his home for work that day. He started his daily inspection of the bank as he had done every morning before opening for business at nine thirty.

Outside the bank Liam and his men had dug a good sized hole beneath the tent that housed them. They had spotted the cables that they would need to cut into and they were already well ahead of their schedule so they stopped for a morning tea break. The rain that Jimbo had told Joseph that he had felt in his waters earlier that morning had started to fall from the sky quite heavily. The bad weather conditions helped Liam because the people on the street started to disperse quite quickly as they felt the rain coming down on them.

Wednesday was always a quiet day for banking which suited Liam down to the ground so he sat back and took in the view of the street through a small tear in the striped curtain. He had a good view to the end of the road which was one way to traffic and he could keep a watchful eye out. His men had put the barriers onto the pavement causing passers by to cross the road so that only the bank customers would come anywhere near to them. Paddy Beirne was his number two and it was he who would go with him on the next part of his mission. Paddy was probably Liam's most loyal man. He too had lost most of his family in similar circumstances to Liam and he had nothing to live for which made him a very dangerous sort. Liam knew that he could trust Paddy who would give his life rather that to betray his leader. The other men would make their own way back to headquarters whilst Si Collier could get the equipment and van back to their rightful owners. They had until at least ten thirty so they got out the cards and started up a game of pontoon like any normal workmen might do at the start of the day.

Joseph had showered and shaved in Liam's flat and he looked every bit the successful barrister that he was. He had phoned around and put all the minor men that he had contacted in the picture of what their part in the job was to be. Mickey Mee had distributed the new clothes to his band of tinkers who would all be getting dressed in them before ten thirty. He had taken delivery of them the night before from a local warehouse. The warehouse had been on their list to rob so to be given the clothes for free was a great bonus for them. Mickey's tinkers were not fashion icons and had been happy wearing their scruffs but freebies were not to be snuffed at. When Mickey had been approached with the idea of kitting his men out in new gear he had jumped at the idea. His niece was to be married just before Christmas and the gift of the new clothes meant that he could put his men out smart for the occasion. If everything went to plan he had also been promised ten crates of champagne complete with glasses.

The tinkers were known to throw a good party and Mickey was glad for the kind contribution to what he planned to be the 'tinker' wedding of the year.

Joseph had spoken to the head of security and he knew exactly which route that Jimmy's wagon would be taking. He also knew that the court would be adjourning before eleven that morning. It seemed that one of the three judges presiding had a pressing appointment at the hospital and the other two who were unsympathetic to the criminals would be happy to take an extra long recess. It was an unusually quiet court with only two cases to be heard that morning and Jimmy was to be the first one up. The appeal should really have been cancelled in the light of Mike Rooney's suicide but Joseph had decided to give the information at the hearing. Had he brought it up earlier the appeal would not had gone ahead for it would have been seen as a complete waste of time. His actions could have possibly brought him a reprimand in the law courts but Joseph had been willing to take that risk.

The appeal had been the only sure fire way to get Jimmy in a position where he would be out of the prison and where he could be rescued without too much danger.

The second appeal was from a rapist who had decided to apologise to his victim as he had read in the papers that it would lessen his sentence. The rapist in question had been convicted of the same offence on different women twelve times in his life time so Joseph had no doubts that both cases would be dealt with in the minimum of time. The European courts gave more rights to the criminals than it did to their victims which all criminals were aware of.

With only two prisoners on board on the return journey Joseph would not know until they had left the prison exactly what form of transport would be used. His guy on security was going to call Joseph as they were about to leave giving all details of the van including the registration number. Although it would be highly unlikely there was always the chance that the wrong prisoners might be sprung for Joseph remembered that happening once many years earlier. Joseph could not afford any slip ups as this would be their only chance, so he needed to be absolutely sure of every little detail. If it went wrong he knew that he would never get another shot at it so everything depended on precision timing and good luck.

He had men posted along the route who would call him to keep him informed on Jimmy's every movement and on the amount of police presence. They needed to know how the land lay ahead just in case there was a sudden unplanned hitch along the way. He had an ambulance and driver with crew who would, on Joseph's order look as though it was in attendance to a road traffic accident. This would cause the wagon to stop in a position that Mickey's boys could work best in without too much outside interference. They had chosen a stretch of road that had no shops or buildings either side of it therefore it would have very few pedestrians passing. It was also somewhere that had lots of different escape routes close by. He had put over ten escape vehicles in place which would either act as red herrings or take Jimmy on to meet Julie and his freedom.

Julie had been on the phone just after eight sounding to Joseph like an excited schoolgirl about to have her first sexual relationship. She was going to meet Jimmy very calmly in a small café close to the airport. There they would greet each other as old pals before leaving for the airport to head for a well earned break and a lot of loving.

Jimmy would be the least of the police's worries and at the time he was due to board the plane there would be no-one looking for him. He had a valid passport and a ticket to take him to Tenerife, all he had to do was to look like someone looking forward to a couple of weeks break in the sunshine.

Joseph had done all that had been asked of him and it seemed as though everything was going according to plan quite nicely. He drove to the back of the courts and parked his car in a space reserved for court officials. He had just turned the engine off when his phone rang and he answered it to hear the security guy telling him the very transport that Jimmy had left in earlier that morning. Joseph smiled as the exact vehicle that his chap was describing drove up the back entrance. It seemed that the caller had been taken into a meeting just as he had been about to phone Joseph and he had only just got out of it himself. At least Joseph knew that the van had arrived and that it was on time.

He called Liam who was still playing cards with the lads

outside the bank and he reminded him of his duty.

"All systems go up to now my friend. I will not be able to be contacted for the next possible hour so I must leave it with you. You know what time to make those calls and I will call you to confirm zero hour as soon as I am able"

Joseph very carefully used no names for from that moment every one of the people involved in Jimmy's plan would be referred to as my friend.

Joseph had been amazed at the number and the calibre of the people whose names Jimmy had written down in his book of favours. Joseph had read and heard all about the famous Alberto Vincente many times in his legal career. He was a modern day Godfather as had been portrayed by Marlon Brando in the seventies but Alberto was real life. He was a highly respectable gentleman whose love of the arts gave him plenty of coverage in the society pages yet he was also a feared gangster of the underworld. One though who had never been convicted of so much as a parking ticket in the whole of his lifetime.

He was also worth a fortune with millions of pounds invested in this country and unknown, copious amounts in his own country of birth. Joseph had spoken to him earlier that morning after he had showered. It had been a straight forward exchange of words between two highly intelligent men with no need for any explanations.

Alberto had showed no sign of shock as Joseph had passed on the part of Jimmy's plan that Alberto needed to know. The bank that Jimmy had allocated for Alberto was the very rich Saudi bank on the South point of his compass. Joseph had suggested that he might have been pushed for time and Alberto had kindly sent one of his men out to collect his mobile phone and stop watch from Joseph. Joseph explained that Alberto would be left to his own devices which seemed to suit him down to the ground and Joseph thought how clever Jimmy had been in planning it that way.

The men that Jimmy had chosen to help him with his plan were all giants in their own rights and Jimmy had not tried to tell any of them how to do a job. He had given them the respect that they all deserved and enabled them to each use their own methods. All that Jimmy had asked of them was to pool together at the end and to follow Jimmy's instructions to the tee.

Alberto was happy to do his bit and he promised to wait for Joseph's call for zero hour before striking then he had got off the phone and made his own plans. Maria Vincente had known that Wednesday was to be the day and that is all she knew. She had seen the glint in Alberto's dark dreamy eyes as he had put the phone down and she knew that he had been excited. They had all the power and money in the world that they would ever need and they had the most beautiful little girl in the world. They also had the most loving relationship that they knew of and they had a wonderful life and a beautiful home. When Maria had first met Alberto he had been one of the lads in a gang the only difference was that his family background had him destined for fame and notoriety. Now Alberto could have anything happen to anyone in any part of the world at the touch of a button. He could even choose which person he wanted to rule a particular country again by picking up the phone and making a simple call. Despite having such powers Maria knew that he missed the danger and thrills of being involved. He had been very hands on when Maria had first met him which was one of the things that had attracted her to him. His jet black hair that was set off by the small patch of snow white hair on his temple was the other. Alberto had a passion that most men would die for and that most women would adore. He was a true red blooded Latin lover throughout.

Whatever it was that Jimmy had asked him for he had risen to with more gusto and enthusiasm that Maria had seen for a long time. He had kissed her so hard and passionately after he had come off the phone that he had bitten her lip. As she tasted the small stream of blood that trickled from her lip she knew that she had a night of passion beyond all comprehension later that evening.

Alberto met his men at the restaurant where he had his phone and stopwatch delivered. He had called in a favour of his own and got a supposed rich Arab friend of his to make an appointment at the bank in question.

Mr Ezair owed Alberto over fifty thousand pounds and was not far off becoming bankrupt. His gambling debts in a Manchester Casino had forced him to sell his wife's priceless emerald necklace that had been in the family for over nine generations. He had gone to Alberto for help when he needed to get the jewels copied before selling them so that his dear wife would not know and Alberto had sent him to an excellent jeweller that he used. Alberto had found Mr Ezair easy to convince.

"I want you to call the bank and to make an appointment to put something into one of the safe deposit boxes there. Your wife's emeralds"

Mr Ezair had gasped in horror of taking the gems into the bank for he was not sure just how good a copy they were and he wasn't sure what his wife would say about keeping them somewhere other than their own safe.

"Book a holiday before making your appointment there for eleven o' clock. Tell your wife that the jewels will be safer in the bank in case you are burgled in your absence. I have it on good authority that the bank will be robbed later in the day"

"But why would I want to put them in a place that will be

robbed"?

Mr Ezair had smiled to himself as he realised what he had just asked and the reason that his friend was giving him such good advice.

"Because my friend your 'emeralds' are insured and because once you are paid you can pay me back that small amount that is still outstanding"

Mr Ezair made the appointment and then he had called Alberto back to confirm what he had done and to thank him for his kindness.

Alberto then arranged for some of his best men to visit the bank not long after eleven for various reasons. Some would call in to order foreign currency, others to change it back. There would be people making enquiries about opening new accounts and other salesmen. Alberto would make sure that when he hit the bank that the only customers in there would be his own men. He also organised to have a van big enough to carry his hoard waiting in the next street to where the bank was, on standby. Joseph had explained to Alberto that only one of his most trusted men would be allowed to follow him on to phase two of the plan and where it would lead him.

Alberto had decided to pick Alphonso for his one man that he could have for he had been with him for most of his life. He trusted every one of his men but he realised that he was only a part of Jimmy's operation and that he had offered his help to him unconditionally. As Alberto had got dressed earlier that morning he had felt a strange thrill run through his body that he hadn't felt for a long while. He had deliberately chosen to wear black Armani jeans and a black silk polo neck sweater. Even his socks were black and they were made of the finest silk that slipped easily into his leather soled soft leather black boots. He had looked into the mirror as he thought that he had reminded himself of the dark hero in the Cadbury's Milk Tray advertisement. Then he had slipped his small silver pistol with its mother of pearl handle into his trouser pocket and he had patted it with his perfectly manicured hand.

Alberto's part of the plan was very much in hand, all it was waiting for was the go ahead that he would get from the phone call. Alberto had kissed his wife passionately before leaving his home to take part in something that already made him feel twenty years younger. It reminded him of the good old days when he first started out and the adrenalin started to rush through his veins with excitement. He took one last look in the mirror and smoothed his perfect hair into shape. He had put a black rinse on the distinctive white patch of hair that he was usually so proud to display. Alberto could take no chances that someone might recognise him so the white splash of hair that Maria loved so much had to be hidden just for the day. Alberto felt better than he had done for a long time and he whistled softly. Even the heavy rain that lashed against his face as he left the house did nothing to break the good mood that he found himself in.

It was raining hard in Levenshulme where Mr and Mrs Rooney were about to leave their son's home for probably the very last time. They had waited in for the van to come from the charity shop which had just arrived to collect Mike's things that they had sorted out for them. Sid Rooney had helped the driver to put the bags and bits of furniture into the back of the van which was just as well for the driver looked about seventy years old and as though he was ready to pop off at any time. The lady next door peered through her curtains as Sid and the driver loaded the van up. She was having a nosy at what they were giving away. She had hoped that they might have let her daughter rent the house from them but the For Sale sign that hung on the wall had told her that it was not to be. There were about twelve black bin bags to go into the back of the van in total and Sid hoped that the stuff would go to good homes. The driver had a good cough as he locked the back doors on his van then he had touched his cap at them and took the bags he had just been given. They would go to the main shop in Piccadilly where they would be looked through by Annie and Ethel who would decide how much to sell each of them for. Anne took one last look around Mike's house thinking that she could have done more to protect her son. She knew that she would never lose her feelings of guilt so she shut the door behind her before they took the door keys to the estate agents. They had called the Superintendent at the station and had promised to pop in and see him before they left to let him know about the funeral arrangements. The Superintendent had told Mr and Mrs Rooney that he was due to go into a meeting which hadn't been completely true but it had meant that his meeting with them would be kept short. Mike's parents got to the station where they spent just ten minutes there much to Superintendent's relief. They didn't want to be there any more than he wanted them to. They were not proud of the way that their son had taken his own life and they felt ashamed to be with men who wore the same uniform that he had. They had decided that Mike should be buried with his grandmother in a family plot so the funeral would be held in Sheffield. This had been good news for the station and the Superintendent had promised that he would contact the Sheffield station. He had promised them that there would be a strong police presence including men that Mike had started his career off with. They both thanked him and then they went back to Sheffield to tell his ex-wife of Mike's death and to help her break the news to their young grandson.

Chapter 19

Joseph had seen Jimmy for a very short spell just long enough to assure him that everything was going to plan. He explained to him that his time in court would be short and sweet and then he asked Jimmy to call him once he had reached Tenerife. Just to let him know that he had got there.

"Thanks Joseph, for everything. If something should go wrong would you look out for D.J. for us"

Joseph had told him not to be silly but he had promised that he would do it even though something going wrong was something that none of them had contemplated. His long law career had taken up all of his own youth and apart from the odd dinner date he had been on, Joseph had no-one special in his life. One of the reasons that he liked being around Jimmy was because that he envied the wonderful relationship that he shared with Julie. To see the way that they looked at each other and the magic in their eyes for each other was the closest thing to a love affair that Joseph would ever get to share.

Joseph took hold of Jimmy and he had hugged him in a way that re-assured them both that everything was going to be alright. More like his friend than his lawyer. Then he went upstairs to the courtroom to face the wrath of the judges. He took his seat as he waited for the court room to fill up and he looked around at the faces, some of which he had seen many times before. He laughed to himself as he thought of the contrast between the man he had been to see earlier and the men that sat in the court room.

It had been a very quick visit to the estate that Fred Nuttall still lived on. Joseph had been surprised at Liam's accommodation which had been much better on the inside than anyone would have imagined from the outside. But Fred's house had been just the opposite. It had looked like a shit tip from the outside and it had been an even bigger tip from the inside. Fred or Satan as he had reminded Joseph to call him looked exactly as Jimmy had described him. He was big and clumsy looking with dull green coloured eyes and a mop of wiry red hair on the top of his head. He had a scruffy stubbly beard on his double chins made up of the same wiry red hair that adorned his head. He had fat lips, yellow teeth and bad breath that made sitting close to him almost unbearable and Joseph made his visit as short as he possibly could. When he told him about the plan to break Jimmy out Satan had got really excited and he had started to snort as he laughed. So when he told him what Jimmy wanted him to do with the bank he had burst into hysterics.

"Wow. Good old Jimmy, what a guy. Is there anything else I can do"?

Joseph went on to tell Satan that Jimmy would like him to cause quite a few disturbances out and around the town centre.

"We need to keep plod busy for the morning and he said that you had a lot of people in your pockets"

Jimmy had actually said low life but Joseph wasn't about to repeat that to Satan for he was feeling quite threatened just being near to him. Satan showed a set of crooked yellow teeth as he laughed his crazy laugh.

"I can keep every station in the whole of Manchester busy for a week if he wants me to. Just leave it with me and thanks for the phone and stuff"

Joseph told him that he would phone him later to give him the zero hour then he had spent another ten minutes explaining to Satan what zero hour was. It caused him to burst into more fits of laughter and Joseph left for he had started to feel quite nauseous in the big man's presence. He had given him the phone and stopwatch and told him an approximate time and he had told him which bank was his.

Joseph just hoped that the big oaf that he had just seen was intelligent enough to understand what he had been told. Satan knew only too well what he had to do and within seconds of the posh guy that Jimmy had sent to him being out of the way he was on his new phone. He called Sally the slapper who looked after his toms for him and he got her to round up all of the girls and more besides.

"Every station in a ten mile radius, are you kidding me Satan"?

Sally had asked when she had been told to get the girls to go into all of the police stations and to complain about the lack of protection that they were getting. Satan had assured her that he was deadly serious and he even offered to sort out the transport costs for them. Sally didn't mind doing it because safety amongst the girls was getting to be a problem. There had been a couple of nasty murders of prostitutes a couple of months before in Liverpool and the girls were starting to get worried. The bodies of the girls had been chopped up and thrown away in bin bags and the girls on the streets were getting scared. Even though the guy had been caught and put away there was always the chance of copy cat killings so she had agreed to do it for him. It would make a nice change for the girls to walk into the stations of their own accord. Satan left it with her then he called up his mates in the National Front party and arranged for them to be active in Manchester for ten thirty that morning. Last minute arrangements were no problem to his Nazi party for none of them worked anyway and despite the weather they were always up for it. One of the gatherings was to be outside a mosque in Levenshulme which would be interesting as the Muslim population was quite high there. Another was to be held outside the City of Manchester Stadium that was home to the Manchester City football team. One of the main ones was planned for outside the Town Hall in Manchester where plans for a new development of housing for asylum seekers was to take place. Then there was to be the one that would take place outside the German Bank which was the one that Satan would head. Satan had intended to do some more meetings that weekend so everything he had needed had been close at hand. Before going out to round up his own lot of men he called up about thirty opportunist crooks that he knew and tipped them off that the police computers would be down and that there would be chaos in town later that morning making it the perfect time to carry out a raid. He also arranged for a couple of no marks to phone in hoax calls to all of the emergency services which had cost him no more than a couple of quick fixes for them. Once that was all done he nipped out to one of his warehouses and geared him and his men out.

He had just had an assignment of rubber Adolf Hitler masks that he was dying to use so he dished them out and sent some over to the other protesters. He got out all his placards that they had used on the last march they had been on in Oldham and he laughed as he remembered the riots that they had caused that day. Satan had been involved with the Nazi party since being asked to leave the chapter of Hell's Angels that he had been with. It seemed that his own brand of violence was even too much for them to deal with. Satan's involvement with the National Front party was slightly selfish because he found that on the marches he could crack skulls for fun. Satan had set his stall up a bit earlier than planned so that he could enjoy a bit of violence before he turned his skills to the bank. He tried on one of the rubber masks which fitted perfectly. As well as providing them all with a perfect disguise the masks would also keep the rain off them. Then he stuck a gun down each of his socks and one in his belt and he put a stiletto blade up his sleeve for good measure then he went out to weigh up his bank job dressed all in white.

Joseph was still thinking about Satan when the usher had entered the room and announced that it was time for them to all rise.

He got up and stood until the three judges had entered the room and taken their seats before him then he had sat down again.

It was ten o' clock when Jimmy was brought up from the cells and Joseph had asked for permission to approach the bench. Once there he explained that he had entered the appeal on the grounds of new evidence that had come to light that unfortunately was no longer relevant. Two of the judges seemed to show annoyance that they had not been told the facts earlier but at least one was sympathetic. Joseph went on to explain that another suspect had been found who had taken his own life rather than face the wrath of the law.

As it was only recognised as hearsay and as forensics had proved that the weapon belonged to Jimmy who still could provide no alibi the judges could do nothing but turn down the appeal. They called Jimmy to the stand to take the oath before delivering the bad news to him.

"Peter James Mackay in the light of what your barrister has just told the bench we are unable to listen to your appeal or change your sentence. We are sorry that you have made such a long journey for such a short hearing but perhaps your barrister can shed some light on that for you"

Joseph recognised the sarcasm in the judge's voice which he knew to be directed solely at him. He waited until his client was taken back to the cells before excusing himself from their courtroom and apologising for wasting their time once again. He bought a black coffee from the canteen which he took out to his car and he drank it slowly as he waited for Jimmy to be loaded into the prison van. Joseph had never smoked a cigarette before but as he sat waiting for the final part of the plan to happen he had never felt more like a smoke in all of his life. With each of the four men that he had spoken to that day he had began to feel more and more important in his new role as Jimmy's man.

Even the man that Lee Won King had sent to collect the mobile phone and stopwatch had stood to attention as he took them from him causing Joseph to feel as though he really did belong to the world of crime that he had vowed to uphold the law in.

Lee Won King had been waiting patiently for Joseph's call that morning. He didn't like to be indebted to anyone and he had owed Jimmy for as many years as he could remember. In a way he was glad that it was now when he was in a position to do anything that anyone asked of him for he really wanted to help Jimmy. He didn't just see Jimmy as someone who had once helped him but he also saw him as a true friend.

When Joseph had told him that he was to take the Bank of Hong Kong it had made it extra special for he had unfinished business with the president of that bank. Henry Chui had doubled crossed Lee six years earlier in a private stock deal and Lee had lost a considerable amount of money on the stock market. He had soon made the money back but his pride had been hurt. Taking his bank would be like killing two birds with one stone and Lee knew exactly which stone he could use for it. He had his own man on the inside who was head of security so Lee had called him up to make sure that it was still the same manager there. Spike Yung had been glad to furnish Lee with information about Mr Chan who was still the manager at the bank and who still treated all of his staff with contempt that they didn't deserve.

Lee had a portfolio of information on him as he did with all of his enemies and he looked up his details on his laptop. He gave Mr Chan's address out to two of his men who set out to wait outside Mr Chan's Prestwich home to keep watch until he left for work. Lee Won King's plan would be a lot easier than the other three gangs for his plan was simply for the manager to hand everything over to his men. Lee had a plan which involved bogus Custom's officers and forged twenty pound notes which would assure all of the staff that when all of the money was taken out of the bank by security guards that it would all be very much above board.

Lee's power and influence in town had also enabled him to help Joseph with the last bit of Jimmy's plan which was to put certain traffic lights and cameras out of action. Lee had assured Joseph that it would be dealt with and he had passed his best wishes on to Jimmy and to Joseph. At ten minutes to eleven Joseph heard the first of the police sirens shooting about town and he knew that Liam must have put his bomb scares through. He listened to ambulances and fire engines hitting the streets and was pleased that they were travelling away from the direction that Jimmy would shortly be taking.

He made a few phone calls to his men along the way who all confirmed that there was a lot of action passing by them.

One also confirmed that the traffic lights on Oldham road were not working which would make the break out so much easier. He had just finished on the phone when he saw two men being brought out and being put into the prison van. One of the men was Jimmy which was Joseph's cue to give the signal for zero hour.

Inspector Harry Thomas at Bootle Street Police Station was having a nightmare of a day even though it was still only eleven o' clock in the morning. For some ungodly reason all of the computers had gone down and there had been reports of traffic problems in the town centre.

For unknown reasons it seemed that all of the traffic lights in the town centre had all gone down at the same time. There had been two bomb scares phoned in earlier that morning which had been taken deadly serious for they had been authenticated with the correct code. Most of the men from his station had been sent to secure the surrounding streets from the public and to assist the bomb squad. They had to take as much care as they could to make the streets safe without causing too much alarm to the general public. The people of Manchester were only too aware of the devastation that a bomb could cause after the Arndale disaster some years earlier. They would have to evacuate all of the surrounding buildings as quickly as they could without causing panic. The Inspector had just taken reports of a National Front protest taking place outside the Town Hall which was the venue for an important meeting that was being attended by some European dignitaries. The mayor's office had called showing extreme concern so he had sent out twenty of his men to try to break it up before the men inside were aware of a problem. The men had only just left when there had been further reports of another two such demonstrations taking place locally. The Inspector had been about to send more men out to disperse them all when his station had been almost taken over with hoards of prostitutes, all of them demanding police protection. The desk sergeant had called for back up to help to regain control in the station when reports started coming in of lots more burglaries and robberies. They seemed to be happening all over the place every couple of minutes. On top of all that it appeared there were five hundred flash mobbers waving daffodils at the docks! He called to Mill Street to arrange for back up but had no luck for they were dealing with a rather nasty race riot that had been started as a result of another National Front march on their patch. Every station that he contacted all seemed to be having the same problems and his manpower was not enough to cope with what was being thrown at him. There were about two thousand five hundred police covering Greater Manchester at one time and that number included high ranking officers and desk staff. With the amount of crimes that were reportedly taking place even if Inspector Thomas had enough officers to catch the criminals he would have nowhere near enough cells to put them in. It seemed that every crook on his patch was out doing all kinds of jobs at the same time. Then just when he had thought that was bad enough he started to get reports about the armed robberies. Two armed robberies had been reported to be in operation at that very moment and an Asian guy with a gun had been reported acting crazily outside a primary school in Eccles. The gun crimes had taken up all of the personnel of the armed response unit that was available in one go. Before long every single one of Inspector Thomas's cars and officers were out in attendance of crimes on and around the streets of Manchester. He had absolutely no idea of what to do next for never in all of his time in the police force had his men been stretched so much. The phone calls were still coming in thick and fast and the foyer to the station was brimming with every tom and old lag that had ever been picked up it seemed. All that was left at Bootle Street was the desk staff and a couple of probationers who were helping to man the busy phone lines. Henry and the desk sergeant were busy holding the fort when news came in of two prisoners going on the run after the van taking them back to the prison was literally overturned. It seemed that two dangerous prisoners had been broken out of the prison van by what was described as an army of men. Henry had called in four of the police escorts that should have been accompanying the prison van back to the station to report for duty only ten minutes before the two remaining escorts were overpowered. He had been so short of manpower that he had sent the police bikes out to four separate robberies that were in progress and he had felt so guilty at leaving his other men so vulnerable when he had heard the news.

"Bloody fantastic that's all we need, now we've got a murderer and a serial rapist on the run in a town that seems to be threatened by everything but floods"

The heavy rain started to hit the windows as he spoke and Henry Thomas had a sinking feeling that his long career was about to come to an end. All of the squad cars and officers were out on calls so the Inspector had left the sergeant to cope with the crowds of people that were queuing up to complain whilst he took to the streets. He even had to take his own car. If the Inspector was to try and salvage his career he would need to be in the thick of it for there was so much going on that he was bound to make a few arrests. As he had been about to leave the station he had passed a couple of his officers. His men were bringing in a few of the Nazi party that had been demonstrating quite forcefully outside of the Town Hall which was desperately in need of more manpower. It seems that the protest was starting to get really nasty and big crowds were starting to gather so the Inspector picked up four pairs of handcuffs before going to assist his men. The meeting taking place was due to end at one o' clock which gave him less than two hours to get it under control before the foreigners got wind of any problem.

Just then a news flash came on the radio giving details of two bomb scares that were happening in Manchester and Stockport.

Joseph had followed the prison van at a safe distance after phoning to his men on the roads to make sure that everything was in place. He too had been listening to the radio and he was amazed at the chaos that they had created. It seemed that all traffic in the centre of Piccadilly was almost at a standstill courtesy of Simon Collier's handy work. The traffic lights being out of action had got cars beeping and tempers rising and there had been reports of many accidents as a result of the confusion. Joseph had watched as four of the six police on bikes had left the prison convoy to attend other crimes leaving just two bikes escorting the van. Then shortly after he had watched as the prison van had come to a halt as it came across a road traffic accident. The driver had radioed to his colleague who was at the back of the van watching the prisoners and he had told him the reason that he had stopped.

"It looks like an accident blocking the road with an ambulance in attendance. Shall we offer assistance"?

"No it could be a scam, let's wait and see. I'll phone in just in case"

The prison officer had no chance of getting through because the phone lines were hot with members of the public calling in with concerns of the bomb scares. He was a cautious chap and he moved to the front of the van to see exactly what was happening. As the driver had told him there were two cars that looked as though they had hit each other head on. There was a young lad lying on the ground who was covered by a big red blanket who looked as though he had been injured in the crash. One of the two officers on motorbikes got off his bike and he walked towards the ambulance to check out what was happening and as he did there was a sudden rush of men. They came from what seemed like out of nowhere and they were all wearing identical clothes like some kind of underground army. The officer on the ground was taken down with a rugby tackle and he was sat upon as others tied him up with tape. The officer on the bike was pushed over with his bike as twenty or so big men jumped on him before he could even get to his radio.

Jimmy could just about hear what was going on outside of the van and he had held on tightly to the bar that he was handcuffed to.

"Fucking Hell Joey what do we do"?

"Sit tight I'll call for help. They can't get us we are bullet proof"

Just then the van started to rock from side to side then suddenly the pushing got much faster and more violent. As it rocked further the driver fell forward and he cracked his head hard against the windscreen and warm blood started to trickle down his face.

The other guard tried his radio but he could get no response when suddenly he too went flying in the cab as the van fell completely to one side. The guards were trapped in a tin box surrounded by hordes of violent men trying to get in. There were about three hundred angry men thumping the side of the van causing a terrific din and the guards started to get worried. The driver shouted to the other guard.

"The police officers have been taken out and we are outnumbered by hundreds. I don't know about you but eight pounds an hour isn't enough to put up with this shit. I'm going out before I'm killed"

The driver had held up a white towel to the front window as a flag of surrender which was noticed and the noise suddenly died down.

As quickly as it had been pushed over, the van was pushed back and the men outside waited for the driver to open the door. Some of the men grabbed hold of the guards and threw them to the floor. Then they taped them up whilst others got to the prisoners who were waiting for them. The bolt cutters cut open the handcuffs and one of the prisoners was free. They were going to leave the rapist behind but then they had thought that if they let him go it might make Jimmy's escape a bit easier. The rapist sat and watched in amazement as some stranger cut his handcuffs to set him free and then pushed him out of the van. He was still dazed from banging his head against the side of the van and he lay on the floor besides it for a couple of minutes.

He had no idea who all the men were that had just broken him out but he was just happy to be free at last that he didn't stop to ask them. He didn't even know where he was and he had no money on him but he was free so he took his chance and he started to run down the road. Jimmy was taken out of the prison van and he was pointed in the direction of an old works van just up the road.

The ambulance had packed up and left the scene and the street was soon filled with hundreds of men wearing black pants and white tops who were running in all directions. Jimmy took the clothes that had been thrust into his hands as he jumped into the back of the van which set off as soon as he was in it.

A solitary police car arrived on the scene shortly after to

find an empty prison van and two police officers and prison guards lay on the ground firmly taped up. There were men wearing the same clothes running like rats into all different directions and the two officers that had arrived on the scene didn't know what to do first. One of them had radioed for assistance as the other had started to untie their colleagues.

"The bastards have taken our bloody bikes. What the hell is going on"?

"It's the Great Escape mate, perhaps we'll be part of a film". No-one laughed because they were all hurt and confused and they had the impossible task of trying to find the men who had carried out the rescue.

"Did you get a description of the men"?
asked the officer as he phoned through for help.

"White, male, hundreds of different builds all wearing identical clothes"!
An A.P.B was sent out on what communication was left but with little to no available officers almost all of the tinkers had managed to slink away and get home to take off their new clothes to save them for the wedding.

Julie waited at the café that she had arranged to meet Jimmy at. She was on her third cup of coffee and she was smoking her tenth cigarette as she watched the breaking news on the bomb scares and the prison break. She lit another cigarette as she sat and waited for Jimmy not knowing how or when he would appear but hoping that it would be soon.

Tulip was in the Trafford Centre when she saw the news flash on a television screen in the window of an electrical store. She didn't know how Liam was involved in it but she had a feeling that he was. He had been far too eager to get her out of the flat that morning and he had even given her money. She had also wondered why they had put such a rich and distinguished guy at their humble abode the night before. She had taken the car and parked it at the back of her friend's house till she was ready to go out shopping to spend the money he had given to her. Trixie had to take her kids into school before she could go out with her friend so Tulip had sat at the window and kept a watchful eye on the flats. Liam had gone out with nearly all of his men whilst the posh guy had stayed in the flat for a couple of hours longer.

A guy on a motorbike had called at the flats and Joseph had given him a parcel and it had all seemed very cloak and dagger to Tulip. Liam had told Tulip that he would be in all day playing a big card game yet he had gone out the minute that he thought that Tulip was out of the way. She had been curious earlier on but now the news of the bomb scares made it all a bit clearer to her. She decided to buy some sexy underwear for herself and lots of drinks for them both to share later. If anything could get Liam to talk it might just be those and Tulip was keen to find out what he had been up to. Trixie was pulling at her to go and look at a sexy white top in a shop over the way so Tulip had kept her thoughts to herself until later at home.

It was eleven thirty in the morning and if all had gone to plan Joseph was expecting a few phone calls to start coming in. He had a lot more driving to do so he started to head down the motorway towards his next port of call and he drove until he reached a Little Chef café where he pulled in for breakfast. He had ordered his food so he sat and waited for it and for the others to call him to tell him that they had completed phase one of the plan. Then Joseph could give them their next set of orders. The waitress bought him his cafeteria of black coffee to drink as he waited for his Olympic breakfast to arrive and his calls to come. He listened to the news on the radio and overheard people discussing all of the strange goings on that were happening in Manchester at that moment. Just as he had hoped most people were putting it down to terrorists.

"It's that bloody Bin Liner fellow if you ask me"
said one old lady as she drank her fourth free refill of coffee and Joseph couldn't help but laugh at her cheek and her naivety. Others in the café were talking about how they had known that he would strike on September 11th even though it was only the tenth but it was good for Jimmy that they felt that way. Jimmy had chosen his date carefully and the fact that it coincided with his appeal date made it all the more right.

Joseph took credit for the flash mobbing though which was a very new thing hitting the internet. He had even used a cyber café to arrange it from and he had just invited people to be at the docks for a certain time and asked them to bring a daffodil as a sign of respect. The fact that they had responded confirmed to Joseph just how many idiots lived in Manchester and how easy they were to control.

Chapter 20

Liam had given the bomb scares as he had been asked to do. He and his men had just cut through the cables outside of the bank when Joseph had called to confirm zero hour with him. They were on countdown and Liam had sent Paddy and Noel inside the bank to explain to the manager the damage that they had just accidentally caused. Mr Arends was furious when the workmen trailed mud into his bank and even more so when they told him that they had cut through some cables.

"We are not too sure which ones we have cut through and our foreman said you should check what is and isn't working"

"Oh he did, did he? Well you can tell your foreman that he can come and see me himself and you can tell him to take his bloody shoes off at the door. Oh! And just for the record I don't deal with the monkeys"

Paddy and Noel looked at each other before going back out into the rain. Going inside the bank had given them a chance to check out what customers if any were in the bank and all that they had seen was one elderly lady that was putting her umbrella up before going back out into the rain. They came out of the bank and they gave the thumbs up sign to Liam and the boys who immediately pulled out the barriers that had been hidden beneath the canvas. They set them up on both sides of the road closing it off completely leaving just two men at either end of the street. The bad weather and the bomb scares made it highly unlikely that anyone would interrupt them at work or try to get anywhere close to them. The news of bomb scares had been emblazoned across television sets around the country and Liam had been informed that the police were very thin on the ground. Ten of Liam's men entered the bank with the last one to go in closing the door behind him. The security guy was just about to inform the manager that there seemed to be a problem with the cameras and security monitors when Paddy had met him at the door. He whacked the guard in the face with the butt of his gun then he pulled his unconscious body behind his desk and taped him up to the solid legs on it. Liam went to the four cashiers who were all sat side by side in a neat row and passed a note to each of them. The note read:

I HAVE A BOMB TAPED TO MY BODY THAT I WILL SET OFF IF YOU SO MUCH AS MOVE A MUSCLE. I WANT TO DIE, DO YOU?

Each of the cashiers slowly shook their heads which told Liam that they didn't want to die. Some of his men had gone into the private offices down the corridor where they had found a couple of mortgage advisors taking a coffee break. Then they had looked into another office where they had found the manager's secretary typing out yet another letter of complaint. There were no heroes in the Bank of South Africa and before long all staff but the manager were safely taped up and unable to move.

Liam headed to the manager's office as his men secured the rest of the staff by taping them securely to their chairs. They lay the cashiers neatly side by side just as they had been seated earlier then four men pulled sacks from down their overalls and started to fill them with what cash they could find in the drawers. The cashiers could do nothing but to lie still as they watched the gang of men ripping drawers out for fun. Paddy didn't like an audience and he had held his gun to the head of the young woman who lay at his side.

"Either look away or say your prayers bitch"

They all turned their heads in the other direction and started to pray anyway for none of them had ever been in such a situation before.

When Liam's men had taken all the cash that they could find they left one man to watch over the cashiers. Then the others went down the corridor to look for their boss. Liam had burst into Mr Arend's designer office only to find him lying on the chaise lounge holding his head.

"How dare you walk in like that, I shall call security immediately"

"Don't piss me off and your security is out of action so don't bother to call him. Now my man said something about you calling him a monkey"

At that moment Paddy and Noel walked into the office and Mr Arends started to regret his choice of words to them. He looked down at his white wool carpet that had cost the bank ninety six pounds a square metre and his heart sank. Ordinarily his carpet remained pristine but all he could see was that it was streaked with dirt from their wet, muddy boots. He went to reach for a panic button and he managed to press it quickly before Liam punched him hard in the face knocking him off his leather chair. The button would have set alarm bells ringing at the police station had the wires not been cut a short while before.

As it was it had done nothing but give Mr Arends an even bigger headache than the one he had come into work with that morning. Liam had admired his stupid courage.

"You have made my nose bleed"
he had said indignantly as he wiped the blood with the back of his hand.

Liam pulled out a filleting knife and held it underneath the whimpering manager's throat close enough for him to feel the cold steel of its blade.

"I will take every piece of skin from your body and I will make a coat for my dog with it if you don't stop getting on my nerves. There is a bomb outside your building that is due to go off in ninety minutes"
Liam took the stop watch that Joseph had given to him that day.

"Make that eighty two minutes. Now you can help us or you can die"
Just like the other members of staff it seemed that none of them wanted to die. Mr Arends could see that his phone lines were out and he had been told that all of his staff had been tied up so he stood up and he took a large set of keys from his desk. The sooner he could get rid of the men that were invading his bank the sooner he could get a letter out to the insurance company to put a claim in for his beautiful white carpet. All but one of Liam's men followed the manager down to the bank vaults to what turned out to be a wonderful Aladdin's cave.

They stopped at two enormous safes that were at least eight foot high.

"Please do not tell me that you cannot unlock these or I will have to kill you. I may be Irish but I am not stupid"
The manager did not dare to upset the man who had threatened to skin him so he opened the first of safes to reveal more money that any of them had ever seen before. More sacks came out and three of the men walked inside the safe and started to fill the sacks with money. Liam waited for the manager to open the second safe that was just as full

and he left another three of his men doing the same. Then he took hold of the manager and shook him.

"Very nice now shall we go to the safe deposit boxes"?

"They are in there but I only have one set of keys. You need the owners to be present with their key also otherwise the boxes will not open"

Liam waited as he unlocked the door to the room that contained the safe deposit boxes and he pushed the manager into the corner as they all entered the room. It reminded Liam of the Crematorium at home in Ireland with rows and rows of steel boxes containing people's ashes. It had always reminded Liam of a prison cell which was why he had let Christine's ashes flow in the wind before being taken out on the waves.

He felt instant hate towards all of the boxes before him so he had pulled a jemmy from out of his overalls and he had started to prise the boxes from the wall. The other two men took out their tools and did the same throwing the steel containers intact onto the floor as they removed each of them from the walls.

"See, you don't always need the other key do you"?

The manager could do nothing but to watch in dread as some of his most important customers belongings were being stolen from under his very nose. Noel nipped upstairs to find that everything was still quiet and told Mickey who was keeping watch, to call for transport then he went back downstairs and taped the manager's arms, legs and mouth. Paddy and Noel carried the sacks upstairs and left them at the front door then went back for some more as all of the others hacked away at the boxes in the wall. Within thirty minutes they had hacked out the lot and all of the men carried the loot to the top of the stairs where it was dragged over to the door. A large British Telecom transit van driven by Psycho Collier pulled up at the doors of the bank and he reversed it up onto the pavement. The back doors of the van flung wide open and two men jumped out and knocked hard on the door as the van sounded its horn.

Paddy opened the doors and all of the men stood in a line as they systematically passed on the heavy sacks and boxes as though they weighed nothing at all until eventually all of the sacks were in the van. The doors were closed shut and Liam had jumped into the driver's seat as Psycho jumped out. Paddy pulled up behind the van in another transit van that he had bought from the auction the day before and he waited for his boss to set off. Liam opened his window and he called to the others to make themselves scarce then he had whispered to Noel for a crowd of them to go back to the flat and set up a poker game.

"If Tulip gets back before I do tell her that I have nipped out to the off licence to get a few drinks"
Liam looked at his watch to see it was twenty past twelve and he had completed his mission without even coming close to losing a man.

He drove away with his man in close pursuit stopping only when he was safely out of reach of the area then he pulled into a lay by whilst he called Joseph.

"Mission accomplished, where to now boss"?
Joseph salivated with excitement, it was the first of the calls that he had been waiting for and it had been a success. He had told Liam to go to Aldershot and he gave him a pin point destination to get to and asked him to call him again when he had reached it.

"Any problems with any of that my friend"?
"None at all"

Chapter 21

The driver for Help The Aged had done all of his collections and he had taken it all to their main shop in Piccadilly for Beryl and Edith to sort out. Most of the other workers in the shop were on community service mostly for traffic offences but Beryl and Edith were full time workers who had been there for years. Edith had a soft spot for Joe the driver and she put the kettle on when she heard his cheery voice as he entered the shop.

"Sorry I've taken so long but the roads are murder today. Everywhere you go there are bloody demonstrations it took me half an hour from Stockport road and what about all of these bomb scares"?

Edith brewed up whilst Beryl and Joe dragged the bags into the back room then they all sat down for a while and had a nice cuppa. Joe told them where all the bags were from and asked them to look out for a nice pair of size nine shoes for him which Edith promised to do for him. He said that he would call back later then left to take the pieces of furniture to the warehouse.

"We might as well open the copper's bags first because there might be some good stuff in there under the circumstances"

Edith and Beryl were both in their early seventies and they didn't pussyfoot around when it came to talking about death. Even the bomb scares that had been on the news had not worried them for they had survived the blitz with hundreds of bombs dropping so a couple of scares meant nothing to them. A good bag of clothes was the best thing that came close to excitement for either one of them so they started to open Mike Rooney's bin bags one by one. Beryl tipped the first bag out onto the table to find that it was full of Christmas decorations and she picked out a couple of nice glass fairies and put them on one side to take home for her little great granddaughter. Then she picked up the next bag to find it was full of the same and she put it to one side. Edith took another bag that felt as though it might have had some shoes in it so she tipped the contents out excitedly before her. Edith had thought about Joe and what he had asked her to look for when he had been in earlier. If he was lucky the copper might have been a size nine. As the clothes and the shoes fell out onto the table Edith picked up a black shoe that she had thought that Joe might have liked and then she had screamed out loud as she had thrown it down again.

"Whatever is the matter dear"

asked Beryl, concerned at her friends sudden outburst.

"Look at the shoe it has got dried blood on it and so have the pants"

Beryl looked down and she saw that Edith was right. There was blood on almost all of the things that had been tied up in that bag and it had belonged to a copper. She reached for the phone and looked for a number then she made a call to the police.

"Which station do you want to speak to"?

Beryl had called police headquarters switchboard and she had been given a choice of stations to be put through to. Joe had told them that he had collected the stuff from Levenshulme so she had asked to speak to someone at Mill Street and she had explained to the girl on the switch the nature of the call. Just like all of the other police stations in and around Greater Manchester all of the men were busy but when Inspector Collins had heard about the call he had been very keen to take it personally.

Beryl had explained to him what they had found in the bags that had been collected from a house in Levenshulme earlier that day and that she believed that they belonged to a policeman who had recently died.

Inspector Collins knew exactly which officer the bag of clothes had come from and he thanked the lady for calling him so soon and assured her that someone from his station would call to collect them as soon as possible.

He cursed himself for not investigating further when Joseph had told him of his suspicions and he felt guilty that Jimmy had taken the rap for a murder that he had not committed. He was very aware of everything that had gone on that morning including the break-out and he had thought how ironic it was for Jimmy to escape from a jail sentence that he should never had been subjected to. The station was busy so he called someone from forensics and asked if they could collect the clothes and analyse them for him although he already knew what the results would tell them.

Jimmy had changed his clothes with the ones that he had been given as he had travelled in the back of the first van that had helped him to get away. He had been amazed at the way everything had gone to exactly to plan. He knew that he was only minutes away from his meeting place and he was scared that his luck might change before he got there. He had changed cars at a petrol station and he was being carried in a Skoda for the final part of his journey. Julie was sat at a table just by the door as she watched the old Skoda car pull up on the opposite side of the road and she was delighted when she saw her Jimmy get out of it. She rushed over to meet him before he even got to the door.

"Thought you said that you would never be seen dead in one of those"

"From now on babes they are my favourite kind of motors"

They both laughed as they hugged each other like very good friends who had missed each other desperately. Then they called for a cab to take them to the airport where they had just a couple of hours to wait before the plane that they were booked on was due to take off. Forty five minutes later they had checked their baggage in and were sat in comfy seats in the executive lounge where they enjoyed free drinks and snacks until just before their plane was due to depart. Julie turned one of the television sets on just in time to see the latest news on the bomb scares.

Mr Ezair had strolled into the Thomas Cook office on Deansgate and he had asked for details of the Cruise to Egypt that was on special offer in the window. A pleasant young lady gave him all the details and before long she was taking his details from him and putting his credit card through the machine. He stood and watched with baited breath as nothing seemed to happen and he had been worried that he might have used all of his overdraft facility up. He had been just about to tell her that he had changed his mind when the machine produced a receipt from it.

"If you could check the amount and sign it for me please"

Ahmed took the receipt and signed it then he passed it back to the girl who gave him a receipt and told him that his tickets would be at the desk at the airport on Friday. Then she wished him a happy holiday and took the last minute bargain sign for the cruise out of the window. Ahmed had walked to the bank where he made an appointment to see the manager at eleven o' clock. It had been quite short notice to get the appointment but luckily there had been a cancellation and due to the nature of the visit the manager had been happy to squeeze him in.

Mr Ezair called into the florist where he bought a beautiful bunch of yellow roses for his wife then he had headed home to surprise her with them and news of their holiday that he had just bought. Their relationship had been a little shaky of late due to the stress that he had been under. He had been very unlucky at the Casino and lost considerably more money than he had in the past. He had done what any true gambler had done and he had speculated to try to accumulate but unfortunately all that he had achieved had been an even bigger debt. He had borrowed fifteen grand from the man at the Casino for which he had to pay twenty grand back. Like any other loan from a shark the interest accumulated on a weekly basis and Ahmed had been in danger of losing his house to pay it back. Alberto had plenty of dealings with the Casino and he had purchased Ahmed's debt for the twenty grand that he owed. Alberto had been a shrewd business man and had promised not to add any interest if Ahmed had left something for security with him. The something that he had asked for had been Mrs Ezair's beautiful emerald necklace that was worth more than twice the debt that it covered. Ahmed had no choice but to hand the necklace over to Alberto but before he had done he had arranged for a perfect copy to have been made by a jeweller that Alberto had recommended. He had sneaked the necklace out one day when his wife had been visiting her daughter and he had managed to give Alberto the real one. Then he had put the fake back into the safe before his wife had ever realised that it had been gone.

Sumi Ezair had been busy baking a pie for their supper when her husband had arrived home. She had long since stopped running to the front door to greet him for in recent months they had barely spoken more than a few words to each other. Since the children had moved out of the family home to start families of their own Sumi and Ahmed had drifted further and further apart. Sumi had known that her husband was a gambler but she had no idea of how much trouble he had gotten himself into this time. Ahmed walked into the kitchen and handed his wife the bunch of flowers. She had been taken completely by surprise by the unexpected gesture but before she could speak he had astonished her even more.

"Forgive me Sumi for causing you so much upset. I have been a very silly man but I promise you that I will make it up to you. Do you think that we can start again"?

Sumi was unable to speak as she started to cry. Never in all the years that she had been with her husband had he ever apologised to her for anything yet he had finally done it with flowers and all. There was more to come.

"I am taking you away on a second honeymoon on a cruise to Egypt and I can promise you now that I will not even be tempted to step into the Casino"

He took out the receipt that the girl in the travel shop had given to him then he had sent her upstairs to do the packing.

"What about the pie"?

"The pie can wait my little apple blossom. Let us go upstairs and look in your drawers"

Sumi and Ahmed had run up the stairs laughing like a couple of teenagers. Both of them were thinking that the bad patch that they had been going through was eventually coming to an end.

"I've made an appointment with the bank manager for eleven o' clock to arrange to leave your emeralds with him whilst we are away"

Sumi started to get suspicious of her husband's intentions. He had come home with a bunch of flowers and a few nice words and all of the time he had been after getting his hands on her mother's necklace.

"The emeralds are fine just where they are thank-you and if you think that I am silly enough to let you take them out of my sight then you must be dafter than you think that I am"

"My precious one please, try to calm down, what on earth are you thinking? We have the appointment, both you and I not just me. Those jewels are priceless and our house insurance nowhere near covers their true value. There has been a spate of burglaries in the area just lately do you think it would be wise to leave them whilst we are away"?

"I am so sorry Ahmed for having such bad thoughts about your motives all I can do is to beg for your forgiveness" Ahmed had patted her on the head thinking how right she had been not to trust him. Upstairs in the safe there was about four hundred pounds worth of fake gems where Sumi's forty thousand pound heirloom should have been. If what Alberto had told him was true Ahmed knew that if he got the insurance money he could buy the necklace back from Alberto and have enough money left to keep him at the roulette wheel for some time. Ahmed lay back on the bed so that Sumi could show him just how sorry she really was and so he could show to her just how forgiving he could be and they had stayed in the bedroom longer than they had for years.

The Saudi bank was very well guarded with two big uniformed guards at the front entrance and boasting a state of the art security system.

Mr and Mrs Ezair arrived at the bank at ten minutes to eleven with Mr Ezair carefully carrying the emerald necklace locked up in a briefcase that was chained to his wrist. They walked past the two guards into the bank and went up to the large reception desk where they had to sign themselves in. The receptionist rang the manager to let him know that his eleven o' clock appointment had arrived and he pressed a button under his desk that allowed the door marked private to be opened in readiness for them. The receptionist led Mr and Mrs Ezair through the door and took them to the door marked 'Manager'. She tapped on the door then waited for the manager to call out and invite them in.

"Enter"

The receptionist opened the door and introduced the new customers to the manager then she went back to her desk. Salik Samir was always pleased to meet new clients especially ones that looked as affluent as the couple that sat before him.

"What is it that I can do for you today"?

Salik Shamir smiled at them giving them a good view of the large gold tooth at the front of his mouth that glinted as the light caught it. Ahmed unlocked the chain from his wrist as he fiddled with the combination lock on his briefcase until it opened. Then he took out a leather bound box that he handed to the manager.

"We are going away on a holiday and we would like to leave this necklace in your safe keeping"

Salik Shamir opened the satin lined leather box that Mr Ezair had just passed him and he gasped in appreciation of the stunning necklace as he took it out from the box.

The necklace was made up of nine emeralds in total with one large stone as a centre piece and four smaller stones in decreasing sizes at either side of it. Each emerald was encrusted with diamonds around the edges that sparkled as the light touched them. Mrs Ezair looked on smugly as she explained the history of the necklace to the manager who was obviously taken with it. Mr Ezair hadn't been quite as sentimental as his wife had and he gave the manager the valuation certificate. The manager put the necklace back into its box before he examined the certificate he had been handed. The valuation had been done in 1998 and it had been valued then at forty thousand pounds. Salik Shamir knew that it would be worth a lot more than that and he suggested that they should get a new valuation done.

"That is very good advice and we will get it done when we get back from our holiday"

Ahmed had almost panicked at the thought of someone doing a valuation and he was relieved that they were going away so soon.

"Do you think that we can see where you are going to keep the necklace please"?

"Of course you may but first of all I need to know what you would like me to do with it. You can leave it in the bank's vault for which you will be charged a monthly fee for as long as it stays there or you can have a safe deposit box. There are various sizes and the cost depends on the size of the box that you take. If all you are leaving is the necklace then I would suggest a twelve inch box. Would you like me to get a price for you"?

Ahmed shook his head.

"I think for the moment that the vault will be sufficient. When we get back from our break we may look at a bigger box"

Mr Samir took out some paperwork from his filing cabinet which he went through with them before getting them to sign it in triplicate. Then he countersigned it and ripped off one copy that he handed to Mr Ezair.

"I will show you just how safe your gems will be with us. Please keep hold of that receipt for these beautiful stones are the bank's responsibility now"

Ahmed shook the manager's hand then he put the receipt that he had just given to him into his wallet and popped it safely in his pocket. Then they followed the manager who was carrying the necklace out of his office and through the bank to the lift that would take them down to the vault. As they walked through the bank Salik Shamir was pleased to see so many new faces in there. He had thought that the news of the bomb scares would have kept people off the streets but it hadn't been the case at his bank. Alberto's men had been watching the bank from the other side of the road. Eight of them were already inside the bank and they had watched as Mr and Mrs Ezair had entered the bank earlier. Alberto had been given the countdown from Joseph and the plan had gone underway. Alberto had given the nod to his men and they had taken up their places. Four of them wearing cashmere overcoats approached the two guards who had been stood on the steps to the bank. They pulled out badges that indicated to the guards that they were with M.I.5.

"We are on a mission of national security, have any of you seen this man"?

One of the supposed spooks pulled out a photograph of Ahmed Ezair and both of the guards gasped as they realised that it was the same man that they had let through about thirty minutes before.

"He is inside the bank with an accomplice and they are with the manager as we speak. He looked suspicious as he walked past us and he had some kind of case chained to his arm."

Alberto's men looked at each other knowingly then one of them spoke into a small microphone connected by a wire that peeped out from beneath his collar.

"The suspect is in the building and the bomb could be attached to him"

The guards both turned pale and looked unsure of what to do next. One of Alberto's men pulled one of the security guards to one side and gave him some instructions.

"We must not panic. The bomb will not go off until twelve thirty which gives us almost one hour. I will call for back up meanwhile try not to look worried and don't let anyone else through unless they show you identification. We already have some of our men on the inside and there is no need to panic. If we can keep our cool we should be able to stop him before he tries to blow us all up. We have been on to him for a while and now he is literally minutes within our grasp. If we are successful you two men will get the recognition that you deserve for being so vigilant"

The guards both smiled and they were obviously pleased to be part of such an important operation. The guard wearing a polished badge bearing the name Richard stayed at the door as the one called Roger went inside.

Roger had been in the army and he was keen to show that he could still take an order so much so that he had almost saluted the guys from M.I.5 He was pleased to see that they had a strong presence in the bank and he did as they had asked him to do and went to each of the members of staff and assured them that they would be safe. He pointed out Alberto's men and explained that each of the staff would be discreetly removed from the bank and the dangers that it faced. He also emphasised how important it was that none of them should panic or call for help. The staff remained exceptionally calm under the circumstances probably due to the fact that they felt that they were in safe hands.

"Right we need to get to the manager without causing any suspicion but first of all we had better look at the security cameras"

Roger naively took two of Alberto's men into the room that was the hub of the bank's state of the art security and he very proudly showed them how it all worked. He explained all about the alarm system and gave them all the codes that they used then he left one of them to keep watch as he took the other to go to look for the manager. Joe Banalle had been left to take care of security and he did just that. As soon as the door had closed behind Roger, Joe had started to take the video tapes from the six video recorders. He took them out and broke them up rendering them all completely useless then he disconnected the alarm system just in case any of the staff panicked. Then he unlocked the back door in readiness for their escape before wiping all traces of his prints from the room. Roger pressed the button for the lift that would take them down to the vaults then he and two of Alberto's men went to find the manager. Once Roger had told them all that that they needed to know he was of no more use to them and Jonjo gave him a head butt that knocked him out cold. Then he had dragged Roger's concussed body into a side room and taped his hands and mouth before locking him in a cupboard. Just as Joe had done he wiped away any of their prints and both men put on ski masks and surgical gloves. Salik Samir had given a guided tour to his new clients and he was just about to take them upstairs when he walked into the corridor straight into the barrel of a gun. One of the men took hold of Mr Ezair and pushed him into the room that he had hidden the guard in and he pushed him onto the floor and taped him up in the same way. Mrs Ezair was shaking with fear as Jonjo took hold of her and did the same with her as he had just done to her husband. As she had lay on the floor next to him all he could hear was her muffled cries from beneath the tape as she had realised that she was about to lose her precious necklace. Salik Shamir was distraught as he was forced to give details of his clients and codes and keys that the men were asking him for and he looked into the camera as he did it. He knew that his security guards would be making one of their hourly routine checks soon and that they would check the monitors. He hoped that if he could stall the men for long enough that someone would notice that he was still with his eleven o' clock appointment. Richard was still stood at the front entrance dissuading what few customers the bank almost had not to enter. He had puffed his chest out as he had explained to the odd few people who had asked him that it was a matter of national security. He had tried to contact Roger to find out what had been happening inside but he had not been able to make contact. He had been about to go inside and look for himself when one of the spook guys came out to him and told him that he would be needed to help them in a few minutes. Richard had assured them that he was on hand for whatever they wanted him for and he waited for them to call on him. Inside the bank the staff numbers had been dwindling one by one. They had been asked to take their belongings and to walk out of the back door as if they were on a lunch break. One by one they had followed one of Alberto's men into the back room only to be pounced on before being securely tied and left in a room that was fast becoming full. All that remained behind the counter in the bank were two ladies who managed to look calm and collected right to the end. It was ten minutes to twelve and Alberto gave the final nod. The last two ladies were led to the staffroom where eventually they were joined by the helpful security guard. The large front doors were closed leaving Alberto's men with a totally free hand in the bank. A brand new black van supposedly holding surveillance equipment had been directed to the back entrance by Richard, the security guard. It had been one of the last useful things that he had done for Alberto before being led into the room that was full of tied up staff. Richard could not see Roger which at least gave him a glimmer of hope that all was not completely lost as he lay on the floor and waited to be rescued. All of Alberto's men were masked and gloved up and all signs of their presence had been wiped away. The manager had been tied up in his own office and the black van had reversed right up to the back door. The men acted quickly and quietly as they emptied the contents of the bank's vault. The manager had provided them with two sets of keys which enabled them to simply open the boxes and empty out the contents into the large heavy weight sacks that they had brought from out of the van. One by one the boxes were tipped up and diamonds and gems galore fell into the sacks. There were bundles of notes and foreign currency and lots of securely tied up packages. There was not enough time for the men to take much note of their haul for they only wanted to be out of there as quickly as they could. The whole thing had been plain sailing up until then and Alberto had wanted to keep it that way. He had four men outside keeping watch and they had reported a bit of police movement passing by so Alberto and a few of his men started loading up the van.

At exactly twenty minutes past twelve the bank had been completely stripped of all of its best assets. The security guard who had assured the staff that they would be alright had also told them that the bomb was due to go off at twelve thirty. As they all lay bound and gagged they looked up to the clock on the wall and every single one of them had started their own personal countdowns. Roger had woken up to find himself tied securely and locked in a cupboard. He had no idea of the time all he knew was that his head just like his pride had been severely damaged. He started to bang his head against the cupboard door in the hopes that someone may hear that he was locked inside it. The other members of staff could hear him alright but could do nothing to help him escape.

As the bank staff watched the minutes ticking away on the clock Alberto and his men had all left the building. The black van had been loaded up with the money and the treasures that Alberto's men had just cleverly stolen from the bank. As he had been instructed to do by Joseph, Alberto had got into the drivers seat of the van. All of his men but Alphonso fled in different directions to head back to the restaurant where they had all been since early that morning as forty other prominent people in society would vouch for them if they were ever asked to. Alphonso went to the front of the building where he had left his car with his mother's disability badge proudly displayed in the window. He waited until Alberto turned onto the main road then he started to follow him towards the motorway. Alberto used the mobile that he had been given that day and he called Joseph who had given him a pin point destination close to the one he had given to Liam.

"Well done my friend, call me when you reach it"
Joseph kept the call short and sweet so he would not miss any other calls.

Two of the four bank operations had been successfully completed and he knew that Jimmy had got away from the news he had been given from the men who had witnessed it. Later reports had given descriptions of the mayhem as what few police that did turn up in pursuit of the escapees had to decide which of the many men on the scene they had to follow. All that Joseph needed now was to get two more calls declaring victory in order to enable them all to move onto the next phase of Jimmy's master plan.

Chapter 22

Joseph had arranged phase two just as Jimmy had asked him to do. There had almost been a hiccup with the absent Major but a few sharp words from the Minister had sorted that out. The Minister could not have cared less what he had to do to get his tape back. He knew that he could not have taken the shame that would surround him if the tape had ever become public knowledge and he had even contemplated suicide. When Joseph had called him it was like a make or break opportunity that he had to take. It would end years of speculation and dread of what would be asked of him and what was asked of him was within his powers. His position in the Cabinet allowed him to be able to arrange what would be classed as a top secret mission without arousing any suspicions. The war in Iraq was still not completely over and weapons of mass destruction were still being sought. Although convoys carrying toxic waste would not be a welcome sight on the streets of Britain they would not look too out of place.

The Minister had arranged for a convoy of military trucks to be sent to an old airstrip where they would be loaded up with toxic materials. The drivers assigned to the mission would be hand picked from the ranks of the Special Forces who were all used to being involved in top secret missions. Each lorry would contain a lead container that would be filled by other personnel who would be wearing protective clothing. The lorries would be filled in a sealed room and only when the boxes had been secured and locked would the drivers be allowed to take charge of them. The whole process would be overseen by the Minister who would pass on details of the final destination of the toxic materials at the very last moment. The convoy of twenty army vehicles would be accompanied by a high ranking Major who would stay with them until the supposed materials were safely locked away. Once the convoy was safely inside the compound the drivers would be escorted back to their own units and the dangerous matter would be put away by the five men in protective suits. Each of the men concerned would be all of those who had been involved in the robberies and all of them were good friends of Jimmy Mack.

The Defence Minister had been able to arrange everything over the phone from his office. There had been a slight hitch which had been when he had tried to contact James Harris. It seemed, he was told by the junior officer who had taken his call, that the Major had some kind of illness and he had taken to his sick bed at his mother's home. He had asked the Minister if anyone could help him.

"No they bloody well can't. This is the Minister of Defence's office and we need to speak to the Major in a matter of national security. Get me a contact number for him straight away"

"Yes Sir, straight away Sir and please accept my apologies"

The person on the other end of the telephone grovelled as he tried to find a number for the Major which he eventually found and gave to him. The Minister called the number right away and his call was answered by a woman.

"Lady Harris' residence. How may I help you"?

"I would like to speak to Major Harris please. I believe that he is unwell but I need to speak to him on an urgent military matter so I would appreciate if you could get him for me please"

The maid had recognised the urgency in the caller's voice so she had gone upstairs to the Major's room and she had knocked on his door.

"I thought I had left orders not to be disturbed. Can't a fella be ill in this house"?

The maid had opened the door just enough to be able to see the Major who appeared to be in one of his bellowing moods.

"I'm very sorry Sir but the chap on the telephone said it was a matter of national security"

The Major dismissed the maid then picked up the telephone by his bed.

"Major Harris, what do you want? This had better be bloody good"

He changed his tone and his manner when he realised just who it was that he was talking to.

"Just one moment Sir"

The Major waited until he heard the sound of the telephone as the maid put the downstairs telephone back on it's receiver then he spoke.

"I am so sorry about that Sir, what can I do for you"?

"They have called in on the favour James and today is the day"

Major Harris had a temperature of 100 degrees and he felt extremely weak. Every one of his muscles ached as though he had been trampled on by a horse in a game of polo.

"What do they want"?

"Meet me at fifteen hundred hours at the old airstrip at Aldershot. Bring twenty trucks each carrying radio active waste containers. The trucks have already been authorised and I have arranged for the drivers to be on standby just awaiting a call from myself. As far as they are all concerned this is a top secret military assignment. If we can get through this James we are clear"

Major James Harris agreed to meet the Minister despite feeling poorly so he came off the phone and took off his blue and white striped pyjamas. He cleared his throat which was sore and dry and he finished off the drink that his mother's maid had brought him earlier. It was a glass of whisky mixed with lemon and sugar and it tasted sweet and sickly but it did help to soothe the sides of his throat.

He took a neatly pressed uniform from out of his wardrobe and he put it on then he took his highly polished boots from his boot cupboard and he did the same with those. Lady Harris had just got to the top of the stairs on her stair lift as her son came out of his room. She was surprised to see that he was fully dressed and she started to moan at him.

"James darling what on earth do you think that you are doing. You are supposed to be a poorly bunny"
James hid his snarl beneath a smile as he bent down to plant a kiss on the top of his mother's snow white hair.

"I have to go out on urgent business mother"

"But darling you are supposed to be ill please don't go out"

"Sorry mother but I need to but please don't worry because I have finished that hot toddy that you had sent up for me and it has made me feel a lot better"
Lady Harris doted on her son who was her only child. He was stubborn and pig headed just as his father had been and she loved him for it. She knew that it would be useless to argue with him so she just put her lift into reverse and followed him down the stairs.

"Will you be home for supper Bunnykins"?
James cringed when her mother called him such stupid names but he put up with it to keep her happy. His mother was eighty nine years old and she was in a frail state of health. When she passed away which he hoped would be in

the next twelve months he was due to inherit the whole of her estate. It was estimated to be worth around four and a half million pounds and once he had got it he intended to get out of the army. Then he could live the life of luxury that he had yearned for and that he felt that he deserved. The only thing that James was scared of was that his mother might get wind of his murky past for he knew that if she did she would disinherit him. If he could pay off the favour that he owed then he could just sit back and wait for the old girl to pop off. Which was the reason that he had to go out in spite of his ill health. Eleanor the maid opened the front door and bent her head respectfully as the Major left the house. He had snorted as he had brushed past her as he usually did and she watched him as he walked towards the garages. She could not understand how such a lovely lady as her mistress could have such a hateful son. Eleanor closed the front door and went to make her mistress a nice pot of Earl Grey tea. Then she would sit and listen as her ladyship went on about what a lovely son she had and how proud she was of him. Major Harris coughed and spluttered as his Range Rover drove out of the grounds. He set his satellite navigation system for a destination in Aldershot where he had arranged to meet up with his partner in crime.

The Minister had called Joseph to let him know that everything had been arranged and it was all systems go.

"We will meet you at the hangar as planned"

"Right, if there is a change of plan I will call you otherwise I will see you later"

Inspector Collin's station was still inundated with lady callers who for a change were walking in of their own accord. Unbeknown to him, each of the girls was getting ten pounds just to come in and complain about the lack of police protection that they were getting. As a result of the tenner that they had been promised the Inspector had girls queuing up outside the station. Most of the National Front members had been brought in and there was a pile of rubber masks on the station floor that had been taken from them as they were booked in.

News had just come in that the bomb in Stockport had just been a hoax but it had taken the army to find that out as they had come in to deploy it. The rain had started to die down when the Inspector's mobile phone rang out. It was his friend in the forensics department who was calling to confirm what he already knew about Mike Rooney. It seemed that the blood samples taken from the clothes that had belonged to Mike Rooney matched exactly to the blood sample taken from poor old Charlie Reed.

This D.N.A. evidence he had just been given linked with the fact that Mike had sent Jimmy Mack on a wild goose chase on the night of the murder was all of the evidence that Peter Collins needed. The fact that his officer had taken his own life with a weapon that had been stolen from the station along with the traces of narcotics that had been found in his bloodstream was more than enough to convict him of the murder albeit posthumously. Superintendent Collins had tried to get in touch with Jimmy's lawyer but communications were not at the best and he had not been able to get through to him. He had imagined that the lawyer would have been out trying to locate the whereabouts of his client who had unofficially released himself from custody earlier that morning. He felt guilty to think of poor Jimmy who must be hiding out somewhere when in reality he should have been sat at home with his lovely wife. He would make enquiries when he had more time and he would try to find out what, if anything he could do to make amends to Jimmy. Then using his own mobile phone he called Mr and Mrs Rooney and left a message on their answering machine asking them to call him when they arrived home.

Jimmy Mack was sat with his wife although it was not at home as the Superintendent had thought that he should be. They were sat in the executive lounge at Manchester airport sharing their second bottle of wine as they waited for details of their flight to be announced. They raised their glasses to each other as they toasted themselves.

"Cheers. Here's to us and them and them and them and them"

Jimmy had told Julie about the compass plan and how it would work. It was probably the first of his plans that he had ever told her about but he felt that she needed to know. He could not be sure that he would not yet be caught and he knew that he wouldn't be home and dry until he was sat in his lovely villa. If anything should go wrong he needed Julie to know what should be happening. Even Joseph's life may have been in danger with the risks that he was taking and he needed to let Julie know just how much he owed to his faithful lawyer. Jimmy was on the run and as such for that alone he was a criminal so without telling Julie any other names or places he told her what he hoped was going on as they spoke. Julie's big blue eyes had lit up in amazement as Jimmy whispered to her about the four hits that should be happening.

Inspector Thomas from Bootle Street Police Station was ready to have a nervous breakdown. There had been a recent prison van break and reports of alarms going off at almost all of the businesses in the town centre. Robberies were happening one every few minutes and he just did not have the manpower to deal with all of the things that seemed to be happening. An officer from the armed response unit had been wounded and a member of the public had been caught in the crossfire and was lying in a critical condition in hospital. The police helicopter had never been so much in demand and the lunatic at the primary school had barricaded himself in the building along with forty two pupils and five teachers.

A report had just come in about the South African bank being robbed and there was a concerned boyfriend at the front desk who was worried about his fiancé who worked for another big foreign bank. He had tried to contact her to meet her for lunch but she had not been answering her mobile so he had called round to the bank that she worked at. When he had got to the Bank of Saudi Arabia he had been surprised to find that it's front doors were locked up. He had spoken to a man further down the road from it who had noticed a black van leaving from the bank's direction rather hastily. Inspector Thomas had put the enquiry on a pile with hundreds of others and he had promised the young man that he would deal with it as soon as he could. His priority was at the primary school and he allocated what few men that he had to join the others there. There were two thousand five hundred police workers on duty at one time in Greater Manchester including high ranking officers and clerics and everyone of them had their hands full. There were so many crimes going on at one time that the police were not able to deal with all of it and the alarm systems that had gone wrong gave lots of false calls and even more irate members of the public. Everyone had been on alert for the days leading up to September 11th but it was only the tenth.

Extra police had been requested to attend the football game at Old Trafford where the England team were due to play that evening. There was news of a thousand pensioners who were protesting outside the Houses of Parliament in

London and racial tension was building up in all of the big cities. The free speech policy that England adopted had allowed for posters to be put up about Muslim meetings that were planned for the next day. The posters were offensive to most of the population as they praised the ones responsible for the September 11th terror attacks and the Home Office had advised for the police to be extra vigilant. The early morning news had been full of news about the suicide bombers in Israel and it felt to Inspector Thomas as though the whole world was about to explode. He also felt that the fuse was about to be lit in Manchester.

Peter Parker was getting plenty of stick about the computer system going down. Not being able to do police checks was making life difficult for all of the officers. He had informed the powers that be that he would do all that he could to put it right as soon as he possibly could. Although he was doing his best to look as though he was concentrating on his work in reality his mind was miles and miles away with his beautiful lover. Justin was going to celebrate his sixteenth birthday on Sunday and Peter had bought him a solid gold bracelet as a surprise present. He had decided that he would tell Madeline that their sham of a marriage was over and he was going to ask Justin to move in an apartment with him as his partner. The programme he had put into the computer system to corrupt it had been so easy for him to do that he knew that if he lost his job as a result of this mess that he would easily find work elsewhere. It seemed that the whole of Manchester town centre was in chaos with alarms ringing for no reason and lots of houses and businesses without power. The traffic lights at the heart of Piccadilly were all out of action as were the security cameras on most of the streets. Simon Collier had deliberately blown up the electricity cabinets which had just added fuel to the bomb scares that had been issued. The few people that were left on the streets in and surrounding the town centre were scared of being blown to pieces for some had been in a similar situation seven years earlier. Hundreds of shoplifters of all ages were taking advantage of the mayhem that was happening in the town and they had shopping sprees galore. Meanwhile hordes of young thieves were just running into department stores and leaving with their arms full of clothes. The lack of police on the streets was the green light that half of the rogues in Manchester had been waiting for and it seemed as though the word was spreading like wildfire. There were several National Front rallies going on around town and Harry Thomas could not help but wonder if the 10th September was a significant date in the war.

"Zeig Hiel"
came the cries from the masked men as they goose stepped up and down the street outside the town hall where officials were having their meeting. The men in masks had got even noisier as they had seen the police men approaching towards them. They had been joined outside the Town Hall by hundreds of England football supporters who were getting psyched up for the International game against Lichenstein that night. They had heard of the protests in town and had wasted no time in getting there to join forces with them for a bit of pre match violence to get them in the mood for later. The soccer hooligans had joined their arms together making a human shield to prevent the police getting past them to reach the N.F. protestors without using force.

There was only a small police presence due to all the other activities that were taking place but the ones there had come well prepared. The senior officer leading the men gave them the nod to take out their new weapons and to use them. The M26 Tasers were brought out and the men used them for the very first time in Manchester. The Taser guns had been on trial in other parts of the country for almost six months and there was already a lot of controversy surrounding them. Under the circumstances and the need to quell the crowds the guns were very much needed in the protest situation that the police were in. The M26 Taser was an American invention it was a laser stun gun that fired barb darts with copper cables attached that could deliver up to fifty thousand volts into a victim. Drastic circumstances had called for drastic measures so the weapons that were brand new to Manchester had been given their maiden voyage at the National Front Rally outside the Town Hall. The police took their aim and fired their Taser guns into the crowds that were preventing them from getting to the violators that they needed to arrest in order to break up the demonstration. Bodies fell to the ground like flies being swatted and the victims cried out in pain as the darts hit their bodies and the electrical charges ran through them. They suffered a temporary paralysis that put them out of action for long enough for the police to be able to break through them. The offending darts would leave them feeling sore for quite some time after. Before the police had the chance to use them for a second time they found themselves being mobbed by the angry crowds.

"You are hitting innocent people, why don't you go and catch criminals, ain't that what you pigs are paid for"

The shouts came from a member of the public who was generally opposed to violence of any form just before he was trampled on by the hooligans.

"The boys in blue want a bit of action, let's see how big they are without their big boy toys shall we lads"?

The officers were instantly overpowered and their precious

Taser weapons fell into the hands of some very dangerous people who added them to their own arsenal of weapons.

The meeting in the council chambers that was deep in the heart of the Town hall carried on with the visitors totally oblivious of the total anarchy that was taking place outside it. They drank coffee and discussed how we could all get on more with each other, regardless of race. Asylum seekers were very much on the agenda and the Mayor of Manchester had just given assurances that the town was in itself very multi cultural and how pleased he was to announce how well everyone got on together. The dignitaries had been brought in on such a route that they had not seen the Muslim posters emblazoning the walls nor had they seen the offensive graffiti that had been daubed over them.

They had managed to get them all safely seated before any of the National Front members had positioned themselves outside the Town Hall and the wonderful soundproofing had prevented them from hearing any of the taunts that were being shouted across the square outside. Inside the Town Hall representatives from member states sat around drinking tea and nibbling on home-made biscuits oblivious of the troubles that surrounded them.

Chapter 23

Satan and his men had managed to insight the crowd outside the German Bank into a heated frenzy. Gunther Muller the manager was sat inside in fear of his life. He had tried to contact the police station but he had been unable to get through to them on the phone line. He had waited for ages as he had tried to get 999 on his mobile but even that was engaged for a while. When he had eventually got through he was told that his report would be dealt with in due course. He was told by the operator that due to the problems that the police were experiencing that it may take some time for them to get out to him. The operator suggested that it might be a good idea for him to close the bank and to leave the premises by the back door. Herr Muller had decided that seeing as they had no customers that it would be a good idea for them all to go home and he called the security guard who had been busy watching through the window and told him to lock the front door. He had been just about ready to change the code on the vault when the protestors broke into his bank. The guard had been closing the front doors when Satan's men had rushed him.

As the others had ran in to claim the bank Satan had stayed at the door. He picked the guard off the floor so that his legs dangled helplessly and he kept him held against the wall with just his left hand. Then he asked him his name.

"Snichz, Hans Snichz"

He said it in a manner that Satan hadn't liked and he put his right hand into his pocket and pulled out his gun. Then without giving it a moments thought Satan put the gun to the guards head and blew Hans Snichz to bits. Everyone in the bank had heard the gunshot and they knew that they were dealing with either dangerous men or lunatics. A senior cashier decided to try and press the panic button only to be gunned down in cold blood by a lunatic wielding a sawn off shotgun. His heroic death had been totally pointless as the alarm had been disconnected by Simon Collier earlier that morning. Petrified by what they had just witnessed all of the others stood not daring to move as Satan's men plundered their bank. Satan had no major plan or strategy he just took what he wanted and if anyone dared to stand in his way he killed them. His plot consisted solely of violence and he had no qualms whatsoever about using it which was obvious to all who saw him.

He was sixteen stone of pure evil who from as long as he could think back to had been subjected to physical abuse from those who should have cared for him. Satan had never known love or affection and as a result he was not capable of showing it himself. Other people's tears did not move him so when a woman cashier had started to cry at the sight of her dead colleague lying on the floor Satan had shut her up. The lady was knocked into unconsciousness as Satan's size ten Doc Martin boots connected with the side of her head. He then went into the manager's office and took the manager down from the coat stand where his men had left him hanging and he frogmarched him into the bank in full view of all of his staff.

"Tell your people to put all of the cash into the sacks for us. Get the men to bring all of the security boxes to us along with a list of their owners and bring them all to the back door. My men will be watching their every move and if any more of your people would like to be heroes I will kill them. If they are German people I will enjoy killing them even more."

"Do you understand Herr manager"?
The manager had been unable to speak for terror had taken hold of him.

"Ve av vays to make you talk"
Satan mimicked the manager using a comical German expression he had seen in comedy films over the years. He had no allegiance to anyone but himself and he enjoyed to kill full stop, regardless of race, creed or colour.

"Every one of my soldiers here is trained to tear people or animals from limb to limb. We are a race of people that like to cause pain and suffering to others so it would be a good idea for you to do as we say otherwise you could annoy us. The manager looked over to where his chief cashier lay still in a pool of blood and he could see that Miss Ryder another of his cashiers was semi conscious. He knew that he mustn't do anything to annoy the bunch of animals wearing ridiculous masks who had taken over his bank. He got his staff to do what had been asked of him as he got the paperwork they wanted. There was a loud bang on the back doors of the bank and one of the masked men opened it to find a large fork lift truck outside. The noise from the nearby protest outside could be heard inside by the bank staff as they hurriedly bundled stacks of money into the sacks.

Satan looked at the stop watch and he hurried his men on for even though he knew that his men outside would give him plenty of warning if the police arrived he didn't like to be cornered. There were an awful lot of sacks and boxes to get out and he wanted to make sure that he didn't leave any behind. He put two of his men at the back door and they started to load up the fork lift truck with the large metal boxes that had been brought up from the vaults. A large battered maroon coloured van pulled up and two masked drivers got out and opened the door as the fork lift truck lifted the boxes into the back of it. At twenty two minutes past twelve all of the cash, bonds and boxes had been put into the van and its doors had been firmly shut and padlocked. Satan's men got the bank staff to form a line and he marched them down to the large vault that he ordered them to walk into. Not one of them had the fight left in them so they had all walked into what might become their eventual tomb and sat down. Satan locked the barred door and left them to whatever fate his number two wanted to give them. Then he went out of the back door and he got into the old van. He ordered the others to join ranks with the members outside the Town Hall where the meeting inside was about to finish and to cause as much trouble as they could. He sat in the old Direct Works van until all of his men had left the bank and he watched as the last one out got into an old battered box van that they had parked up earlier. Mark Skelton was the last of the men to leave the bank. He took off his mask and the rubber gloves that he had almost set fire to as he had lit the petrol bombs that he had thrown into the bank as he had left there just for good measure. Satan called Joseph who was driving on the motorway but his hands free kit enabled him to take the call and he was delighted to hear that Satan and his men had finished their job. He tried to give Satan his next location by giving him a destination point on a map but map reading had never been one of Satan's few talents.

"What the fuck are you talking about mate. Just tell me where you want me to go and I will be there but don't tell me in fucking numbers."

Joseph had not anticipated that any of the men would not

be able to follow his simple instructions but he had not reckoned on Satan's lack of scholarly skills. He formed a quick mental picture in his mind of the area that they were all to meet up at and he directed Satan to the nearest Shell petrol station that he could think of.

"Call me when you get to the garage my friend and well done!"

Joseph smiled as he marvelled at how someone with so little education could have pulled off such a big bank job as he had.

He was glad that he hadn't written the instructions down for he was sure after just speaking to him that he probably couldn't read either. A plane had just taken off from the airport and Joseph wondered whether Jimmy had managed to get there and if he had how long would it be before he left the country. He longed to call Julie to find out but he knew that there would be a lot of questions to be answered in days to follow. It would be unwise at this stage to do anything that might jeopardise the otherwise perfectly constructed plan. Jimmy and Julie sat waiting in the lounge at the airport getting more nervous as the time went on. Jimmy had noticed the two men that had walked into the lounge a few minutes earlier and he didn't like the way that they kept looking in his direction. Paranoia made him think that they were detectives and he hid behind the Daily Telegraph where he could keep a watchful eye on them from over the top of it. He didn't recognise any of them but they were suited up and they didn't seem to carry any hand luggage. Julie sat next to him wearing a pale turquoise satin suit that complimented her sparkling blue eyes and dark tanned complexion.

Under the jacket she had on a white lace top that just about contained her large heaving bosom that brimmed over the top of the vest. As she got up to fetch a plate of snacks

Jimmy noticed the two men watch her every move and he started to panic as the bigger of the two men walked towards her. He watched as they spoke by the bar and he was relieved to see her laugh at something that he had whispered to her as he had handed her a card. The man accompanied Julie back to the table then he gave Jimmy the thumbs up sign before leaving to take the Amsterdam flight that had just been announced on the loudspeaker.

"What was all that about and what did he give to you"?
Julie laughed at him as she passed him the card that the man had given to her and he looked down to see that the card belonged to some porn king.

"He only asked if I fancied being in one of his bloody movies, the twat"
Jimmy had smiled and he put the paper down thinking just how lucky he was to have the kind of girl that turned men on and how, once they got to Tenerife he would make a little porn film of his own with her. Even after all the years they had been together Julie was more woman than Jimmy would ever need and he loved every lovely inch of her for it.

Mr and Mrs Rooney had just got in and they had checked their answering machine for messages.

There had been one call from Patsy another from the bank and the last one had been from Inspector Collins. Anne Rooney tried to call the police station in Manchester but it seemed to be totally engaged so after ten minutes of trying she gave up. She called the bank only to find it had been just a courtesy call about home insurance and then she made them both a nice cup of tea whilst she sat down and thought about what she would say to Patsy.

"You will have to tell her sooner or later"

"I know dear but can we make it later. I think I would like to speak to the Inspector first just in case it concerns the funeral. I'll call her tomorrow"

Simon Collier picked up the British Telecom van and took off the dodgy plates and replaced them with the real ones just before the police called round to investigate the report they had taken about a supposed robbery.

Bootle street had taken so many bogus calls that it had started to send out Special Constables that they had called in to assist them when they had realised the enormity of the crimes that had been happening there.

Special Constable Hill had been working with the police for over six months although normally she would have been assigned to office duties. Once she had chased a shoplifter all the way from Kendals to Piccadilly Gardens and she would have caught him if she hadn't been tripped up by a lad outside the Wimpy bar. She didn't usually work on Wednesdays but she had popped in to drop something off for someone there and immediately the sergeant had nabbed her and he had got her to work. She had spent an hour filling in complaint forms for the ladies of the night before being sent out to check and eliminate bogus robbery calls. The double doors at the bank were closed and she couldn't see through the windows that were all too far off the ground for her to be able to reach them. It was pointless trying to telephone for half of the lines in the area had been put out of action so she walked around to the back of the bank to see what she could find. A tramp was rummaging around in the bins and she asked if he had seen anything suspicious. He looked at her as though she was mad.

"Do you mean as well as the bomb scares and the guys waving guns in the air as they ran out of the bank? No I don't think I have"

The tramp turned his attentions back to the bin where he

pulled out a half eaten burger. The Special Constable presumed that he was taking the mickey and she didn't fancy getting close enough to him to question him so she left him to finish off the burger and she went back to the front door. She looked through the big brass letterbox but she couldn't see a thing. She was just about to go back to the station with nothing much to report when she thought that she heard a noise from within the bank. It was a kind of banging and it was coming from the main body of the bank. She tried the door handle and was amazed to find that the door had been open all along. She radioed in for assistance as she entered the bank alone and she peered round the corner. What she saw caused her to get back on the radio for urgent back up and to call for an ambulance for there were bodies tied up lying on the floor. She waited for a moment as she listened out in case the robbers were still there but it was quiet apart from the tapping sound so she went in. She ran to the first of the cashiers that was taped to her chair and she started to pull the tape from her mouth.

"I think they may have killed the manager they had him in his office"

Special Constable Hill took the tape from the cashier's hands and legs and she told her to untie the others as she went to look for the manager. Taking out her truncheon she walked slowly and quietly up to the door down the corridor with the shiny brass plaque with the name 'Manager' on it and she pushed the door open.

Expecting to see a gruesome sight in the office she was pleased to find the manager taped up on the floor. His eyes bulged, his face was bright red and he was struggling to breathe as she tore the carpet tape from his mouth. He began to cry as he realised that he had been rescued and as soon as his hands were free he threw his arms around her.

"It's alright Sir, help is on the way"

She passed him a glass of water that she poured from a jug on his desk then she left him as she went back to check on the rest of the staff.

Mr Arends cried even more when he saw the state of his beautiful white carpet that was mud stained and filthy. He drank the water then like the captain of a ship he went to check on the health of his staff. All of the ladies were crying whilst the men were giving macho accounts of how they had tried to stop the men then one of them mentioned the bomb.

The Special Constable got back on the radio and called in a bomb scare then very quickly she got all of the people out of the building. Mr Arends looked around in despair at the state of his bank which had broken drawers strewn across the floor and paperwork that looked like confetti. He had to be forced to go outside into the cold damp air where he had to wait for the police to arrive. An ambulance pulled up outside and all of the people were treated for shock and covered with foil blankets by the busy paramedics. Only one of his tellers had been badly affected by the experience which was a man in his fifties who suffered from angina. The rest of his staff were still in shock and would probably be putting in a lot of sick days. The ambulance took as many of them as they could officially carry in their ambulance and they took them to the sanctuary of the hospital to wait to be questioned about their recent ordeal. Two officers in a van eventually got to the bank and they went back inside and helped Mr Arends to check out the damage and to help him to lock up. It seemed a pointless exercise as the bank had been emptied of everything of value. Even the petty cash box and Mr Arend's solid gold pen set that he had been awarded for long service had been taken. Special Constable Hill was still shaken at what she had found and she was disappointed when she radioed in and was told that her next job was to go and help to supervise a N.F. Rally.

Mr Arend's description of the robbers could have fitted a thousand or so men. The only thing that he had been sure of was their nationality, for their broad Northern Irish accents had been unmistakeable. The Inspector had been in on the interview and he jumped up as he listened to that.

"The bastards, there never was a bomb scare it has all been one big scam as a cover up whilst they took out the bank. I bet it was those buggers that put out our communications too. I need to speak to the Home Office"

Mr Arends sat sipping second rate coffee from a paper cup thinking that if it had been the I.R.A. that had robbed his bank that he had been lucky to escape with his life. He had no idea of how he could explain to his clients just what had happened. The cash of course was safe for it was insured but the contents of the safe deposit boxes were known only to their owners and some of them had belonged to some of the most powerful men in the world. On Monday he had taken a call from the president of the bank that told him that he and one of the bank's most prolific clients were to be coming in to look at the bank. The president had requested that Mr Arends made especially sure that the bank would be in pristine condition. In the light of how much money had been used up in floor coverings alone he had told his manager that he would expect it to be. The distinguished client wanted to take some important papers from his safe deposit box and the man was so important that he was being accompanied by the bank's President. Mr Arends sat and contemplated taking an early retirement before being given the sack.

Chapter 24

Lee Won-King and his men had been up since very early that morning. He had sent a courier round to pick up the mobile phone and stopwatch that Joseph had bought for him and he had two men watching the house of Mr Chan. At eight thirty his private phone rang and he picked it up to hear that the manager of the Bank of Hong Kong had just left his home.

"Wait for five minutes then go in and call me to confirm it"

Spike and Lee Wong left their car in a lay by as they walked round the back of Mr Chan's detached house. Mrs Chan had just filled the dishwasher with the breakfast pots and she was busy making up her new baby's bottles. At thirty seven she was seen as a mature mother and she was finding motherhood quite difficult so she was glad of what time she could snatch on her own, without her husband and son. She was just about to sit down for a cup of herbal tea when the front doorbell rang.

She went to the door to find a man stood in the porch holding a letter in his hand. She left the safety chain on as she opened the door slightly to find out what the man at the door wanted.

"Good morning. I have some important papers from the director of the bank for Mr Chan"

"I am afraid that you have just missed him. He left for

work but you can leave them with me if you like and I will make sure that he gets them"

"I am sorry but there are important papers in here and if I leave the envelope I must get a signature or the director will crucify me"

Mrs Chan had heard all about Mr Chui the director and she had heard that he was a very strict man. The man at the door looked like he was soaked to the skin so she took the safety chain off and took the envelope from him. Before she had a chance to even glance at the envelope he had handed to her the man who had been stood at the door pushed past her.

She had just been about to scream when she felt a hand cover her mouth as a second man entered her home. She was bundled into the front room and pushed into a chair where she sat and waited for them to tell her what they had come for. As if reading her mind one of the men spoke.

"Please do not make a sound. We do not intend to hurt you or your baby"

Mrs Chan had gasped when she realised that they knew that she had a baby and she wondered just who they were and what it was they wanted.

"We will sit and keep you company until we have spoken to your husband and provided that you do as we ask you will not be hurt"

"My husband is at work he won't be back until five o'clock"

"Yes we know and I expect that he will call you on your mobile phone in a few hours. If he calls you before that I would advise you not to answer your phone. Now is that herbal tea that I can smell"?

Mrs Chan nodded and she took another two cups from the cabinet and poured two more cups of tea out. Mai Chan was not the devoted wife that they had expected to find and if they had asked her she would have joined ranks with them for the hell of it. Mai had been given to her husband in exchange for thirty thousand pounds that her father had owed to the bank. They had been about to for-close on the loan when her father had come up with an alternative and he had offered his beautiful daughter to him. Her husband was nasty and cruel towards her and he forced himself onto her in the bedroom. He liked to tie her up and when she refused his advances he would beat her into submission.

The only good thing that had come out of their marriage had been the birth of their beautiful baby son and if it had not been for him Mai would have walked out on her husband. Her father had passed away the year before and she no longer had his word of honour to protect.

Suddenly the baby's cries could be heard through the baby monitor and Mai waited for permission to go and fetch him. Lee's men gestured for her to get up and Spike followed her up the stairs. As they walked into the bedroom Spike could not help but notice as the manager's wife tried to kick something under the bed. She picked the baby up from out of his crib and she carried him out of the room and down the stairs. Spike followed her into the kitchen and watched as she struggled to take the bottle from the fridge as she held her baby in her arms. He reached out to take the baby from her and he saw how she winced when his arm brushed her own. There was something very sinister and sad about Mrs Mai Chan. Spike took the little baby into the lounge whilst Mai Chan warmed up the baby's bottle and he held it tenderly close to him.

The baby was about four months old and he had a mass of jet black hair and tiny black eyes. He was sucking his fingers frantically and he reminded Spike of his own son at that age when he had been hungry.

Mrs Chan brought the bottle in and she took the baby from

Spike's arms and she sat in the corner in a nursing chair where she started to give the hungry baby his feed. Spike went back upstairs to see just what it was that the frightened woman had not wanted him to see. He reached under the bed and pulled out a large piece of lint that stank of T.C.P. lotion. There were blood stains on it as if it had come off a wound and the blood appeared to be fresh. He bent down to get a better look under the bed and he saw a box pushed right underneath it. Curiosity made him crawl further under the bed and he pulled the box towards him then he stood up and put the box on the bed. He opened it up and what he found inside the box sickened him for it was full of pictures that would have been at home in a torture chamber. The pictures had all been taken with a Polaroid camera and they showed just the torso of a woman. It looked as though the body had been ripped to shreds and Spike knew exactly how the red wheals had got there. He picked up a small leather whip from the bottom of the box and everything started to make sense. He put everything but one of the photographs back into the box and he ran downstairs to show Lee what he had found.

"This is you isn't it"?

Spike put the photograph under Mrs Chan's nose and he waited for a reaction from her. She looked down at the floor in shame and Spike could see her tears as they ran down her face. He kept looking at her until eventually she nodded to him that it was her on the photograph.

"Why do you put up with it? the man is nothing but a demon"

"He is my husband and he owns me"

"Bullshit he is a monster and if I ever see him I will give him a taste of his own medicine and see how he likes it. Are you in pain now"?

Mrs Chan had nodded for she no longer had to hide the

fact that she had been beaten. The men who had broken into her home were nothing but criminals but they were not cruel men and they were the only ones to have shown any compassion towards her. Spike took the baby from her and put him on his knee as he gave him the rest of his feed.

"Go upstairs and take a warm bath and put table salt in the water, it will help to heal your wounds. Don't worry we will not harm your baby the only person that you need to fear in this house is your husband"

Mai Chan nodded gratefully to Spike and she went upstairs and ran a bath like the kind man had suggested that she did. She slid into the warm bath water and she cringed as the salt water stung as it entered her wounds. They were new ones that he had inflicted on her that morning before taking his shower that smarted as the T.C.P. lotion sank into her skin. Spike had fed and winded the baby like a true professional then he lay him down on his blanket so that he could have a kick. Lee could see that his friend was annoyed at the photographs that he had seen for Spike's own mother had endured similar treatment at the hands of a maniac.

Spike had murdered his step father by chopping him up with a machete and he had just spent twelve long years in prison for doing it. Seeing those photographs had just reminded him of the horrors that his mother had endured before he had freed her from her life of terror and it had upset him. Spike was a very dangerous man when he was upset and Lee needed to alert Lee Won-King about his friend's state of mind. He called the boss on his mobile and he filled him in with everything that they had just found out about the manager's secret life.

"Is there a fax machine at his house"?

Lee looked into a small room off the lounge and saw that there was a fax machine so he told Lee that there was one.

"Good, we will still make him phone you on his wife's

mobile phone but as he speaks I would like you to fax the photographs that you speak of to the bank. In a way it gives us even more of a hold on him now put Spike on the phone I need to speak to him"

Lee handed Spike the phone and he watched his friend nodding as he spoke to the boss. He was smiling as he came off the phone.

"Mr Chan is to get what he deserves, the boss has just promised me"

Mrs Chan came down the stairs looking a lot more relaxed than she had when she had gone up them. She smiled at her two captors and asked if they would like some tea.

"Sit down with your baby and I will make it for you. How are you feeling now you have had a bath"?

"A lot better thanks to you, what is going to happen"?

"Well to start with your husband will never hit you again but if I were you I would divorce him and take half of everything that he owns"

"He would never allow that for I came to him with nothing"

"You came to him with everything and he has abused you. If you like, when all this is over I will help you to get rid of the evil swine"

Mai Chan smiled at Spike and he had felt his heart flutter. His own wife had left him when he had been locked up all of those years ago and when he got out he found out that she had taken his baby son with her to China. He had never thought it possible that he may ever find true love again yet the look in Mai Chan's eyes had given him a hope that he thought he had lost forever.

Lee Won King sat in his office wondering what punishment he would hand out to Mr Chan. He thought that he would wait to see the offending photographs before making a decision but he had promised Spike who was a trusted friend and Lee Won-King's word was his honour. The security guard at the Bank of Hong Kong owed Lee a lot of money and he had sent one of his men round to see him before he had left for the bank. One of the things that the guard was asked to do was to make sure that none of the twenty four hour video tapes would be recording and the other was to do whatever his men asked him to do.

The guard had agreed and he had promised Lee that his men would be safe in his bank. The men would wait in one of Lee's restaurants around the corner from the bank until Lee gave them the go ahead. All Lee had to do was to wait for zero hour to be confirmed by Joseph. A Group Four security van would be on hand to take away the spoils and every one of his men would have a cast iron alibi for their whereabouts. There had always been a problem with the hostage situation with the wife and baby but if what the other Lee had said was right even that wasn't going to be a problem for them.

Lee Won-King had got the go ahead from Joseph and he had passed it on to his men. It had been Lee himself that had entered the manager's office at eleven thirty precisely twenty minutes after he had taken a call about their alarm being tested. An operator claiming to be Telecom 150 had called to say that the alarm system would be tested at eleven fifteen a.m. In actual fact the 'operator' who had phoned the bank had been one of Simon Collier's girlfriends on the phone and at fourteen minutes past eleven precisely Simon had cut through an underground cable and disconnected the alarm causing it to go off. The manager had informed the staff and customers not to be worried at hearing the alarm sounding as it was a routine test to check that it was working.

When Lee's men entered the bank they were safe in the

knowledge that the security cameras were not working and that all alarms and panic buttons had been deployed. They also knew that they had the bank manager one way or another and that he would do as they told him to.

It was a wet windy Wednesday morning and the streets of Manchester had been short of pedestrians and cars because of a bomb scare. Many of the major streets had been cordoned off and the broken traffic lights in the town centre had left what cars remained on the road in turmoil.

Lee had entered Mr Chan's private office without even knocking and he had walked over to him and had taken a seat on top of his leather bound desk much to Mr Chan's anger.

"How dare you walk into my office that way I shall have you removed"

Lee Won-King remained calm as the manager reached below his desk to sound the alarm. He stared menacingly at the manager who was no more than a snivelling little wife beater and he grabbed hold of his boney arm.

"Mr Chan I would like you to call your wife on her mobile phone and I would like you to listen to what she has to say to you"

"There is a fault with the telephone"

"Then use your mobile phone to call her and do it now if you want to see her or your son again"

The manager picked up his phone and called his wife but she didn't answer it even though she was sat on the knee of the man who did.

"I would like to speak to my wife please and I must say that if you try to harm her you will be in trouble"

Mr Chan was keeping up the pretence of that of a loving husband.

Mai Chan had been enjoying the company of Spike who she found she was becoming increasingly fond of with every minute that they spent together. She jumped off his knee and went over to the fax machine where she sent copies of the photographs showing the damage that he had done to her that very morning. Mr Chan could hear the whirring of the fax and knew that something was coming through but he had no idea of what it would be.

"What did you say Mr Chan, don't harm your wife! I think that we both know that I couldn't possibly hurt her any more than you already do. If you don't believe me why don't you take a look at the photos you are receiving right now on your fax machine"

The manager ran over to the fax machine to see that the copies coming through to him were from his home address and at a glance he could see that they were the photographs that he had taken himself that morning. Even in black and white the photographs looked terrible and he went pale as he saw Lee pick them up to look at them himself.

"What do you want from me"?

"There is a security van calling to your bank in less than one hour. When the security guards come in I would like you to give them everything!"

Mr Chan ended the call and looked at Lee who had seen the photographs and who did not look happy at what he had seen.

"I can explain, she likes that kind of thing she gets a kick out of it"

Lee pushed his head into Mr Chan's forehead and looked into his eyes.

"Do you think that you will keep your position in this bank when the newspapers get hold of this story? I happen to know that the president of this bank might be a bastard but he is a family man bastard and there is no way that he will keep you on here. As for the police I am not sure what they would say but you would definitely be looking at a prison

283

sentence"

Mr Chan had no choice but to go along with the men who appeared to be blackmailing him and he had to do it in such a way that his staff did not know what was going on for his reputation and his job depended on it. He took four of Lee's men along to the private room that held the safe deposit boxes. It was a long clinical looking room with a white ceiling full of bright spotlights that made up for the fact that it had no windows. The safe deposit boxes were set into both sides of the wall which they filled every bit of space of. He took the men into the room and gave them the keys to the boxes then he left them alone as he had been ordered to do. As he walked past the security man he mouthed the words 'help' to him that he hoped that the guard had noticed. If he didn't let the guard know that he was being forced into helping these men to rob his bank then it might be thought that he was in on it too. The manager was told to take as much cash as he could from the tellers drawers without arousing their suspicions. Two of his men accompanied him in the guise of stock takers as the manager explained that they were being investigated by Customs and Excise and that all monies on the premises needed to be checked. He went on to tell them that forged notes in big quantities had been reported as coming from his bank and that sample notes thought to be fakes would have to be removed. The way that it was explained to the staff made them all feel guilty of being part of it themselves. Four more of his men took large crates in that had to be wheeled in on trolleys into the room where his men were taking out the safe deposit boxes. Two other of his men took turns in interviewing all of the staff one by one and the bank was closed whilst it was under investigation

This went on for almost an hour when the security men came in to take the 'evidence' away which was put into the security van that parked legally on double yellow lines due to the nature of its business and the large amounts of cash that it contained. Even the traffic warden waved to the driver as he walked past him and his van. His ticket book was tucked safely away in his pocket as he went to give assistance in the town centre where the police were in need of his services for once.

Inside the bank the staff had been told that they would be taken to the station where they would be asked to make formal statements regarding the fake notes. They had all of their personal possessions including mobile phones taken away from them as they were left to wait in a room. One of Lee's men waited with them to make sure that they didn't try to make up stories and unbelievingly they all naively believed such a tale. With all of the staff out of the way the security guard started to work alongside Lee's men as they helped the 'Group Four' men load up the Security van. It was nothing unusual to see the boxes being taken out of the bank and being placed in the van for it was a common sight that took place a couple of times a week. Although usually it was for nowhere near as long as the time that it was taking that morning. The amount of men that Lee had working on it and the fact that they had as much time as it took made it a very straight forward job.

Lee remained with Mr Chan in his office as he tried to make sense or understand why Mr Chan had treated his wife so cruelly but try as he did Lee could not understand.

"Take your clothes off"

"I beg you pardon I will do no such thing"

"Take off all of your fucking clothes before I rip them from your body with this and I'm not too steady at the minute"

Lee took out a meat cleaver. It was the same one that he had used to cut the bollocks off the bastards that had killed his mother. The manager took one look at the shining silver blade and he started to undo his shirt.

Before long Mr Chan was down to his boxer shorts and he looked at the man who was now sat in his chair expecting a bit of leniency. Lee had shook his head and watched as Mr Chan stood before him in the buff.

"Now lie face down on your desk. You do like leather don't you"?

Lee took twine from out of his coat pocket and he tied the manager to the desk legs using enough twine to ensure that it would cut through his flesh before coming loose. Mr Chan was totally exposed and Lee's only regret was that he hadn't brought a whip out with him. He heard Mr Chan whimper as he watched Lee take the thick leather belt with the large silver buckle from around his waist. Lee picked the mobile up and he called Mr Chan's wife so that she could share a special moment with him. Spike answered the phone to hear loud screams from the other end.

"This one is for you my friend"

Lee left the phone turned on so that Mrs Chan and Spike could listen to Mr Chan taking the kind of punishment that he had dished out himself for years. Lee picked up the crumpled pair of boxer shorts from the floor and he shoved them right inside Mr Chan's noisy mouth.

Then he brought the belt down on his scrawny back again and again until there wasn't a strip of skin that wasn't covered in his blood.

The security van was loaded up and Lee's men took the staff into the back yard outside the bank where they were put into two groups and told that they would be collected. The staff had no idea whether what was happening was the correct procedure. None of them had ever had dealings with the Customs before other than the times that they had brought extra duty free home from holidays.

"I've heard that they are even more powerful than the police and the government so I wouldn't be surprised if this is the way they work. I don't know about the dodgy notes though I can't remember seeing any"

One of Lee's men stayed with them in the yard just long enough for all of the others to get well away. Lee had got into the security van wearing a Group Four uniform and one of his men pulled up behind him in a small box van.

The last of Lee's men told the staff that he would call the station and he left them standing in the yard as he made his get away.

The staff waited for almost twenty minutes before any of them had the nerve to go to look for the Customs guy that had left them in the yard. It was a new member of staff who was on a works trial with them that eventually walked into the bank to find that everyone had gone and that they had taken the contents of the bank with them. He shouted to the others to come in then they went to find the manager who had passed out on the top of his desk.

A senior cashier opened the door unaware of what she might find there then she fainted at the sight of Mr Chan's shredded body. It was tied to the top of his desk and she had not noticed the nakedness of it which was disguised by all of the blood. One of the others called for an ambulance and the police to attend urgently as they all realised that they had been taken in big style. The security guard's body was found behind the toilet door where he had been knocked unconscious and left. Someone covered the manager's body with a clean white towel then they called his wife on the mobile to give her the bad news about his ordeal.

Lee Won-King called Joseph on the mobile as he waited at the traffic lights. Joseph answered after only two short rings to hear the last of the four men tell him that he had completed his mission which had gone well. Joseph gave

him the destination that he needed to reach and he asked
him to call him when he got there. Unless anything went
wrong all five men including Joseph should reach Aldershot
on time. It was twelve forty and Joseph had estimated that
they should be leaving the airstrip by seventeen hundred
hours at the rate they were going they would be bang on
time.

Inspector Thomas had just had two more calls about bank
robberies that had been confirmed by his own men which
had brought the total to three within the hour. The Police
Commissioner had been on to him and the Mayor had been
distraught to find a National Front meeting in full swing
when they had left the meeting that they had been
attending. The fire brigade had gone out to a fire at the
German bank only to find all of the bank's staff locked in
the vault suffering from smoke inhalation. With the other
jobs that had been reported it brought the total of bank jobs
on his patch to four in one hour. As well as the banks there
had been two post offices held up, thirteen jewellers robbed
and endless accounts of petty theft and muggings.

There had scenes of angry clashes which had incited race
riots which had been witnessed by the visiting dignitaries
and as well as that, reports of over two hundred road traffic
accidents. Road rage had become commonplace in the town
centre as tempers frayed at the busy junctions that had no
traffic lights and where none of the parties would give way.
None of the drivers wanted to stay in town longer than
necessary and panic mode was beginning to set in. It was a
case of the bigger the vehicle the higher priority it got.
Shoplifters were out in their hundreds doing a bit of early
Christmas shopping and the streets of Manchester were
experiencing looting on a big scale for the first time since
the war.

10th September 2003 was a date that would go down in history for the downfall of the Greater Manchester Police and in the demise of Inspector Thomas. The army had been called in to assist the police who were seen not to be coping and more senior officers were drafted in from surrounding areas. Crimes curiously seemed to be getting fewer as the day went on. Despite all of this less than fifty petty criminals had been arrested in all and with the computers out of action the majority of the criminals caught had been named after cartoon characters frustrating the police even more. All of the complaints from the toms had been duly registered for on top of everything else the police had to be seen to be fulfilling their duties to everyone under the Human Rights Act. The computer systems had been corrected with the fault being put down to a nasty virus that was prevalent worldwide but the backlog of checks would keep the police busy for days to come. The apparent power failures had been put down to the same problem that the National Grid had experienced a couple of weeks earlier in London and it appeared that a workman had accidentally cut through some important wiring causing many of the traffic lights and cameras to stop working. The bomb scares that had forced many of the shops and offices to close for the day had been proved to be cruel hoaxes and the race riots had been exactly that. The Inspector could only put it down to terrorists for whoever had masterminded such a day of chaos was obviously a very clever and devious man. It had to be, in his mind the work of a madman or a bloody genius.

A BOOK OF FAVOURS

Chapter 25

Joseph's hire car was the first one to arrive to a point on the bridge from where he could see the three vans arriving. He had chosen a busy lay-by where the vans would not look out of place and from where they could leave in a convoy. The first of the vans to arrive was the shiny black 'surveillance' one driven by Alberto with Alphonso in close pursuit. Joseph watched as he saw Alberto using his mobile phone and he picked his own up in readiness for his call.

"I am here my friend, what would you like me to do now"?

"There is a truck stop café 300 yards down the road, tell your man to take a well earned rest there. We are waiting for the others to arrive but once they are here we will be gone for about three hours. Tell him to wait for you there until you get back and tell him there is to be no alcohol. An old Direct Works van with a battered red box van pulled into the lay-by just ahead of Alberto. Although the two vehicles pulled into the lay-by together neither of the drivers acknowledged the other. One of the men got out to stretch his legs whilst the one sat in the van started to read a newspaper which told of a big robbery!

Liam called Joseph just as Alberto had done and Joseph told him very much the same as he had to the first man as well as explaining who was with them.

"The Black van behind you is one of us and we must wait for one more to come then we will go to meet the fourth.

Your man can wait for you in the café and we will see him in a few hours time. I will call you as soon as our other man turns up and I will give you your final destination. Well done, stretch your legs and chill out."

Liam could have killed for a drink but he knew that alcohol was definitely not allowed on this mission. Knowing that he couldn't have one made him want one all the more and he compensated by chain smoking. He walked over to the van behind him and asked the driver for a light when he probably told his driver where to wait for him. It was ten minutes later that Lee Won-king turned up but there was no sign of his number two who had got stuck behind a trail of caravans further down the motorway. Everyone knew that they must proceed with caution and try not to draw any attention to themselves so Lee had sat patiently and waited for the caravans to turn off which had been only at the junction before.

He called to Joseph who sat watching from the bridge above to make sure that none of his men were being followed by the law.

"I am here my friend but I have a problem because I have lost my number two. I haven't seen him for the last twenty minutes or so"

"Is he driving a small red van"   "Yes"

"Then take a look in your mirror he's pulling in behind you now"

It wasn't the type of van that had alerted Joseph's attention to him but the fact that the driver was Chinese was just a bit of a give away.

"Right, three of the five big vans parked up are ours. Tell your man to go to the truckstop up the road and to wait for you to return which will be in a few hours time. I am driving a blue Vauxhall Vectra and I will sound my horn as I pass you so that you and the others can follow me. I will pass you in five or so minutes then I need to pick the last of our drivers up from the petrol station who will follow us to the final destination. We are heading for the old airstrip that is about fifteen minutes up the road so my friend our task is almost complete. See you later my friend"

Satan was waiting at the petrol station stuffing his face with chocolate and soon all four of Jimmy's compass points would be in one place. Joseph's heart beat fast and his pulse raced as he turned on the engine of the car and left to head his convoy. He sounded his horn as he passed the lay-by and as planned all three vans pulled out and followed him as he headed for the petrol station that was a mile up the road. Joseph called Satan to let him know that they were on their way and he told him which other vehicles were involved.

"I am in a blue Vectra saloon car there is a white transit van, a black Mercedes van and an old Direct Works van. We are heading to the old airstrip about five miles down the road. Are there any problems so far"?

"Only that the windows don't open in this old rust bucket that I am in and I've got a very bad case of the wind."

Joseph watched in his wing mirror as Satan joined the convoy then all five of them headed for the old airstrip. It was almost four in the afternoon and they were bang on time and on target. At the airstrip the Minister and the Major waited patiently for the men to arrive. The army vehicles had been left in an old hangar waiting to be filled with their 'special' cargo whilst the chosen drivers sat inside.

The Major despite his obvious ill health told them of their next mission and he reminded them of the secrecy connected to the one that they had just completed. Afterwards as the men drank coffee the Minister and the Major conferred secretly in the corner.

"Are you sure that this will be the end of it all"

"As far as I know it will be James. I have just taken a call and the men will be with us shortly. I will go out to them as soon as they arrive whilst you stay with the men. I will contact you when the cargo is loaded"

"Have you any idea what the cargo is that we are carrying for them"?

"Not a clue and I don't want to know. Whatever you do don't complicate matters. What we don't know can't hurt us but what they know could crucify us"

The Major agreed to stay with the army drivers as the Minister went to wait for the visitors. There were only two guards at either entrance to the airfield which was very rarely used. Terrorist alerts had forced all possible means of escape by air to be monitored but the airstrip was close to army barracks and thought to be quite secure.

Joseph and his convoy approached the airstrip and the guard unlocked the gate as he had been instructed to do by the Minister. Lee hummed "The Great Escape' as he followed Joseph's car through the gates and he smiled to himself as he looked at the sentry who stood erect saluting each of the vans as they passed by. It was a strange assortment of vehicles that passed by the sentry but he knew that on certain matters of security the most ridiculous modes of transport could be used. The army vehicles that he had let in earlier had all displayed signs to indicate radio active materials so it was obvious to the guard just what kind of cargo the vans would be carrying. As soon as the last of the vehicles passed through the gates the guard locked them just as the Major had instructed him to do earlier. The Minister greeted the man in the first car that was totally unknown to him but who he knew that he shared a mutual acquaintance with. He directed the vans to the furthest corner inside the hangar next to a line of twenty army trucks. Joseph got out from his car and he took the five lots of protective clothing that the Minister held out to him.

When the Minister had left the building Joseph gestured to all four men to get out of their vehicles.

One by one they got out and walked over to Joseph who handed them a suit each. Only Lee and Satan knew each other from school and from the estate but the others were complete strangers to each other. The men followed Joseph's lead and put on a protective suit each then they waited for Joseph to speak and to make the introductions.

"Right then men, this is us. As we speak Jimmy should be on his way to the freedom that he deserves. He told me to tell you all if we got this far, well done to you all! We need to move as quickly as we can in putting the hauls that you have each managed to secure into the lead boxes in the back of each of the trucks. It doesn't matter if we mix the things up because it will be equal shares for every one of you here today. Once you have unloaded your own van please help someone else to empty theirs and once a container is full just put the lid down. The cases are impenetrable and the lids are self locking so once they are closed you will not be able to open them without the right equipment. When everything has been locked away and the trucks are secured I would like you all to step into the shadows whilst the drivers come in to claim their vehicles. No-one will try to look into the containers even if they had the means to for they think that they are dealing with highly toxic materials. The convoy of trucks will be taken to its final destination where it will be left to be unpacked and secured by us. The hauls will be left and we will return in twelve months time to uncover exactly what we have got away with today. Are there any questions"?

Satan was the only one to say what they probably all were thinking.

"What about if one of these men comes back before the

year is up and takes the lot? We don't even know what we have taken and it would be easy for someone to rip us off big style"

"That could not happen I can promise you and I will show you all why when we get there but for now you must trust each other. I know that Jimmy has personally handpicked you four because he knows that he can trust you, but you must trust his judgement too. Can you do that"?

"It ain't Jimmy that I don't trust but I don't even know two of these guys and we are talking big money"

"Then let me introduce you in a way that will keep your true identity safe.

This of course we shall call quite simply East"

As he spoke he pulled Lee Won-King to his side and pointed to him.

"This is South and this is North"

He pointed to Alberto and Liam as he said that.

"I guess that makes me West does it but tell me my friend what do we call you"?

"Just call me friend and from now on these are the names that we shall be known to each other as. Now let's get loading these bloody trucks up"

All four of the men ran to their own van and they started to unload the goodies and put them into the containers as Joseph had ordered them to.

Then they shut the heavy lids that clicked into place as they closed and they locked up the back of each of the trucks. All five men stepped back into the shadows in the corner as they waited for the army drivers to come in to take their trucks away. Joseph had informed the Minister that the cargo was ready for collection and he ordered the men to take them out. As the twenty military trucks waited in the grounds for their drivers to take their orders Joseph explained to the men what would happen next. He had arranged for himself and Alberto to go with the Minister whilst the other three would travel with the Major. The Major pulled up in his Range Rover and Lee, Liam and Satan got into the back seat still dressed in their protective clothing which served as a good disguise should anyone wonder who they were. Then a shiny black saloon car pulled up and Joseph and Alberto got in it to find the Minister in the driving seat. The Major drove to the first of the army vehicles and he passed on directions to the driver then he drove to the very end of the convoy just at the back of the Minister.

The sentry unlocked the gates to let them through and the trucks started to form an orderly queue on the road outside when suddenly two police cars with flashing lights pulled up by the first of the trucks causing Joseph to catch his breath in fear.

"Please God not now, not when we have got this far"
Joseph had not needed to worry for the police were there on the instructions of the Minister who had authorised a police escort for his 'hazardous materials' whilst they were in transport.

"Fucking Hell man they are giving us a fucking police escort, I don't believe it. Who says that there is never a copper about when you need one"

Lee and Liam laughed out loud at Satan's last remark but could see exactly why he had said it. The police cars positioned themselves at the front and rear of the long convoy not to arrest them, but to assist them. The police officer in the front car had taken directions from the driver of the first truck. When he was sure that they were ready to go he set off for the secret destination that they were heading for with all of the other vehicles in tow. The hideout that they headed for was only about fifteen miles from the airstrip hidden behind large trees, metal gates and high fencing. It was an old stately home that had been seconded by the Government and it was used for training Special Armed Forces. It also had an underground shelter that was to be used by important Government officials in the wake of a nuclear attack. There was also a large storage room that could be used to house some of the country's treasures if such an attack occurred. It was in the storage area that the supposed 'radio active materials' were to be stored. The vehicles pulled up outside the magnificent grounds and the police officer in the first car got out and spoke into the intercom that the party they had been expecting had arrived. The big heavy gates creaked as they opened up and the military convoy drove into the massive grounds.

The police officer stood to attention until all of the vehicles had passed by him then he got back into his car and he and his colleague sped back to the motorway to deal with rush hour traffic and the problems that it caused. The trucks drove to the back of the building to await further instructions. The Major sent the drivers inside for refreshment as the cargo was unloaded and as soon as the soldiers had vanished from view Joseph's men got out of the cars that they had travelled in.

The Major took them down in a lift to what must have been old dungeons at one time and showed them where they could leave their stuff. He opened the locked boxes for them before he went inside to join his men and the Minister. Joseph told the men to work as quickly as they could by moving all of their hauls from the containers into the underground cache. He instructed them to work as a team and he joined in using a fork lift truck for the heavier stuff. Most of the things were still locked in steel boxes but there were vast amounts of cash and papers and lots of items of expensive jewellery that lay in the bottom of the sacks.

Without stopping to inspect any of the things that they had stolen the men loaded up their haul in record time. Every last one of them poured with sweat due to the fact that they were roasting in the protective clothes that they were still wearing. Each of the men worked fast and furious in their quest to finish off and very soon that quest was done. The five men looked at each other smugly and waited until Joseph took off his head gear then they all did the same making it easier for them all to breathe easily once more.

"Now what was it that you were going to show us"
asked Satan who was still very cynical about leaving all of the gear behind especially after just seeing how much of it there was.

"Watch very carefully my friends. First of all we must say goodbye to all of this until next year which is when we will see it again"

The men still looked a little unsure but they listened to what Joseph had to say to them. Joseph pulled the door to until it was almost closed and he pointed to the width of the door and asked the men.

"Just how wide would you say that door is my friends"?

Liam was the first to answer for measurements were a speciality of his. When he had fought for the cause he had been expected to remember a whole room layout, dimensions and all after seeing it for only five minutes.

"Fourteen centimetres of solid steel that would take eight pounds of Semptex to wrench it from its hinges"

"Well done my friend that is exactly right and I must congratulate you on your skills but this room will not be accessed by anyone other than our-selves next year. The Minister has assured us that it will be very much off limits to everyone except ourselves next year"

"But how can you be sure that the two army guys won't try

to rip us off"?

"Because my friends, of these"

Joseph banged the heavy door shut and the sound echoed around them all then he produced four large heavy duty keys and he pointed to the four locks on the closed door.

"Four keys to fit four locks and only one key fits one lock which means that the only time that this door can be opened is if all four of you are present and you are all carrying your key. If just one of the keys are missing though then the door will not open. Today the five of us are sworn into a pact that cannot be broken, a pact that means that not one of us dare to speak about what we have just done here. There will be massive rewards offered by the media as soon as tomorrow that might tempt your own men to betray you. All men have their price and we can not afford to take chances.

Each of you is solely responsible for your own men and if at any time you think that any of them will betray you then you must kill them. Will you all be able to do that if the need arises"?

The four leaders that stood before Joseph, all knew that they could trust their own men implicitly. Provided that no-one else got to know of what they had done each of them felt that they would be able to trust them. All of the men that had been involved in the robberies would be rewarded greatly for their work and each of them would die for their leaders if they were asked to. They all nodded to Joseph as they knew that the need to kill one of their own men would never happen.

"Before we go from here I need to know that everyone of you and your men have all got good alibis for today. There are bound to be investigations and by the law of averages one of us, if not all of us are bound to be pulled in for questioning"

All four of the men assured Joseph that they had cast iron alibis that would stand up in any court of law and that their men were trustworthy.

"Then my friends our work here is finished for now. Jimmy will call me when he is safe in Tenerife and I will be able to tell him that his plan went well and that he should be proud of his good friends. You will be contacted on the ninth of September next year and you will be given a new set of plans. Please, none of you put this operation in jeopardy by getting yourselves arrested will you"?

"If we do I know a bloody good lawyer"

Liam joked but Joseph could tell by the way that he spoke that he had meant it and he felt quite honoured by the compliment.

"What do we do with all the stuff that we robbed and how do we share it out equally"?

"We will come back here and Jimmy will join us, then in the privacy of these walls we will share out the goodies taking as long as we need to"

"How exactly will the boxes be shared out between us"? asked Lee Won-king.

"Who the fuck gives a toss there is enough spondulas to keep us all out of work for the rest of our lives. It will make honest men out of the lot of us"

"The cash and bonds will be counted and shared out equally as will the foreign currency. Most of the boxes are unopened so it is like a lucky dip as what each of us will find so they will be distributed between us until they are all gone. Then all of the expensive jewellery that is just lying at the bottom of some of the sacks will be tipped onto the floor for picks"

"Does that answer all of your questions and if it does are you all happy with it"?

Liam and Satan did a jig around the room to show just how

happy they were whist the others stood laughing as they watched them. Joseph handed each of the men a key as he told them.

"Guard it with your lives for without all four keys we have nothing"

Each of the men secured their own key on their bodies then they took off their protective suits and gloves. They took turns in shaking each others hands firmly and respectfully for the five of them were joined in a pact that could change all of their lives. Joseph spoke one last time to them all.

"Right my friends from this day until we all meet in twelve months time none of us should meet or speak. If any of your paths should cross by accident there must not be any sign of recognition. Do you all understand how important it is for this plan to work and do you all agree to the terms? I am sure that you all understand so now you will be taken back to a point where you can be easily be collected by your number two's. Say nothing to your men but congratulations for the good work that they all did today"

Joseph looked at the four men as they waited for the two cars to take them back to where they had come from and he knew just by looking that these men would not be likely to bump into one another. They were four very different men with different beliefs and very different lifestyles. All that they had in common between them was Jimmy Mack, their friend. They got into the same cars that they had been brought in and not one of them spoke a word to the others on the journey home. Both of the cars had the radio on and it was full of news of all of the daring raids that had been carried out in Manchester earlier that day. The bank jobs had been likened to 'The Italian Job' and although they never spoke, each of the men swelled with pride. The men were dropped off at locations far enough away from each other but still close enough for their men to collect them from. Joseph was let out at the place that he had left his hire car and just like the others he got out of the car without even a goodbye.

The truckstop café had been busy all day but fat Marie behind the counter couldn't help but wonder who the four new faces were. They were certainly not together and none of them had acknowledged the others even though they had all arrived within minutes of each other. One of them had done nothing but eat all day as though he had been starving whilst another of them had pigged out on cakes and doughnuts. The fancy one had drunk gallons and gallons of black coffee and the yellow one had asked if they served herbal tea of all things.

"We do P.G.tips teabags love in a mug, you know the one that is advertised with the monkeys on the telly. I can put in a request for you to the owner but somehow I can't really see herbal tea being on the menu"

Within minutes of receiving calls each of the men left as they had come. Each of the men headed off in different directions to collect their bosses and to take them home relieved that they had finally turned up safely.

Joseph sat in his car as he did a mental check list in his head.

'Mission completed ? - Yes!'

'Evidence disposed of ? Yes! All but this hire car that will meet its maker at the scrap yard later on'

'Men briefed on what they can and cannot do in the next twelve months?
Yes'

'Jimmy safe and well in Tenerife? Hopefully, to be confirmed later'

Joseph turned his radio onto Classic F.M. and he drove

back listening to Bach, Beethoven and Chopin. He made sure that there was no-one around as he let out a large whoop of joy. Joseph had finally made it!

All he needed to know was that Jimmy had made it also.

Mrs Rooney managed to get through to Inspector only to be told the terrible news about her son. Her husband had listened to the pain in her voice as she spoke on the phone and watched as she sat down in shock after putting the phone down. He knew that something was wrong but he waited for her to tell him.

"That was Inspector Collins, he has found out the reason that Mike took his life and it isn't very nice"

Mrs Rooney burst into tears and was unable to say any more to her husband. She knew that he would have no sympathy and she felt as though she could take no more. Her husband held her close to him as he assured her that whatever it was that he would be there for her. He knew by the way that she spoke that it must have something to do with Mike for even now he could manage to come between them and he cursed him inwardly as he consoled his wife until she was able to speak.

"He killed someone Sid, an old man. He battered him to death with a brick on that last time that he phoned me. It was the night that he asked for you to forgive him when he said he was going away"

Sid Rooney swore beneath his breath. He had never felt anything for Mike but he had never thought that he could do something as cold bloodied as murder.

"We must tell Patsy and Ben before they read about it but what do we say"?

Sid really didn't know what to say to his wife and he had no idea what they would say to their grandson. He didn't know how to explain to a young man that his father had killed someone and that then he had cowardly taken his own life. It was hard enough for Sid to accept the news so he had no idea how Ben would take it but he knew that they must see Patsy before she heard it on the news. He put on his jacket and picked up the car keys then he passed his wife her handbag. Anne Rooney wiped her eyes then she followed her husband out to the car.

She turned away from her neighbour as she passed her in the street and wondered how she would cope when everyone knew the truth. They lived in a small close knit community and Anne knew that the news would spread like wildfire once it was out. Only then would Anne Rooney know who her true friends were. They didn't speak on the journey to Patsy's home and as they pulled up outside Sid took hold of her hand.

"I'll tell them, just try to be strong for Ben"
Ben had been looking out of the window and he ran to the front door to greet his grandparents. For all of the years that his father had ignored him his grandparents had done their best to give him what they could. He knew that they were on a pension and that they didn't have much money but his grandmother had been one of the only people to talk about his dad and she always brought him little treats. He had just left school but had not yet got a job and he had started to hang around with a gang of boys that his step father called hooligans because they hung around on street corners. The visit from his grandparents cheered him up and he flung his arms around Anne Rooney's neck.

"Mum look who is here put the kettle on quick"
Patsy came to the door and she smiled at her ex in-laws then went in the kitchen to put the kettle on. Dave Martin her husband of six years had got up and walked out of the back door before the Rooney's saw him.

He had been drinking heavily and he was sure that they would notice. Patsy had nagged him enough for both of them and he had been forced to shut her up with a good hiding. The last thing that he wanted was for any one else to get on his case so he had gone back to the pub before they got the chance to. Patsy apologised to them that Dave had been called out.

Anne Rooney smiled for she had far more important things to think about. She noticed the marks on Patsy's neck and she wondered if her ex daughter-in-law would try to explain those away as well but she didn't.

"I don't suppose you've heard from him have you"

The 'him' referred to Mike for Patsy could barely bring herself to mention his name these days. It may have been that she blamed his leaving her for all of the bad things that had happened to her since even though it was her adultery that had forced him to go. Ben had asked her many times why his dad had gone away and every time she had lied to him. She had told him that he had never loved them and that his work was more important to him than they were. She had even thrown away the birthday and Christmas cards that Mike had sent to his son and told Ben that his father couldn't even be bothered to remember his birthday. It had been easier than telling him the truth and it had made Patsy seem like the martyr in the relationship. Patsy felt guilty when Mike's parents came to see her but she had even managed to convince them that Mike was a rat. She brought in a tray of teas and sat down hoping that they would not notice that she had been crying. If she had looked directly at Mike's mum she would have noticed that she too had been crying. Sid got hold of Patsy's hand and sat her on the settee as Anne put her arm around young Ben.

"We need to tell you something Patsy and it isn't easy for us"

Ben looked scared and Anne squeezed him trying hard not to cry herself.

"Mike's dead Patsy, he killed himself this week"

Ben jumped up shouting out in denial as he ran up to his bedroom.

Sid tried to follow him but by the time he got up the stairs Ben had locked himself in his room and would not unlock the door despite his grandfather's pleas. Sid went back downstairs to find both women in tears and he put an arm around each of them in an attempt to calm them down. Meanwhile Ben sat crying on his bed holding a photograph of him with his dad that his grandmother had given to him years ago. It was old and the corners were turned but Ben had treasured it secretly. He had kept it in his drawer so that he wouldn't upset his mum or annoy his step dad but he suddenly felt that he had a right to take it out and look at it. Ben had never understood how his dad could have just forgotten about him the way he had.

He had grown up hating him for it but as much as he had hated him part of him had also loved him and Ben's poor head was in pieces. He had intended to leave home once he had got a job and then he was going to confront him and find out why he had just walked out on him but now even that had been taken away from him. Ben took one last look at the photograph that he had treasured for so many years and he tore it into two pieces and threw them both on the floor. Then he got up from the bed and started to kick the door. Each kick represented the anger that he felt inside and he kicked the door until all of his energy had been drained from his body and he fell exhausted onto his bed.

Downstairs the tears had stopped as they listened to the anger that Ben was showing upstairs and suddenly his young grief put their own in the shadows.

"He should have been there for him, he should have stayed

and took his responsibilities seriously instead of walking out the way he did"

Patsy felt guilty and she was just about to explain to them that it hadn't all been Mike's fault but Sid told her to listen to what he had to say. Then he explained the full horrors of what Mike had done including the murder and his suicide. As he spoke they were all unaware of Ben sitting on the stairs listening to it all. Ben didn't know how to feel, he should have felt glad it was finally over but he knew that it wasn't. Patsy listened in horror and disbelief but she could tell by the way that his parents spoke about it that it was true. She jumped when she heard the back door bang shut and she got up to see who it was. She looked out of the window to see Ben running across the field at the back of the house and she had been just about to run after him when she noticed her purse lying on the floor. She picked it up to find that her son had taken every last penny that she had and she threw her purse onto the floor in anger. Anne walked in to find Patsy crying and thought that it was over her son so she left her alone to get on with it. Sid went upstairs to find that Ben had disappeared and he came down to tell the women the bad news carrying the two pieces of torn photograph he had found on the floor.

"Will you be alright if we go love"?

"Yes thanks Anne, I'll wait for Dave to get back then I'll go round to our Ben's mates. I'll give you a call when he gets back, and Anne I am really sorry about Mike"

"I know that you are love, give me a call if you need to talk"

The Rooneys left Patsy to head for home and as they drove through the Manor estate they looked out for Ben as they passed the street corners. They didn't see him and if they had they wouldn't have recognised him.

Chapter 26

Paddy Beirne dropped Liam at the off licence while he went to get rid of the van at the scrap yard. It had been a good days work all round and Paddy had been gagging for a drink so he had called Mick at the yard telling him to expect him. Mick sorted out the van whilst Paddy watched then he dropped him off on Hyde road where he nipped in the nearest off licence that Liam had shopped in not long before. Liam got back to his flat just after half time of the England game carrying a shit load of cider in his arms.

"What have you been up to till this time"?
asked Tulip as she walked out of the bedroom where she had been waiting for him to arrive.

"Who the fuck do you think you are, my bloody mother"?
Liam gave Tulip one of his looks that usually preceded a good hiding so she kept her mouth shut. She watched him as he sat down at the table with the others and picked up a hand of cards as though he had been in the game from the start. Tulip knew that he had only just arrived home but she thought that if he wanted her to think that he had been there all night then that was exactly what she would do. She had become an expert at deceit. She walked back into the bedroom and put on her new sexy underwear then she covered it up with another of her new outfits that she had bought that day. Then with a quick coat of her new lippy and a spray of Obsession perfume she went to join the boys

in the front room. She poured herself a drink and sat down to watch the rest of the football.

"What's the score"?

Liam started to give her a blow by blow account as though he had watched every single minute of the game and she secretly applauded his ingenuity. If she had not been watching the others as they returned as she sat in her friends flat she could have easily been convinced that he had been at the flat all day. Liam could lie without even trying to and he carried on playing his cards while keeping one eye on the football. He had listened intently to the first half of the football on the radio so he was more than qualified to talk about the game as he had. He knew that if he was pulled in that it would help his alibi which would be an afternoon of boozing and a good session of cards as a build up before the big game.

Out of all of the gangs Liam's was probably the safest for the promise of immunity that Liam had been given by the Home Office still stood. The bad news was that Liam's fortress of a home was soon to be demolished and he knew that he would need one hell of a place to accommodate all of his men. Maybe the proceeds from the bank jobs would help towards buying the land and help him to build his own place from scratch. Paddy Beirne turned up just in time to hear the final whistle being blown. He had an arm full of booze which he held up in the air.

"It's party time. I think we all deserve to have a good session boys"

"Why, what have you done"?

"Well we've just won the football and we've got a good game of cards on the table"

"None of you are bloody English so what's all this we"?

"Damn Tulip you are a bloody cynic, this is our second home is it not?

Or would you rather us support the bloody asylum seekers"?

Tulip gave up and joined the boys in their drinking games which went on until after midnight. The drink managed to loosen tongues enough for her to know that something had gone down that day although exactly what she could not find out. She opened a couple more of the buttons on her new top which showed just enough of her new underwear to get Liam in the mood. She knew that if she quizzed him any more that he would snap so she waited until the others had left before sitting astride him on the sofa. Liam gave Tulip no information but what he did give her was the best sex that she had ever had in her entire life. Whatever he had been up to that day had certainly got his adrenalin running and Tulip enjoyed it far too much to complain. She decided that she would bide her time and keep an eye on the news and listen to the radio. She would watch all of the men and wait for just a spark of a reaction and then she would decide what to do. Tulip fell asleep contentedly after a good days shopping, a lot of booze and some great sex. Liam lay awake as Tulip slept beside him thinking that he hadn't felt as good as he was feeling today since the time that Christine had first told him that she was pregnant. Liam knew that he had made a bloody fortune that day and he wished with all of his still broken heart that he had someone proper to share it all with.

Alberto Vincente pulled up outside of the Old Trafford ground and waited for his man to come out to him. Carlo had been sat in his box at the ground since before the start of the England game impersonating his boss and Alberto had just called him to let him know that he was outside the ground. The two men exchanged a quick conversation as the noise coming from inside of the ground reached their ears. Alberto put on the long cashmere coat and the dark sunglasses that Carlo had been wearing and with his mobile phone to his ear he walked back to his executive box. He picked up his glass of champagne that had just been poured for him and thanked the waiter that had served it. All eyes had been on the game and not one of the people in the crowd had even noticed that a swap had been done as one well dressed Italian looked pretty much like the next. Alberto settled down to watch the rest of the game and he made a quick call to Maria to let her know he was safe. Maria could barely hear Alberto above the noise of the crowds but she heard enough to know that he was back and he was safe and well. Young Violletta played happily in her bedroom and she looked up excitedly as soon as she realised just who it was that her mama was talking to.

"Was that papa on the phone"?

"Yes princess, he called to say that he is watching the football with some colleagues of his and that he will be home later. He said to tell you that he loves you millions"

Violletta laughed out loud and her deep violet coloured eyes sparkled like gems as she spoke.

"I love him trillions and trillions"

"I know that you do sweetheart, I know"

Maria Vincente was almost jealous of the loving relationship that her husband had with their daughter. Of course she knew that he loved her madly and that he would never be unfaithful in their relationship but Violletta was almost like an obsession with him. She looked at their daughter as she played with her dolls and she couldn't blame Alberto one bit for loving her the way that he did. Violletta's long dark ringlets fell across her beautiful olive skin making her look every bit the Italian princess that she was. She even had Alberto's white streak at her temple which proved to Maria just how like her husband her daughter was. Maria remembered the terrible night that she had been stolen away from them and she knew that whatever it was that Alberto had done for Jimmy that it would never be enough to repay him for what he had done for them, not in a million years.

Lee Won-King got back to China town just before nine 'o clock. He got washed and changed then he went to one of his restaurants where birthday celebrations had been going on all day, for him. Lee had not bothered to mention to any of the others that it was his birthday that day. The buzz that he had got from pulling off the job had been his best present ever and he couldn't wait until his next birthday when he would get to unwrap some wonderful gifts. The restaurant was crowded and provided the most colourful display imaginable as firecrackers went off around them adding to the excitement. All of the guests wore beautiful satin outfits of vibrant reds and yellows and there was a brightly coloured twenty foot dragon in attendance too. Lee picked up a silver goblet and he held it up in the air as he made his toast to the guests.

"Thank-you all for coming to my party and thank-you for everything"

The men that had been with Lee that day knew only too well that the second part of the toast was directed at them and they all raised their glasses back to him as Lee continued.

"Also I would like to toast absent friends, on this earth and the next"

Lee spilt some of the drink onto the floor as a gesture of respect to his dead mother and father then he smiled as he looked at the scar on his wrist that reminded him of his other absent friend, Jimmy.

"Absent friends" shouted the crowds. The party went on until the very early hours of the morning with singing and dancing being the order of the day and everything seemed to be going well. None of his men had dared to mention the bad news that they had heard for fear of spoiling Lee's birthday party. Even when Lee had mentioned that it was strange that Sammy Yung had not attended his party no-one told him that Sammy Yung's body had been pulled from the canal earlier that day. No-one dared to tell him that the sign of Dakar had been carved into Sammy's chest before his heart had been cut out. It had been a good day for Lee and his men and none of them wanted to spoil it any sooner than they needed to do.

Satan arrived home to an empty house that was in darkness. Only the Rottweiller dogs in the back garden were there to greet him. He pushed open his front door and found three sweet wrappers on the floor and he knew that Tyson had been to see him. Tyson was his nephew or so everyone but him thought when in reality he was his son. Once when his brother Rick had been locked up for the night Tina, his missus had called round to his house to find a shoulder to cry on.

After a bottle and a half of Vodka Tina had got a lot more than a shoulder from Satan and as a result she became pregnant with Tyson. Satan hadn't felt guilty about laying his brother's missus for he didn't have a conscience not even when she told him she was up the tub. Rick had been playing away for years and he knew that he hadn't been there but he had no idea that it was his brother's sprog. Rick was just happy that it was white. Tyson Richard Nuttall had been one of the ugliest babies ever to have been born at St. Mary's hospital. He had a big fat nose and piggy little eyes just like his uncle Fred and a mass of red wiry hair that made him look just like a cabbage patch kid.

Despite his looks he was the only thing in the world that

Freddie as Tyson called him really cared about and he had grown up just as rough as his uncle had. Rick and Tina split up when Tyson was only two years old and Freddie was the only male influence that Tyson had other than the string of one night stands that his mother constantly had. Fred had no skills to pass on to young Tyson other than to show him how to throw a good punch but he did have a place that Tyson could run to if he needed to. Tyson had needed a safe haven the night that one of his mother's boyfriends had tried it on with him when his mother had passed out in a drunken stupor. Tyson had kicked the guy hard in his bollocks just like his uncle had showed him to and ran away from him. Then he had called Freddie on his mobile and had found him in the local pub. Fred had left his drink as soon as he had got the call and he had ran out to his van to call round and see the guy in question. Not having been able to satisfy himself on the boy John Jessup had turned his attentions to the mother and he had raped her whilst she was unconscious. He was just walking out of the gate fastening his flies when Freddie turned up. The angry uncle threw just one big punch that was enough to knock John Jessop out cold. Then he picked him up and threw him into the back of his van like the dirty old dog that he was. By the time that the guy came to they were parked up on the moors and he was out of the van in the open air. He wasn't able to move for his hands were tied firmly to a metal spike in the ground and he had no idea what was happening to him.

Freddie or Satan as he was better known was busy getting his tools from the back of the van. He was nicknamed the 'plumber' for the way that he carried out his punishments and the types of implements that he used. John Jessup screamed out loud as he saw the twenty stone angry. lunatic approaching him carrying the copper tubing and the barbed wire. No-one would be able to hear the cries which Satan liked to hear especially the ones that came from someone who had been crazy enough to try to rape his nephew. He usually saved such treatments for 'grassers' who were guaranteed never to grass on anyone again after enduring the treatment. That is the ones who survived. Satan ripped down the perverts's pants and underpants and he inserted the copper piping into him as roughly as he possibly could. Then he took the barbed wire and passed it through the tube and then he pulled the pipe away. As the barbed wire entangled itself around John Jessup's intestines, he passed out with the pain. Satan pulled out the stake from the ground and left the man where he lay. He picked up his tools and set off to find his nephew to assure him that he would not be bothered again and he never was. Satan didn't feel like being on his own so he called Tyson on the mobile that he had bought for him and told him that he was back. The football was about to finish so he got out the Play stations and waited for him to show. Tyson called back to say that he couldn't come and he sounded upset but he asked Freddie not to call round.

"I'll tell you tomorrow Freddie, it's a bit bad"

Satan was sorry that Tyson couldn't come round and he was worried what could be so bad to keep him away but he was hungry and thirsty so he went to the pub. By the time that he got there the rest of the lads were all bladdered and he had to knock back the triple Vodkas to try to catch up. They played pool, drank and ate endless bags of crisps and partied until midnight when they went to collect their curries that they had ordered earlier. Fifteen of them took their food to the park where they sat and ate it all in record time then they played on the swing above the river. Soon they were falling in the water and stripping off and before long they were comparing their peckers. Satan always won the biggest dick competitions even though he wasn't that well endowed for he had the biggest hands. He had great fun pummelling all of the others into submission and by two in the morning they were all ready for their beds. Only one of his men was daft enough to ask Satan about the haul that they had taken that day turning a happy night quite sour. Satan took hold of the man roughly and he shoved a handful of notes into his mouth.

"You did a good job today and it was for charity that is all you have to know. Now get out of my sight and don't ever mention today again, as far as you are concerned, it never happened"

"Right boss, sorry for asking"

he said as he took the fifty pound notes from his mouth. Satan gave all of his men similar amounts of cash and it was never mentioned again. He eventually fell into his bed in a drunken coma feeling very pleased with himself with his days work but concerned about his nephew for he was sure that something was very wrong.

A BOOK OF FAVOURS

Chapter 27

"Good afternoon ladies and gentlemen. Just to let you know that we have begun our descent into Sophia Airport and we shall be landing in approximately fifteen minutes time. May I take this opportunity to thank you all for flying with My Travel. On behalf of the cabin crew and my-self we hope that you have enjoyed your flight and we look forward to seeing you on your return journey. You will be happy to know that it is not raining and the island is currently enjoying temperatures of twenty seven degrees centigrade"

Julie shrieked with excitement as she squeezed Jimmy's hand and kissed the side of his head, much to the amusement of their travelling companion.

"Did you hear that babes, we've made it, you are a free man"

Jimmy nodded and smiled at the same time. Even now he wasn't as sure as his lovely wife was but she looked so happy as she spoke to him that he didn't have the heart not to share her enthusiasm. The plane shuddered as the wheels hit the tarmac and Julie threw her arms around Jimmy and held him tight until the plane had come to a total standstill. The chap in the aisle seat undid his seatbelt as soon as the light on the sign went out and he stood up to retrieve his hand luggage from the overhead compartment. He wished them both well on their honeymoon which he presumed that they were on due to all the kissing and canoodling that had been going on for the last four hours or so. Julie and Jimmy laughed at the thought but the smile was soon wiped from Jimmy's face as he looked out of the window of the plane. A group of armed police officers were lined up outside the aircraft and they seemed to be waiting for someone. Jimmy's heart skipped a beat and he looked straight into Julie's eyes but he didn't say a word. He didn't have to for his eyes said it all. The chap in the aisle noticed them too and made a comment as he started to walk down the plane.

"Looks like they are out looking for the terrorists again" Jimmy and Julie waited until most of the passengers had got off before they stood up. Jimmy wanted to spend as much time as possible with his lovely wife before they locked him up again. Julie followed him down the aisle of the plane until they almost reached the exit door then she pulled him towards her and whispered in his ear.

"Let's make a run for it, I'll start taking my clothes off to distract them and you run to the perimeter and jump the fence. If you get away I will meet you later in the mountains, I'll keep looking until I find you"

Jimmy kissed her gently on the lips as the air stewardesses watched on in amazement then he held her close to him.

"Babes, I love you so very much but I can't ask you to do that for me. If they are waiting for me I want to go gracefully and I want you to go to the villa and take a holiday as planned. Promise me that you will do that for me and promise that you will be brave for I need you to be really strong. If you love me babes you must do what I ask"

Julie started to cry for she was terrified of what would happen when they stepped off the plane. She also knew that she could never promise to be strong for Jimmy not the way he wanted her to be. She held his hand tightly as they started to walk down the steps not daring to look over to where the police were standing. If she had looked over she would have seen that the police were no longer there. Jimmy started to look around, his eyes scanning every square inch of the airfield and it looked fine.

"Julie chin up babes they've gone, the bloody police have gone"

Julie couldn't believe her ears or her eyes but Jimmy was right all she could see was hundreds of holiday makers just like them. They walked through customs as though they were passing through a stile at a football match with no more than a passing glance from the officials who were stood there. All of the other passengers from their flight queued up to wait for their luggage but Jimmy and Julie had nothing but their hand luggage so they headed for the exit and towards the sunshine. They had just stepped outside and Jimmy was about to flag a taxi down when he felt a hand on his shoulder and his heart sank.

"Senor McKintyre, could we have a word please"

Jimmy turned to see a rather large respectable Spaniard pointing to a door marked 'Privado'. He took hold of Julie's hand as they followed the official into what they presumed to be his office. He ushered them through the door then walked back out of it and closed the door behind him. An Englishman in a white suit sat in a captain's chair that was facing the window and he turned to face them once the door was shut. Jimmy gave out a massive sigh of relief as he saw who the man in the chair really was.

"Jimmy Mack. Welcome to Tenerife you son of a gun"

Then he got out of his chair and walked over to Jimmy and hugged him like a long lost son as Julie just stood and watched on in amazement. When the hugging had eventually stopped Jimmy introduced his friend to Julie.

"Sorry babes I haven't introduced you this is Mark Walton, Mark this is my beautiful wife and my very best friend Julie"

Mark took hold of Julie's hand and kissed it like the gentleman that he had turned into. Many years ago he could have got into a lot of trouble if it hadn't been for Jimmy who had managed to get him back on the straight and narrow. Mark worked for Intelligence now and when he had heard the latest about Jimmy he had wanted to be the one to tell him the good news for he felt that he owed him at least that much. Jimmy had heard that Mark was quite high up now and he wondered what he was doing at the airport. He was just about to ask when Mark volunteered the information that he was seeking.

"I must say Jimmy when you break out you do it big style who the hell were all your accomplices? You never did do things by half did you?"

Jimmy was confused and not sure whether he had got away with it or nor. Mark was one of the only favours that he had not used up from his book so he decided to ask him outright.

"So what happens now Mark? Do I stay or do I go?"

"You go you daft bugger and you have the time of your life"

"You mean until the police find out where I am?"

"No, I mean forever. Don't tell me you haven't heard the news about Mike Rooney"

It was obvious from the way that Jimmy and Julie stood with puzzled expressions on their faces that they hadn't heard the news so Mark put them both out of their misery.

"The murder that you were set up for was done by the dead Detective Inspector Rooney and they have forensic evidence to prove it. That means you are innocent Jimmy so just enjoy your holiday with your beautiful wife"

"But the break-out?"

"It doesn't count because you shouldn't have been in custody in the first place and don't worry I've checked it out myself. There was a bit of controversy about the way the break out occurred but I put a few good words in for you. After all if you can't do a favour for an old friend, who can you do one for?"

Julie went up to Mark Walton and planted a great big kiss on his lips.

"Thank- you so much"

"It was my pleasure"

Mark blushed as he said it for Jimmy Mack's missus was a bloody good looking woman and if she wasn't his wife he would have fancied the pants off her.

He could tell that they were eager to get off so he walked out with them and got one of his men to take them to their destination. He bid them good-bye as they waited for the car then they both got on their mobiles to pass on the good news. Julie phoned D.J. who whooped with joy as he heard his mother tell him the words that he had known all along. That his dad was innocent!

Jimmy had just one call to make and Joseph jumped as his phone rang out. He was soaking in the bath tub sipping an expensive Brandy as he waited for Jimmy to call him.

"Joseph, we've made it. I'm in Tenerife and all charges against me have been dropped, can you believe it?"

"Yes I know Jimmy, I heard and you are right Jimmy we have made it one hundred per cent. I'll call you tomorrow"

Jimmy was the happiest man in the world. He knew what Joseph was telling him – All of his favours had been repaid!

ILL GOTTEN GAINS
(Part Two Of The Trilogy)

It is twelve months after Manchester city centre was hit by the biggest simultaneous crime spree in history.

The police are still baffled as to the identities of those responsible and despite massive rewards posted by the 4 major banks, no-one has come forward with any useful information.

The time has come for the 'Brothers' in crime to meet up again to share out their spoils. None of them know what they have stolen or to whom it belonged!

The dangerous waters on which they are about to embark will carry them on a treacherous journey – claiming lives along the way.

Will their 'Ill Gotten Gains' be worth the wait ?

———

To reserve your copy in advance, log onto
www.abookoffavours.com
or write to Lionheart Publishing